STILL LIFE

TRACY TRIPP

STIL LIFE
ISBN: 978-1-943789-79-5

Cover design and layout by: WhiteRabbitGraphix.com

This is a work of fiction. Any characters, names and incidents appearing in this work are entirely fictitious. Any resemblance to real persons, living or dead, is purely coincidental.

This book may be purchased through

Amazon.com and Amazon Kindle;
Taylor and Seale Publishing.com
www.taylorandsealeeducation.com
Barnes and Noble
Books-A-Million

Taylor and Seale Publishing, LLC.
Daytona Beach, Florida 32118
Phone: 1-386-760-8987
www.taylorandseale.com

Dedication

Still Life is dedicated in loving memory to my father, John Robert Sheehan, Sr.

PROLOGUE

Still Life, by definition, is an art form that uses mostly inanimate objects so that an artist can position them perfectly, thus allowing the objects to be studied, looked upon in the beauty or the horror their precise position in time creates. The subject may be a flower perfectly placed in a vase; a banana lying across a bowl of fruit, a shattered glass across a floor. A still life is a slice of a story based on placement, with no thought to past or present. People are seen less frequently in a still life, possibly because of the belief that people cannot be perfectly positioned, that they move through time driven by their will, that they get up and go when they choose, unable to live in a moment, by nature always looking into the past or the future. Despite that, there are the moments when a still life happens. When people are frozen in time, a time they never foresaw. They were placed in time, maybe only moments earlier, until life refused to stay still any longer, until the moment when the lens drifts onto another frozen object and they are forced to decide their future.

Chapter 1

Jacob

There are moments in one's life that change everything, that knock a person off a path like a giant meteor colliding with a planet. Maybe if the victim had known it was coming, he could have done something to stop it, but then again, who can really stop a meteor destined to find him? Jacob sat at the red light, tapping his finger on the steering wheel and watching the rain pelt the glass in the blinding way it likes to do at times. He was unaware that the meteor had already crossed into his atmosphere as a fiery ball with a predetermined target.

The light switched to green, and Jacob hit the gas to try to time his speed with the next green light. Why was it always when he was running late that he ended up out of sync with the switching signal? Why was it always when a room full of colleagues sat waiting in a conference room did his wife, Samantha, have a rambling to-do list she needed to review with him before he could get out the door?

1

Didn't she realize that with the chaos of the kids and his mind half at work already, he would be capable only of half-listening to anything she was saying, yet somehow he would be held to one hundred percent accuracy of each detail?

Distracted by his thoughts, Jacob didn't see the light turn red until it was almost too late. Slamming on the brakes just in time allowed the small amount of hydroplaning to have its way with his car. The horn behind him screamed obscenities as only car horns can.

Although Jacob wanted to avoid eye contact with the finger-wielding woman in the car behind him, he failed when she decided to pull up next to him. After a quick glance her way that said, "Whatever, lady," the time on the phone blared in the dark car, 7:45. There was no getting around being late for the meeting with his boss—his father-in-law—in-an ironical position that meant Jacob was held to higher standards as well as being ensured of higher rewards. Before the light could change, a text came through, as expected, from his father-in-law: "Meeting in fifteen minutes."

With his hands resting on top of the steering wheel, he quickly responded, "Be there in ten," he lied. *Deep breath*, he told himself. In the office, people knew him as the put-together, calming leader. The office didn't make him lose his temper, but combining a hectic morning, being late, the pouring rain, and a woman with an attitude watching his every move while he tried to get his morning back on track, made him feel insane. In for seven, hold for four, out for eight, or at least that's what he remembered of the breathing pattern he used to calm himself.

Jacob could feel the woman's glare as he laid the phone on the seat next to him and watched the light. As soon as the light turned green, he sped up just a bit faster than necessary to escape her. Noticing the closeness of the next green light, he continued to accelerate, hoping to outrun another encounter.

His phone buzzed, forcing him to glance down. Not her again. Somehow, by trying to make things right, he had created an impossible situation. Maybe the texts were innocent on her part, but he always suspected otherwise. Complaining to Samantha about the unwanted texts from this other woman would only ignite a war that didn't need to be fought. No, he would handle this on his own.

What was she saying this time? He picked up the phone to help his eyes read it a bit more clearly.

"Great new stock tip. Give me a call."

True, some of her tips ended up being useful both professionally and financially, but he could figure out the information on his own. It's what he did. Jacob alternated glances at the phone and the green light as he contemplated his response.

Once again, he took the polite route, continuing a habit that could go nowhere. "Call you later."

Jacob saw the woman coming up on his right, the light turning yellow. She was watching him. He could feel it rather than see it.

I won't be stuck at the next light being glared at by a stranger with an anger issue.

Jacob sped up just enough, he thought, to make the light. The rain picked up as well, and he let the phone drop on the seat while his hand fumbled with the wiper blades. When the light changed to red, he was going too fast to stop in time and barreled through the intersection. He felt a definite thump, a curb perhaps? Debris? Jacob glanced back. He could see nothing through the now-pounding rain except the angry woman stopping at the light.

May I never see you again.

With his attention still half on the woman behind him, Jacob crossed the next intersection. The sound of squealing tires split the air before the truck hit him. In the blurred moment before his head impacted with the side airbag, one confused thought drifted through his mind: *The light was green, wasn't it?*

Chapter 2

Samantha

Samantha tried to maneuver through the morning drop-off line. On sunny days, she walked her children, Sydney and Ryan, to the crossing guard and let them walk the rest of the way on their own. When the weather involved any unpleasantness—too cold, too hot, and definitely rain—she, like the many other pampering parents, drove the short distance and let them off under the covered entrance, protecting them from the elements.

In the background, her children began to bicker for the third time that morning.

"Kids, seriously, it isn't even eight o'clock yet. Could you give it a rest?"

"But Mom, all I said was that he couldn't read a historical fiction if it's supposed to be a nonfiction, and he swung his lunchbox at me," Sydney whined.

Ryan immediately retorted, "You don't always have to try to be the boss of me!"

Samantha knew he was growing increasingly weary of Sydney's constant corrections.

"Sydney, why don't you let me handle Ryan's reading requirements and you..."

Samantha saw the seething looks pass between them as they both crossed their arms and turned to stare out their windows. She let out a sigh and turned the radio up to calm the atmosphere and, for a moment, let her mind drift toward what she needed to accomplish.

Is that what Mom felt like the countless times I fought with my sister Haley? God, I still love Haley, in spite of what she thinks about me. Samantha remembered the envy that began to suffocate her every time she watched Haley play the piano so effortlessly.

I was just the "cute" one, while Haley had all the talent and brains. The report-card days proved it over and over. The quiet conversations she had overheard between her parents embedded in her memory. Her parents' pitiful attempts to praise her for her honor accomplishments did nothing but demean her even more. They demonstrated just a bit too much forced pride and probably never realized how much their praises hurt.

Samantha's blond hair was the first thing people commented on when they met her. The second was her blue eyes that her mom said she'd inherited from her maternal great-grandmother, a gene that somehow skipped both her mother and her sister. Haley had medium brown hair, that some might call mousy, and brown eyes, the kind of brown that was so everyday that if someone asked what color they were when they weren't standing next to her, they would have to think about it. They were that unnoticeable. Yet, Samantha could remember pictures by their pool of the two of them, arms wrapped around each other, their wet hair slicked back and sunglasses covering their eyes. They were undeniably sisters—so similar and yet so different at the same time.

The memories still stung the child inside of her, and she pushed them to the side settling instead on adult matters that did not involve solving the petty problems of the youth, yesterday's or today's. For the next six hours, she could be lost in her thoughts, accomplish things that would not be immediately undone, and enjoy blissful quiet. Some days, she desperately needed those six hours to prepare for the next round of homework, fights, and drama.

She slid into the row of cars letting the children out as the song whispered its final notes. Routinely, the masculine radio voice began going through the morning's traffic problems. Since Samantha's daily business kept her close to her neighborhood, she didn't need to know, so she tuned it out as she said her goodbyes.

Ryan popped his head between the seats. "Bye, Mommy." As always, he made sure he kissed his mother before leaving the car.

"Bye, baby. Have a great day. I love you."

No one heard the radio sounds which mingled with their goodbyes. "Broad Street at Pemberton is closed due to an accident with a fatality…." "The eastbound lanes will be closed for rush hour. You'll need to find an alternate route if you are traveling in that direction."

Ryan shimmied to the door with his overloaded backpack weighing him down while Sydney gave an irritated wave from the sidewalk.

"Bye, Sydney. I love you."

No response, as usual. Samantha was quickly learning that motherhood took thick skin, and she suspected the older they became, the thicker her skin would need to be for survival.

As the door shut behind them, she watched them both avoid each other as they entered the school. Maybe Ryan shared her personality, feisty and determined fueled by a bit of envy, but she understood Sydney as well, just as she understood Haley, to a degree. Both of them had begun their lives feeling just a bit superior, looking down at the ones who just didn't get it quite the same. Haley, maybe with good intention, became the mothering type, trying to help Samantha feel better and smarter than she was while unknowingly making her feel smaller with every intervention.

Sydney was just annoyed with Ryan's occasional incompetence and had not yet practiced any form of patient mothering. Samantha just hoped that one day her children would figure out how to be friends before they realized the hard way that it was not a guarantee.

She carefully inched forward, switching the channel to a song that would allow her to get lost in another world. "I'm Giving Up On You" filled her pearly white Lexus SUV, making her quite sure that someone somewhere existed for her to give up on, but she had no clue who it could be.

Samantha pulled into the driveway. The silence chased out the last of the mystical melody. She stared at the front of the house knowing within it were the remnants of her family's morning. Strewn across their home would be the oatmeal already solidifying on the bowl, the towel left hanging on the bedpost, the brush drawer frustratingly left open by one of them. The familiarity was both comforting and somehow so monotonous it hurt.

She sighed and stepped out of her SUV her husband had bought after she had experienced a mild midlife panic attack. She had adamantly declared the minivan to be sucking the last bits of youth out of her, leaving her a claustrophobic mess, suffocating in the mundaneness of life.

Turning thirty-eight had brought with it sudden anxiety attacks as she watched forty dangerously approaching at a rapid speed. She had overcome the last premature crisis in slightly over a week, but apparently Jacob had heard her loud and clear. Only a minute amount of guilt remained to riddle her consciousness that slipped away every time she melted into the driver's seat.

Once inside, Samantha searched her playlist until she settled on a station playing Zac Brown, allowing his words to make her feel like vacation was only a chore away. As she dumped the last of her coffee down the drain—three cups would be plenty for the day— she smiled at finding one last spot in the dish washer.

The phone rang. The caller ID listed the police department. Just the day before the police had sent out an Amber Alert, so she expected to hear a recorded voice after her hello. It was not the recording.

"May I speak with Mrs. Truax?" It was a man's voice on the other end, curt and seemingly ready to get to the point.

"This is Mrs. Truax." Immediately, she felt the weight of things to come.

"This is the Henrico County Sheriff's Department. There's been an accident."

Silence followed as the officer allowed her time to prepare for the meteor to hit its second target.

"Is Jacob all right?" her mouth uttered before her brain could even register what the officer had said.

"Your husband is at Henrico Doctor's hospital with non-life threatening injuries, broken ribs and a concussion, is what we are being told. They expect him to regain consciousness shortly," the officer said flatly.

"Oh, thank God! Thank you for telling me. I'm heading down to see him immediately. Thank you again." Samantha foolishly thought the worst they were going to face were bandages and a good deal of time healing before continuing on with their lives.

"I'm afraid there is more to the accident than Jacob's injuries, Mrs. Truax."

"Was someone else hurt? Oh my goodness, was the other driver injured?" Samantha asked, and she really did care.

She truly did, but she was still feeling the burst of relief that her husband was going to be fine, a relief so strong that it would not let someone else's pain destroy her moment.

"We believe your husband hit a woman while she was crossing Broad Street and then fled the scene. It appears he was T-boned at the next intersection after speeding away from the incident."

"Jacob? No, you have it wrong. Jacob would never do that."

"I'm sorry, Mrs. Truax, but there are witnesses that saw the accident and saw him texting behind the wheel right before the incident occurred."

"No, there has to be another explanation. Jacob would..."

"Mrs. Truax, that's the information we have at this time." Conversation over or at least her part in the conversation.

The last statements were a blur of mumbled nothingness and then the phone was silent. Charges would be filed. The future she had envisioned for so long faded away leaving only an unknown darkness.

Chapter 3

— — — — — — — — — —

Jacob

What was it that awakened him? Was it the excruciating pain on the left side of his head, the bruised feeling up his torso, or the sound of beeping machines and unfamiliar voices? His eyes were heavy and did not want to open. They struggled to stay closed. He felt they somehow knew it would be better that way, but he refused to listen to their warnings. He had to know where he was and why.

A blurred vision began to form: IVs, a nurse adjusting the bag, empty walls.

"Where am I?" he rasped out.

"You're at Henrico Doctor's Hospital, Mr. Truax. You've been in an accident," replied the young nurse.

Jacob's eyes skimmed over her, judging her lack of capabilities only by the flawless skin of her youth. She turned to him, and with seeming reluctance, made eye contact.

"Does my wife know?" his eyes pleaded. Dread and need washed over him.

"Yes, she has been contacted. I think she's on the way." The nurse paused, fiddling with a towel, and he sensed something—sympathy maybe, but something else hidden behind her eyes.

"Does she know I'm okay?"

"She's aware of your condition," she replied while adjusting the IV again.

"And what is that?" Jacob asked.

"A couple of broken ribs and a concussion. Other than that, you will most likely feel pretty sore everywhere from the jarring your body took."

"That would explain the pain up my side, I guess."

She smiled softly, as if this was part of her job requirements she was forced to perform before adding, "There are some officers here who have been waiting to speak with you."

"Now?" Jacob winced as he tried to adjust himself in the bed.

"Don't try to move." Jacob noticed her badge read Kelly as she leaned over to gently press his shoulder back toward the mattress. Her eyes once again gave a look he couldn't quite understand. "They're ready to see you as soon as you're ready."

Jacob looked over his body, assessing the damage. He decided his parts appeared intact enough to answer questions. Knowing he would never remember the events any better by waiting, he told her he was ready.

"Okay then, I'll send them in." As she headed toward the door and peered back at Jacob, he began to recognize her expression. It was the same one his mother would use when his father walked into the house after a long day at work and had learned of some childhood mess-up Jacob had managed to do at school.

Jacob thought back to the angry woman, the rain, the text, and then that moment when he realized the collision was inevitable. He wouldn't be able to tell them much about the vehicle that struck him other than the fact that it was a dark color and, from where the headlights were, he assumed it was a truck. Jacob knew the light was green. He remembered that for sure—but as the moments clicked away, he began to doubt everything.

Panic welled up inside of him as he slowly realized he could not prove it. The only other car he had paid much attention to was that of the one carrying the pissed-off woman, and from the interactions they had, he was quite sure she was not going to come to his rescue. In fact, she would most likely paint him in an unfavorable light. Maybe there was a camera? Somewhere deep within, he felt the rise of doubt again, and he swallowed the hazy memory that made him hope there wasn't a witness. Everything had happened so fast. How could anyone be sure?

As he let a myriad number of thoughts ramble through his mind, two uniformed officers walked into his room. One of them, rather large, seemed to take up the whole doorframe. The other, much younger, looked like an apprentice rather than an officer. He quickly thought, *He must hate having a partner with that presence making him feel so inferior. Or maybe he likes it, knowing he isn't very intimidating on his own.* He noticed neither of them was smiling. *You would think they were the ones who had the bad morning.* Or maybe this was a sign there wasn't a camera watching, and he would be defending himself more than he had hoped.

"Morning, officers." Jacob again tried to shift higher in the bed, letting his painful grimace settle between them.

The larger one nodded his head. "Mr. Truax," was all he said while the smaller one lingered behind him.

"Well, this wasn't the start of the day I was expecting," Jacob grumbled.

"I would hope not," the large officer retorted as he took another step toward the bed.

As silence filled the room, Jacob felt his heart rate increase. Did they notice it on the heart monitor like a makeshift lie detector? But he wasn't lying, was he? The officer, now towering over Jacob, studied him, not saying anything for a moment before continuing, but the air was changing. Jacob's heart began to slam against his chest. If he could only calm himself, if he could just go back to the moment when he knew he was innocent—but hadn't he heard of innocent people being charged just due to bad circumstances?

"I'm Officer Talbot, and this is my partner, Officer Jordan. We responded to the calls about your accident this morning." Officer Jordan nodded like a puppet in the background.

Officer Talbot paused long enough to pull a chair up next to Jacob. Somehow, being eye level did not lessen his presence in the room. "Why don't you start by telling us about your morning and how you ended up here, Mr. Truax?" He then crossed his arms and leaned back as if to say, "Impress me," and then sat silently.

Jacob shifted under the weight of Talbot's stare. The pain of his broken rib radiated through his body, making the sweat begin to form on his upper lip. "Take your time. We've got all day if you need it."

Talbot's face was rigid. No sympathy hid in his unblinking eyes. The long pauses between their responses began wearing on Jacob, and he found himself cowering into the pillow. The younger one, Officer Jordan, pulled out a pad and prepared himself for writing.

"Well, it all happened so fast. I was driving through a green light." Jacob felt the need to rub his aching forehead as the image of the accident appeared before him. "It was raining so hard that I was watching the lights carefully, so I know it was green, and then I saw two headlights. They were about at truck level, and then I woke up here."

"That matches up with the other guy's story and the witnesses' accounts." Officer Talbot remained in his position, with his pen in his hand, as if waiting for more.

"Well, that's good. Keeps things simple. So I guess that means the other driver is okay as well." Jacob's growing fear lifted. The light was green. Other people agreed. He let out the breath he didn't realize he was holding.

"Bumps and bruises, but he's not in danger," Talbot replied stone-faced.

Jacob waited for them to wrap it up but they both stood watching him. What else could they want? The stories matched up. Everyone was going to be fine. He wanted them to leave and to stop looking at him with that look.

"I guess I'll just contact my insurance today, and they can take it from here, then." Jacob looked from one officer to the next.

"It's not that simple, Mr. Truax." Talbot leaned in closer.

"No? Why not?" Jacob rubbed his forehead again. Every part of him seemed to be screaming in pain.

"You said you were watching the lights carefully," Talbot locked eyes like a predator before the pounce.

"Yes," Jacob replied as the sweat began to bead on his forehead again.

"Were all the lights green when you went through them?"

What were they trying to do? Were they seriously so short on their ticket quota for the month that they were going to track him down in the hospital for running a late yellow light? For God's sake, hadn't his morning been bad enough?

"I'll ask you again. Were all the lights green that you went through?" His voice rose only slightly for the first time.

"Are you serious, officers? I'm in a hospital bed. I have a concussion and broken ribs, and you're going to ticket me for being a little behind a yellow light? It was raining hard, and I wouldn't have been able to stop in time. I did what I thought was the safer choice." Again, he looked back and forth pleading for one of them to show understanding.

"I'm afraid you made the wrong choice, Mr. Truax."

Chapter 4

———— ———— ———— ———— ———— ———— ———— ————

Samantha

Samantha raced to the hospital and through the parking lot. Her hands were shaking; her thoughts were spiraling. She needed to calm herself. She needed a minute to stop hearing the officer's voice in her mind uttering the ugly truth. "There are witnesses... saw him texting... your husband hit a woman... fled the scene." She wasn't ready. So instead of rushing to Jacob's room, she found herself in the cafe. *Breathe,* she told herself. *Get yourself together.*

She found a quiet corner, sat, and allowed thoughts of their last family outing to flicker through her mind until the memory took over, a memory that held more significance than she had ever dreamed would be possible.

***

It was just the weekend before, yet a whole life-time ago, that the family was driving down to hike around the James River. Samantha had packed a lunch, blanket, and towels to lay out on the rocks. She had a perfect picture in her mind of the afternoon.

"I'm hungry, Mom," Ryan whined in that voice that cut to her bones.

"We're almost there, Ryan, honey. You can make it, I'm sure," encouraged Samantha in her best mommy voice.

"No, I can't. I'm really hungry."

Deep breath, Samantha told herself. "How about we listen to three songs, and if we're not there by the time we hear three songs, then you can have some crackers."

"Okay," Ryan responded in his defeated voice.

Problem solved. Samantha was feeling pretty good about her parenting, and then Jacob spoke.

"You know I'm pretty hungry too."

Samantha saw Ryan sit up straighter in the backseat ready to resume battle. Samantha glared at Jacob with fire, hoping he would sense his mistake, but then he continued.

"Could I have one of those yogurts?"

"Are you kidding me?" Samantha replied.

Jacob looked at her as if he was completely unaware of her frustration or rather her reason for it.

"What's the problem with having a little snack?" Jacob asked.

"Yay, Dad. I want some crackers, please," Ryan exclaimed.

"I give up." Samantha dug into her neatly packed picnic bag and retrieved the wanted items. Even Sydney, who had held out a bit just to do the opposite of Ryan, ended up reaching her hand in the box of crackers. Traitor.

"Can you hand me a spoon?" Jacob asked. Without thinking, Samantha handed over the spoon, and then watched as Jacob proceeded to open his yogurt and eat while driving with his knee.

"Are you kidding me!" Samantha stared in disbelief as Jacob took down the yogurt in about four bites and handed her back the container.

"No worries. I'm a pro at hands-free driving," Jacob replied with a smile.

Less than charmed, Samantha turned toward the window. If she said anything, it would be louder and uglier than she would want it to be on a day she had reserved for special memory-making. After all, it was a battle she had given up on, knowing she would lose. Instead, she let her anger simmer inside of her as she privately recalled Jacob's other reckless habits.

Too many times, Jacob would glance at the phone, always for a good reason he would say, never letting her just read the text for him or help copilot by reading the directions.

She would jokingly say, "What are you hiding on that thing? What are you so afraid I'll see?" fully trusting there was nothing.

His confidence was part of what had drawn her to him from the beginning, not to mention his strong jaw-line, full head of wavy, brown hair and hazel eyes that could make her forget the words she was trying to speak, even when she was angry. Sometimes, while he was driving, she would watch how his hands gripped the wheel and his forearm muscles moved under his toned skin, and she would picture how later that night they would be wrapped around her.

But at that moment, all that could not outweigh how annoyed she was at how his confidence and strength made her feel little. And even though it was such a small part of him, a minor character flaw that only occasionally made her forget all the things she adored about him, it became at times all that she could see.

With great effort, she allowed the moment to pass hoping to regain the image of what their day was intended to be, not knowing that the memory of his cocky smile would soon try to destroy more than a weekend outing.

When the officer first spoke that morning, Samantha was sure she had lost Jacob. He had been her world for the last fifteen years, through the sparks and butterflies, the morning sickness and sleepless nights, and finally the partnership of raising two children. She thought of Sydney and Ryan, and their tired faces as they had dragged themselves to the breakfast table. Both of them had inherited their father's brown hair and similar eye color. They made beautiful babies together. It was undeniable.

As with other couples fortunate enough to see it through, truly dependable love became the concrete that bonded the forming memories together. After all the years together she still found herself crazy in love with him between the moments of comfortable companionship. Isn't that all anyone could hope for in a relationship meant for a lifetime, moments of brilliance against an otherwise quiet backdrop? They would have their fights, but they were brief, and they both fought harder for a solution than to be right. Being at odds meant feeling unsettled. Unsettled was the first step to crashing. Crashing was not an option.

She had worked too hard to allow anything to come between them.

So many people bustled around the cafe, some with walkers, some in scrubs, some with portable oxygen tanks. They all had their own worries, their own agenda, their own reasons for being right there in that café breathing the same air as she was. Were any of them sitting there the way she was, avoiding the person they were supposed to be consoling?

Samantha's mind raced between the past and the future. For some reason, watching her spouse turn into a criminal had never even entered her mind as something she needed to fear. Job losses, heart attacks, affairs; everything had crossed her mind at least once. Even when they fought over not texting and driving or eating yogurt while driving with his knee, it was for their own safety. Why had this never been a fear? Could there not have been a sign, a crazy nightmare she described over breakfast, something that would have made her stand her ground when he waved a hand at her paranoid passenger seat comments?

Upstairs in some hospital room, probably alone, he was still here with her. He was still of this world, in regular human form, yet she was scared to see him, scared to see the new "him," the destroyed person left behind. Over and over in her mind she told herself he would just need time to heal. This day would torture him for the rest of his life, but they would survive. She would be there for him.

Samantha knew she needed to face the man who would now somehow feel like a stranger. She feared she wouldn't know how to communicate with him or worse, the anger she was feeling would be the only emotion she could express.

After ordering a coffee that would be left untouched, Samantha went back to her quiet spot in the corner. Just a moment more was all she needed. *Breathe*, she told herself, but the air came out in stuttered desperation. The dam was breaking, but she wasn't sure what emotion would come spilling out through the cracks.

The image of him cockily holding his phone as he stole glances at the road in front of him was too fresh to see beyond. Comforting him when she felt so angry would be impossible. His bullheaded nature had destroyed everything. She wanted to crawl back into her mundane life, to curl up in the dirty laundry that littered the laundry room floor. She wanted to cherish it for what it truly was, life being lived—a life she had taken for granted, and now they could lose it all.

The line between criminal and civilian, good and evil, love and hate had become irreversibly blurred, leaving her stranded in the hazy state of human imperfection. He would need to know she loved him, that she forgave him, that it would be all right. She couldn't lie yet.

A large flat screen hovered above her, only capturing her attention when a picture of a beautiful blond woman appeared smiling down on her. Samantha couldn't take her eyes off her. Barely audible over the din of bustling people, she heard the words, "...killed this morning in a hit-and-run accident. Ava Johnson was the mother of two children, ages one and three. The driver, Jacob Truax, was believed to be texting."

The coffee slid from her hands and splashed across the floor. All she could do was run. The exit lingered in front of her, as it does in nightmares, seemingly at a fixed distance. The letters blurred behind her tears as she fumbled with the door, pushed it open, and was struck with an uncommonly hot spring day—a heat that the morning rain had not chased away.

Samantha found a bench away from everything and stared over the water. The hospital shadowed the pond where two ducks swam innocently. She stared out at the willows that grew on the banks and watched the branches sway in the slight breeze. She curled her legs up to her chest and hugged her small frame, a frame not sturdy enough to tackle the world alone.

Surely, the many passersby would think she had lost a loved one, being that she sat outside the hospital. Instead, she had become the wife of a careless murderer. Jacob and she were one. If he was a criminal, then she, too, would be perceived as a criminal. And what of Sydney and Ryan? How would people treat them? Not her babies. Why,

Jacob? She asked him silently until she realized no answer was coming.

***

In and out of reality, her mind drifted until the sun cast a new shadow across her face, making her aware of the passage of time. Samantha attempted unsuccessfully to hide the puffiness of her eyes by reapplying her make-up with a flip-up mirror. On shaky legs, she began making a steady but slow progression toward the hospital entrance leading her to her husband. She was about to audition for a part that was way out of her league.

The door to his room was like a boulder, and she pushed it open with a feeble arm. Jacob lay with his face toward the window. He did not turn to see who had entered. For the first time, she realized she felt an incredible sadness for her husband and not just for herself. She walked slowly to the side of his bed and slipped her hands around his. She had always loved his hands, so masculine, so safe. Her hand used to look small and feminine next to his, which was something she had loved. Now they just appeared feeble.

He didn't look at her, but she saw his body begin to shake quietly. "I'm here, Jacob. It's going to be all right." A tear rolled down her cheek, chased by another. "I promise you we will get through this."

"I'm so sorry, Samantha. I'm so sorry." Samantha awkwardly curled up next to him, restricted by IV lines and the narrowness of the bed.

She heard herself repeating the words, "I'm here, Jacob, I'm here," until she let the sound of the staggered breathing and muffled whimpers say what words could not express.

She stayed beside him until she sensed he had fallen into a sleep that could momentarily rescue him from the nightmare of being awake and knowing, knowing that he had changed everything. She felt the rise and fall of his chest and the warmth of his body. A fractured rib, a small concussion...

Carefully, she slid off the bed, reached for her purse, and watched him as he slept. How could she stop his pain? An ache rose like a tidal wave, making her head spin. She would do anything. Suddenly, she thought of the one person who always had the impossible answers. She needed to call her sister.

Samantha dialed Haley's number, not wanting to share her tragic story with her, but somehow she knew it was Haley's as well. The phone felt like a brick in her hand as she counted down the moments with each ring, moments that seemed to hold far too much significance.

"Good morning, Bradley's Bouquets. How can I help you?"

Samantha pictured her sister behind a vase of cascading flowers, tweaking each placement to perfection. Unsurprisingly, Haley made her life beautiful even when Samantha stole the color out of it.

"Haley," Samantha uttered. "It's Jacob." She fought desperately to hold back tears, letting the silence do what silence does best sometimes, speak.

"Oh my God, Samantha, what happened?"

"Did you watch the news this morning?" Samantha asked.

"No, I rushed out the door to get here. For God's sake, Samantha, tell me! Is he all right?" A possessive feeling crept in but was quickly pushed aside. Now was not the time for that.

"He hit someone with his car. He killed her." The tears came again in choking sobs.

"Where are you? I'll come right now," Haley's voice cracked with emotions.

"I'm in the hospital parking lot. He was sleeping and I just needed some air. I can't be alone right now."

"I know. I know."

"I'll wait in my car until you get here."

"Fifteen minutes. I'm closing the shop."

The phone went dead. Samantha held onto to the steering wheel, losing all control again. When would it stop? She had only a few hours until her children would be home. It was too little time for the many tears waiting to fall.

She thought of Jacob up in his hospital bed in and out of sleep. She thought of his tired, desperate eyes and hoped he wasn't searching the room for her and finding it empty. Samantha wanted to go to him, but much like a blind man cannot force himself to see, she could not deny her inability to fix the unfixable.

When Haley arrived at the hospital, an unnerving wave of relief washed over Samantha. Haley took Samantha in her arms, forcing her to feel like the child she had never matured from, and she unwillingly cried on her shoulder.

"You need to be strong for Jacob and the kids, Samantha. Do you hear me? Cry now and then you need to be strong. I called Dad on the way here, and he's calling his lawyer. He'll be talking to you as soon as he gets some things sorted out. Your job is to be strong for them."

Samantha was being scolded, scolded for being incapable of anything of use. Why had she called Haley? She knew the answer. She was incapable. Samantha let her take her hand and walk her back to the hospital room like a child that had avoided her punishment. She stood watching as Haley went to Jacob's bedside and quietly spoke of the discussion with their father. Samantha could sense the emotions of her husband as thick as mud in the air, shame and relief—a relief that they didn't need to shoulder the nightmare alone.

When they were finished speaking, Samantha heard Jacob whisper a heart-wrenching thank you, and Haley left his side, leaving room for her to approach. Together they sat in the sterile room as nurses came and went and Jacob went in and out of sleep.

After some time, Samantha took his hand and apologized that she couldn't stay any longer because of the kids. She kissed him on his cheek and headed for the door expecting Haley to follow. Instead, she held her ground and let Samantha know she would be calling her later.

"Aren't you walking out with me?" Samantha asked.

"Bradley can cover the shop. I think I'll stay for a bit or at least until Dad gets here," Haley replied.

Samantha looked down at her watch one more time. There wasn't a choice. After one last glance at the two of them together, she walked out feeling as though she was leaving something vital behind.

Chapter 5

————————————————

Samantha

The day Samantha was born, Samantha's mom, Liz Gorman, recalled two things that were described to Samantha countless times through the years. The first was that she came out with the softest tuft of golden hair that people stopped by the nursery to admire her, then they would return with more people as if they had discovered a magical creature hidden in a tomb.

The second was that Haley, who appeared by looks and size, and according to her birth certificate to be only twenty short months older than Samantha, became a mother herself that day. She wobbled into the hospital room carrying her favorite baby doll that never seemed to leave her side, saw Samantha, and was never interested in her imitation baby again.

If Liz tried to change a diaper, Haley was there. If Liz tried to feed Samantha, Haley went to the drawer and grabbed a second spoon to take over the process. And so it continued each step of the way, each first day at school, learning to ride her first bike, pulling the first tooth. Liz, with pride, told how she sometimes felt as if she observed more than parented. Haley was an old soul ready to give her wisdom to anyone who would listen and learn, or in Samantha's case, anyone who could not avoid being subjected to it.

To have the good fortune of growing up in the Gorman home was envied by many, and for the most part, the good fortune bestowed upon both Haley and Samantha did not go unnoticed by either of them. The sweet smell of spring with the wet ground sprinkled with the perfumes of azaleas and dogwoods, was the kickoff to the many social functions Tom and Liz Gorman would host. Liz liked to say that her home glowed with nature's lanterns, flowers giving brightness to their world. Every year she painstakingly planned where each addition would be planted. Samantha observed as if her mother were an artist creating a landscape with a magical paintbrush.

When the doors opened, inside and out would glisten with perfection. Their guests would be met with their glass of wine, maybe a Ramey Sonoma Coast chardonnay, quickly followed by a tray of smoked bluefish pâté or a Christian Moreau chablis, followed by smoked salmon. Through the years, Liz had even begun to pair some appetizers with certain ales since, as much as it made her secretly cringe inside, some of her guests did not understand the meticulous effort that went into the wine and appetizer selection and would disappointingly ask for a beer instead.

As Liz effortlessly drifted throughout her home welcoming new arrivals and serving yet more drinks, the guests would take a moment to notice the dark mahogany cabinets stretching, and nearly reaching, the high ceilings. They would carry their drinks through the double-wide doors to an outdoor kitchen built of stone and adorned with a flat screen television used to show the game of the day, family night movies, or instead it might just sit quietly yet speak volumes about possibilities. On this night, only a soft background music would dance between the guests, chasing away any daytime stresses.

Even though the pool was heated, it would not tempt any of John's colleagues to dive in. Instead, the guests would mingle around it to enjoy the show of multicolored lights illuminating the fountain. It was an honor to be included in the Gorman circle of friendship and warmth, and the feelings seemed genuinely reciprocated. The blessings of wealth were only appreciated if the Gormans could shower their friends with the finest of everything they possessed.

It was John Gorman's success as a financial investor that allowed their family such pleasantries and allowed Samantha's mother, Liz, to raise Samantha and her sister while she dabbled in her own interests. Those interests led to one of the best-decorated homes in the Richmond area. Her zest for decorating soon poured into the community, making her hobby somewhat of a career of its own. Liz's talents were yet another blessing John couldn't resist showing off. He boasted to co-workers, friends, and the occasional stranger of the talents that his wife possessed.

When Samantha and Haley were younger, their nanny, a slightly heavy-set woman with an accent that hinted of British but had been watered down through the years, would have them upstairs in the bonus room playing games and watching movies while their parents entertained. Gertie was always good to them, but distant. She completed her job as a checklist. Give quick hug in front of parents, check. Help with homework and give appropriate compliments, check. Make sure they brush and floss, check.

All this was fine with Haley and Samantha, since they were not wanting for affection from their parents in ways that some of their friends were. Samantha's best friend at school, Tessa, saw her CEO father only as a silhouette in the dark that would kiss her on the forehead after she had waited groggily for his return from work. The kiss was so dependable that Tessa knew even on the nights that she could not stay awake that he had come in to say goodnight, or at least that's what she told Samantha. Stories such as Tessa's made Samantha content with the lack of affection Gertie bestowed upon them. Her parents refused to be only silhouettes in the dark.

After Gertie had them put on their most adorable, and usually matching nightgowns, brushed their teeth, and combed their hair to its silky best, they were allowed to make a quick appearance at their parents' parties. The girls would be reintroduced to less familiar friends and fretted over by the more familiar ones.

"Oh, that Samantha gets prettier every time I see her."

"How's Haley's piano coming along? She plays like an angel and so smart too. You must be so proud."

After their nightly showing concluded with a good-night kiss, Samantha would smile and hurriedly race back up the stairs, not yet comfortable with the attention she would one day learn to demand.

Haley had asked for twin beds as a young girl, an open invitation for friends. They seldom came. Samantha often found herself one of the only other occupants. Gertie tucked them in before heading out for the night, knowing they would never dare descend the stairs again until morning. Wearing matching pajamas, they would curl up, barefoot. For Samantha, their conversations were like being kissed by the sun, addictive and comforting, yet always leaving her wondering why she couldn't be the sun instead of the sunbather.

"Would you like me to teach you the piano?" Haley would ask.

Samantha felt a little wetness forming in her eyes as she thought about the many times she secretly sat on the hard, unwelcoming piano bench staring at the notes in a book that refused to speak to her. She would gently hit the keys trying to find her sound, but instead found a deafening array of gibberish, a language not fit for anyone.

"That's okay. The piano's your thing," she would reply.

"What's *your* thing, Samantha?"

Samantha thought long and hard before answering. "I'm not sure. Maybe, it's the drums." She had never actually thought about the drums, but beating on something seemed like a great idea.

She heard Haley laugh like a wind chime hit by an unexpected breeze. "You're so silly, Samantha. You look nothing like a drum player."

"What's a drum player look like?"

"I'm not sure, but I think you need a tattoo."

"Oh." The thought of needles and the unknown flashed through her young mind. "Well, I'm still deciding."

"Good night, silly Samantha."

"Good night, Haley."

***

By Samantha's ninth year, Haley, at the ripe old age of ten, held all the answers, but Samantha quickly learned that by admitting that was inviting far too much help from her well-intentioned sister.

Once Haley begged Samantha to audition for chorus with her. The week leading up to it, Samantha sang in the shower, in the back of the car to every song, to the songs that Haley played on the piano. Haley cheered her on, trying to sing just a bit softer so that Samantha's sound could be heard.

"It's going to be so fun to be in chorus together," Haley chimed on the way to the audition.

Samantha practically skipped beside Haley, her ponytail bouncing with each step.

"I can't wait. What song do you think they'll have us sing?" Samantha asked.

"I'm not sure. I wish we could choose our own the first day. I hope they have you sing 'Somewhere Over the Rainbow.' You're really good with that one."

"Thanks, Haley. You're good with that one, too." Samantha was secretly thinking that Haley was good with all of them, but she didn't want to give overwhelming compliments to a person she felt was well aware of her gifts.

The teacher had them all take a seat. Samantha began to sweat more than a girl in the fourth grade should. She could feel Haley watching her and forced herself to smile back at her.

"You'll be great," Samantha saw her sister mouth silently from a few seats over.

"Thanks, you too," Samantha replied.

One by one, the teacher called them up to belt out their tune in front of the whole group. Much to Samantha's dismay, the teacher did not choose "Somewhere Over the Rainbow," but instead chose "Happy Birthday". Everyone knew the song and had unknowingly been practicing for this moment for years.

Haley was called before Samantha, and she sang the everyday lyrics as if it were perfume wafting through the air that met your ears and mingled with the other sounds in the room making them all sound better. Samantha was proud of her sister then, yet could not deny a little envy, for she knew the words would be missing some of the magic when they came from her lips.

After about twenty children had taken their turn, Samantha heard her name. In the few moments leading up to her audition, she had begun to feel her throat dry from nerves. No matter how much she tried to swallow, nothing seemed to help

Finding Haley's reassuring face in the audience, she belted out the tune as if she were the prized guest at her best friend's party shouting the silly song in front of a large group of peers. Yes, her voice cracked several times. Yes, she felt a bit as if she was shouting, but what else should the teacher expect of a silly song being sung in front of a large group of peers by a nervous fourth grader?

The next morning, Haley and Samantha ran into the music room to see the list of kids chosen for the first cut. Samantha immediately saw Haley's name. With panicked desperation, she continued to scan for hers. When she felt Haley's hand on her shoulder, she knew she would not find it.

"I'm sorry Samantha. It was a stupid song to have us sing."

"It's okay. I really didn't want to do chorus anyway. I was just doing it because you asked me to." Samantha could feel the burn of a cry in the back of her throat.

Just then the chorus teacher came up behind them. "Mrs. Carroll," Haley pleaded, "please, let Samantha sing 'Somewhere Over the Rainbow' to you. She sings it so well. That just wasn't her song."

"I'm sorry girls, but all decisions are final. I'm very sorry, Samantha." With that she opened her door and quickly disappeared behind it into her classroom.

"I'm not coming back for the second audition. If they won't take you, then I'm not doing it either."

"I won't speak to you if you do that. I don't even like chorus. You do. I'll do something else." Samantha turned away and went to class. Haley went on to sing in the school chorus, and Samantha watched every concert with her parents. It might not have been the first time she felt the bitter taste of jealousy, but it was the moment when applauding became impossibly painful.

***

Samantha's childhood was doused with memories, almost all of them involving Haley. They were like siamese twins, but Samantha felt as if she were the defective twin. Her memory of Christmases would always involve the trips to the local nursing home to decorate and breathe life into the stagnant air with arrays of floral arrangements. At eleven, Haley, was already skilled in creating the beauty of the arrangement. Funny how Samantha could still see her proudly placing them upon tables and nightstands. She also remembered her mother carefully adjusting random, out-of-place stems behind hers. Maybe the bouquets needed it, or maybe, Samantha thought, her mother also sought out some need to control something in the path of one that could control everything.

Samantha watched from doorways and distances as the elderly inhabitants glowed when they viewed the vivid colors of the flowers and the exuberance of Haley's youthful face. Her ability to make them happy seemed to feed her.

When the nurses asked Haley to play on the piano and wheeled in residents that could no longer walk, Samantha would find a quiet corner and observe how some would stare, lost in their world, and others would clap, sometimes out of rhythm, and praise Haley between each song. She watched as her sister closed her young eyes and became one with the song her fingers created. What would it be like to have such beauty flow from her fingers? Her mother beamed with pride watching Haley, already more of an adult in her preteen body than Samantha would hope to be for a very long time.

In the far corner sat one woman not staring at Haley but looking through Samantha as if she could see her very soul. Samantha recognized her. She was the resident her mother had forced Samantha to introduce herself to earlier that day— Mrs. Bailey. When Samantha awkwardly took her hand and said, "Hello, my name is Samantha Gorman," she felt her face becoming increasingly flushed to the point she was quite sure the woman would be able to see steam rising from her pores. The woman took Samantha's hand, not with the tenderness of a loving grandmother, but with the urgency of a Catholic nun with a lesson that must be taught for the survival of mankind.

"Do not blush, girl. It is a sign of pride."

And just as quickly as the woman had taken hold of her, she dismissed her like a hopeless soul.

At Samantha's young age, there was no hope of understanding what the woman was trying to tell her with her statement. How was it a sign of pride when Samantha was sure she had nothing to be proud of and nothing to make herself feel as if she were better than anyone? She would ponder the question for many years, struggling for an answer she felt she was somehow meant to find.

Now, from across the crowded room, Mrs. Bailey once again scolded her, but this time with her eyes. What was it that the woman was trying to say? Samantha attempted to pinpoint the feeling that the woman's eyes screamed at her in almost a warning. Samantha remembered a time her mother had a friend, Mrs. Beverly, visiting when Samantha returned home with her latest math test. Another C. When her mother asked her how she did, Samantha proudly said," I got a seventy-five."

Her mother understood the triumph. She gave her a quick hug with an, "I knew you could do it." When Samantha looked over at Mrs. Beverly, she had that same expression. Samantha thought the answer was clear. It was pity.

***

When Samantha was thirteen, she sat at her vanity chair and played with the small amounts of make-up she was allowed to own. Mascara and light lip gloss were her go to's. Samantha, when she thought no one was looking, would pretend in her mind to do Covergirl commercials. She was beginning to appreciate what she saw staring back at her. In the privacy of her bathroom, she was trying to learn who she was and what she had to help her survive in a world that often made her feel defeated and small.

But in those private moments, she started to feel hope in the midst of her imaginary advertisement until she looked up and saw Haley watching her in the doorway. Hope became embarrassment. Immediately, she prepared herself for the humiliation of the conversation to come, but instead Haley just stood quietly for a moment with a look on her face, a look Samantha would never forget, it was admiration, maybe even jealousy. Samantha ignored her, and grabbed her lipgloss and began applying it slowly and evenly.

"You look beautiful, Samantha," Haley said as true and honest as words can be.

"Thank you," Samantha replied as if it were just words. But it wasn't just words. It was the moment in Samantha's life that she decided her one asset, the one thing that would give her an edge, was beauty, and from that day on she began to master how to use it to its full degree, forgetting to dig any deeper for what lay beneath. And not realizing at that delicate moment that she had clung onto a gift that would always demand to be fueled by those around her, yet, on its own, would offer little of worth in return.

Her new-found confidence made her feel invincible, and she began to want to prove to herself that she was. Samantha brewed coffee at the age of fourteen as if algebra would make more sense to her if she stayed up past midnight to solve problems that had no meaning in her life and had never made sense up to that point. Haley, after a slight knock, entered Samantha's room with her own cup of coffee, Haley hated coffee, and sat down next to her on the bed.

"I'm here if you need me."

Samantha lay on her belly staring at the textbook while faking an understanding of it. She looked up at her sister and studied her face in awe. She had such a plain face that she blended into the background. It never seemed to bother her that Samantha easily could outshine her look-wise. That trait was maybe what Samantha envied most. If someone complimented Samantha for her beauty, Haley would be smiling at her with such love that Samantha should have beamed back with the warmth Haley deserved. Instead, it became a smile that Samantha interpreted once again as more pity, and it only made her feel more angry.

Yet still, there was Haley, smiling down on her in her time of need saying, "You can count on me," without uttering a word. Haley didn't care that her beauty was the kind of beauty often overlooked. Even though Samantha didn't want to admit it to herself, it was part of what made Haley so beautiful and untouchable. Bad haircuts, acne, glasses— nothing could ruin her because she didn't count on it the way Samantha did.

"I don't need help. Thanks anyway. It's really starting to make sense."

"Are you sure?"

Samantha looked back down at her textbook, letting a blanket of blond hair drift between them.

"Yes, I'm sure."

She got a D and spent the next few months of Saturdays with a tutor.

Chapter 6

—— —— —— —— —— —— —— —— ——

Haley

Haley tucked her chiffon dress under her legs as she adjusted herself on the piano bench. Next week she would be turning thirteen, a teenager at last. Haley always took herself seriously, walking behind her mother like a shadow that sometimes stretched out larger than the source itself yet never quite feeling that she could shine with the same brilliance.

Since the girls were young, their mother always brought them to charity events, desperately wanting her girls to have the hearts of the Disney princesses they had seen a million times. It was what gave their mother the joy behind everything she did.

Haley would watch her every move— whether it be in the kitchen or the garden. Her mother would stand back and look at her accomplishments, covered in mud or flour, and see the beauty in everything. If one of her flowers didn't blossom quite right, she never gave up. She pruned and fertilized until it blended in with all the other colorful foliage. Never give up, never stop pruning, never stop smiling. It became Haley's mantra.

She had been playing the piano in front of elderly people since she was little. Haley was sure it was part of what caused her to feel just a bit older than the other children her age, forcing her to be stuck in a place between pride and awkwardness.

Once she was settled on the piano bench, she would take a minute to look out over the sea of wrinkled faces hiding their stories. Some of them still glowed with joy, and some of them watched, slumped over and defeated.

At her young age, she couldn't imagine what could crumple a person into a balled up sack of skin and bones, living only because their hearts were still beating. Haley closed out their faces by shutting her eyes as she prepared to play, allowing the feeling of the music she created to leave her fingertips and spread like a ripple across the sea of people.

Haley liked to begin with something easy to calm her nerves. The head of the nursing home, Mrs. Forsey, announced that Haley would be playing Johann Sebastian Bach, March in D major from the Anna Magdalena Notebook. The room grew quiet and Haley placed her fingers on the beginning keys.

She felt like a diver standing at the end of the diving board each time she began a concert. The audience had no idea what her capabilities would be. Would she spring from the board quickly forming into a cannon ball and shouting yahoo until she broke the surface of the water, or would her body spiral into flips before forming the perfect arrow that would enter the water without a splash astounding the onlookers?

For her it was a moment she held a secret that tasted like sugar on her tongue. Finally, she released her secret. Her fingers grazed over the keyboard like a feather blowing in the wind effortlessly. When she finished, she always had a slight urge to stand and say, "Look what I did. The one you thought nothing of. The one you didn't notice when she walked in the door," but, of course, she would never.

Haley moved onto a fun classic, Robert Schumann, "The Happy Farmer Op.68 No.10" from the *Album for the Young*. Once she felt the energy herself, she allowed herself to glance again at the audience, watching how even some of the ones that would not show the slightest smile, could not contain the desire to dance.

She craved the response like a normal child craved candy, the small movement of a foot, that had just before stood rigidly. Just once, she would have liked to see Samantha be moved, but unless it happened in the moments that Haley closed her eyes to become lost in her own music, it never happened. Not once.

Haley finished with Robert Schumann, "Knight Rupert Op. 68 No.12." Before standing to bow. Mrs. Forsey walked to the piano and put her arm around her. "Let's give Ms. Haley a big round of applause for her beautiful playing." After allowing time for the their response to dwindle down to a couple of unaware clappers, she continued. "I would like to have Mrs. Gorman and Samantha join us on stage."

Samantha walked so close to their mother that Haley thought she might like to disappear beneath her mother's skirt.

"Mrs. Gorman, thank you again for the beautiful flowers and for bringing your girls to brighten up the residence." Everyone applauded again. Mrs. Forsey turned toward Samantha. "And little Samantha, thank you for brightening up our home with your beautiful smile."

Beautiful smile? thought Haley. Samantha hadn't smiled. She didn't even want to come.

"Your parents must be so proud," Mrs. Forsey continued.

Haley could see the older women share admiring looks with each other, their eyes saying, "What a beauty." Except for the ones that didn't, the slumped-over defeated ones, the ones that maybe had some talent that never mattered enough compared to their beautiful sisters that just showed up. Samantha never had to do anything but just show up.

Most times, Haley wanted nothing more than to be that kind of big sister that was respected and loved because she was always there for the younger sibling, always willing to do anything. Haley envisioned a life-time of being able to give advice and to cheer Samantha on with whatever she did. Maybe she would even be able to teach her the piano someday.

She strived to be that sister, but as the years passed, Samantha grew distant, and the need to please began to fade. Sometimes Haley liked to pretend that Samantha was the wicked stepsister watching Haley the way that Anastasia and Drizella watched Cinderella as she stopped time by walking down the flight of stairs to her prince. For Samantha often had the look of the angry stepsisters, as if she was wishing for Haley to trip on her glass slipper and tumble down the stairway. Haley tried to push the ugly image of Samantha out of her mind, telling herself she was creating it, but sometimes it was hard to believe that.

Haley seldom allowed herself such feelings —partly because she felt that they were not very princess like to attribute such evil characteristics to one's sister, and partly because she loved Samantha and felt Samantha loved her as well. But it was hard to smile when it seemed that no matter how kind, how talented, how smart Haley was, she was never going to be the one that got to be the princess.

Chapter 7

Samantha

Samantha finished up college with a business degree and was still job searching and living at home while Haley had an apartment in the Fan District and made an unfair income selling pharmaceuticals. Her piano playing never became anything beyond something only family and friends could enjoy on holidays and the ongoing Gorman parties that both girls occasionally still made time to attend. At twenty-two, Samantha was enjoying the comforts of home again before having to start paying her own rent. The Gormans, afraid of how empty their home would feel when she did leave, gratefully opened their home to her for as long as she desired. She often wondered if it was their love for her or their lack of confidence in her that made them so willing.

With the dogwoods in full bloom, the party season began to pick up as well, and even though they could easily afford the help, making their home meticulous was something Liz needed full control over. Orders were dictated, and they worked side by side accomplishing the list of "to do's."

Samantha spent the morning shining everything from faucets to windows. When she finally finished and was sent on an errand to pick up fresh flowers from the florist's, she could not resist slipping into the nearby salon for a mani-pedi. She felt a certain excitement in the air about tonight's party that Samantha could not quite put her finger on, a secret smile that hid in the creases of her parents' lips. She lay back, letting the chair knead muscles slightly exhausted from her morning of maid service. She let the mystery half-heartedly bounce around her mind until she decided she didn't care enough to figure it out anyway.

The night finally arrived and, as usual, the aromas of the evening's *hors d'oeuvres* mingled with the clean spring air. Samantha applied her lipstick, a slight pink gloss that would only draw attention to her lips without drowning out her other features. She smiled at herself in the mirror, pleased with the outcome. For just a moment, the quiet, mysterious smiles drifted into her thoughts again, but she let them go without much thought.

Samantha came down the staircase, walking with ease in her Kate Spades, another benefit of her father's good fortune. No guests had arrived yet, but she heard voices drifting up the stairwell from the kitchen—her father's, her mother's, and Haley's.

"Dad, I appreciate it, but I feel very uncomfortable being set up with someone you work with, really, I am uncomfortable being set up in general. I'll meet someone when it's meant to be," Haley pleaded.

"Don't think of it as being set up, darling. You're just meeting a colleague of your father's. If there's no spark, then that's fine," her mother replied, trying to sound calm, but her voice held an urgency as well.

"His name's Jacob Truax. He started with our company about six months ago, a true gentleman. Always on time, always willing to work late, and apparently has some decent morals, since every girl in the office is throwing herself at him and he avoids them," her father added.

"Well, you know what that must mean," Samantha chimed in.

Disappointed looks met Samantha as she entered the kitchen. Haley looked back at her parents, disregarding the last statement.

"Well, then why do you think he would be interested in me? I'm not usually the one that the guys all go crazy over. Why don't you set him up with Samantha?" Haley pleaded again.

"There'll be other men for Samantha. I just knew after the first time I met him he was perfect for my Haley. Just wait and see," her father replied.

Samantha wondered if sounding supportive would change things. "Haley, he sounds great. Give it a chance." Meanwhile, she felt a jealous bitterness. Why couldn't she feel happy for a sister that had always been good to her?

"Okay, Samantha. But you better be there for me. Fake sick for me if I need an out. I'll pretend I need you to drive me home."

"I'm already feeling a bit ill so it won't be hard," Samantha retorted with a forced smile.

"Really, honey? Is it your stomach? Head?" Liz looked ready to run for the thermometer.

"I'm fine, Mom. I'm just messing with her."

***

The fifth ring of the doorbell set the night in motion. Jacob Truax entered Samantha's life.

She waited and watched, mingling and conversing, knowing when to listen and not speak for fear of exposing her limited knowledge, all this while sneaking peeks and sizing up the man that would change everything.

He wore a blue button-down shirt and khakis. Maybe something five other men were wearing that night, but somehow they took on a whole new form as they fell across his toned body. He had wide shoulders, and Samantha felt certain that, even if not perfect, there was an existence of six-pack abs waiting to be discovered. She silently scolded herself for drifting into waters where she had no permission to navigate. She took a small sip of her champagne, determined to remain in complete control.

Mr. Simpson, one of John's subordinates, stood next to Samantha's father and rattled on about something she couldn't care less about, possibly job prospects for her. She nodded her head and mumbled what she hoped were appropriate responses while sneaking glance after glance at Jacob.

Jacob's wavy brown hair fell perfectly and casually out of place. How could that be? His lips, she watched as they formed words she couldn't hear through the din of the crowd, but they seemed to taste the air they touched. Again, she forced herself to look away.

The next time she looked over, Jacob had made his way to another small group of men and women. She could immediately see how the ladies stood straighter as he gave his attention to their group, but mainly speaking to their husbands.

He made his rounds as if he'd done it a million times; as if being the center of attention was what he was born to be.

His confidence drew strangers to him, and Samantha tried in vain to remind herself she was not the one who was to be drawn to him.

Haley had yet to meet her possible future, and Samantha caught sight of her in the kitchen watching and smiling with their mother as though she already owned him.

Shouldn't the parents that supposedly thought of them as equals bring them both to the table for the taking? Her mind wandered to the conversations that must have gone on about her father's other daughter, the one less gifted. Was Samantha's name even mentioned before he quickly brushed the idea of her aside? Anger started to build inside of her with every thought that forced itself into her mind until something else began to form.

Samantha couldn't play the piano, converse with the pompous, over-educated population, soar through college sober and always successful, but there was something she could do. With one quick flick of the wrist, she emptied the champagne glass she had proudly resisted for a rare ten minutes of self-control, straightened her shirt and headed across the room. It was one thing she was sure of— he would notice her.

It was how it worked with Samantha. Effortlessly, she floated out into the crowd knowing he would look her way, and that's all she needed. She passed in front of him as he stood talking with an older partner and watched as his hazel eyes were diverted in her direction.

She caught his sight for only a brief moment and let her lips drift into a smile so faint he would wonder about its existence. Not until she passed him and was well on the way to the bathroom did she let her smile blossom, knowing that whatever else happened that night, he would remember her smile first.

Chapter 8

―― ―― ―― ―― ―― ―― ―― ――

Jacob

Jacob was still fairly new to the office when John Gorman threw his first office party of the year. The office was bustling with excitement on Friday. Apparently, the parties were quite the event, and a great opportunity to mingle with the higher ups in the company, including John, of course.

In the office, John was firm, demanding, but not intimidating. There was a respect for him along with the desire to please him, and that's exactly what Jacob planned to do. From the get-go, John seemed to take Jacob under his wing, grooming him for more important things. It wasn't until the Friday of the first party that Jacob began to realize that more important things might not just mean office positions.

"So I hear you're going to be an honorary guest at this weekend's party," Justin had remarked.

Justin was a good decade older than Jacob and had worked in the office long before Jacob knew what his major in college would even be. He was always friendly to Jacob, but this friendliness always seemed mixed with an air of competitiveness as well. "What are you talking about? I'm not an honorary guest," Jacob insisted.

"Oh, but I think you are mistaken young man. There is more than you know riding on tonight," Justin said with a smirk.

"Feel free to stop talking in riddles any time." Jacob shuffled a few paper on his desk, trying not to look too interested.

"Why do you think John has shown you so much attention, a young man straight out of college with all these tried and true men surrounding him? He's sizing you up to see if you're fit to meet his daughter," Justin smirked.

Jacob swiveled in his chair in order to make eye contact with Justin. It was too impossible to fake disinterest. "John has never mentioned his daughter beyond a few minor tidbits here and there. I think you're wrong."

"Not one other person in this office would agree with you." Justin paused with a cheshire cat smirk across his face. "You're a lucky man, Jacob, a lucky man." He paused again. "Unless, of course, you screw it up and then not one of us here would wish to be you." He turned and walked away, leaving Jacob with the burden of possibilities.

When he entered the Gorman home, he began to envision his future. Christmases, Sunday dinners, it was a life he had dreamed of but not just because of the money. There was a warmth contained in their walls that he wanted to be able to swim in, to call his, a warmth he had always craved.

Jacob had one brother, Brent, from his father's second wife after his mother had passed away. Once his brother was born, their attention seemed to drift to new beginnings, and Jacob became an outsider. His father eventually moved to Canada where his new wife had come from. Beyond a couple of visits a year, the relationship became distant at best. He now decided he needed to keep impressing John. He wanted what he had.

The night began with John's wife, Liz, greeting him at the door and offering him a beverage. He accepted a glass of wine, since he sensed that was what she was pushing. Not used to drinking much, he would need to be careful to keep a clear head.

As she walked away, his eyes lingered on her. Liz wore cream pants with a thin, airy blouse. Her heels clicked across their hardwood floors confidently, and her shiny, chestnut brown hair bounced enthusiastically as she asked each person she passed if she could get them anything. Jacob asked himself one thing: *If she looks like that, what treat lies in store for me in John's daughter?*

Quickly, he found Justin and began to make small business talk, letting his eyes scan the room for the daughter that could soon be his. Not until that moment did he start to feel the first pits of panic rising. What if he wasn't pleasantly surprised? What if he found it impossble to like John Gorman's daughter? He hadn't even realized how special John treated him in the office until that moment when he understood how easily it could all change.

"So it looks like I'll lose that account all due to a small bump in the market. People need to understand the long term here. That's today's problem. No one has patience," Justin rambled on while Jacob continued to scan the room. And then there she was, the most beautiful woman he had ever seen. Her blond hair glistened like a halo around her face, and he could hear her soft giggle as it danced through the air while she made her rounds. It was a sound Jacob was quite sure could make a man happy for a lifetime.

But what sold him wasn't the glowing blond hair or the sparkling blue of her eyes, but the nervous way she held her glass, the almost unnoticeable shift in her feet, as they tried to decide when they could run. Where would she run to? Where was she wishing she could be? Jacob, was sure of one thing—wherever it was, he wanted to follow. It took forever before she looked his way. It was so momentary, just a flicker in time in a much larger eternity, but nothing in his life would ever be the same, nothing could compare to the moment when a person first locks eyes with the other half, when they first realize they were missing something all along.

"Enjoying the view," Justin elbowed Jacob as he approached.

"Excuse me?" Jacob replied, trying to play dumb.

"That's Samantha. She's the younger one of John's daughters," he explained.

Jacob turned to watch her disappear down a hallway, and just as he was turning back to the crowd, he felt the hand of his boss settle on his shoulder.

"Jacob, I want you to meet my daughter, Haley. Haley, this is Jacob Truax," John announced with a certain pride in his voice.

"It's nice to meet you, Jacob. My father has told me so much about you." Haley held out her shaky hand to him.

Jacob could not resist the urge to glance back at the hallway. The other daughter was no where in sight. "It's nice to meet you as well, Haley. I've heard great things about you," his mind raced to remember the tidbits of information John had shared with him, "piano player, pharmaceutical rep, your dad is very proud." For the first time that night, Jacob had to force a smile to form on his lips.

Haley's smile beamed back. Her mousy brown hair was cut shoulder length and almost matched the color of her eyes. There was nothing wrong with her, and yet there was nothing that stood out either. Maybe, had he not seen the other daughter right before, then this moment would have been different, but only for a short time. Jacob locked eyes with John who was glowing with excitement. All Jacob dared to do was give him a smile of approval even though he knew that it was the first step to disaster.

Chapter 9

——— ——— ——— ——— ——— ——— ——— ———

Haley

Haley chose to remember their first date as amazing, the way every fairytale romance begins. And for a while, she was able to keep the memory blinders on, focusing in on only the moments that kept pace with her dreams. Jacob took her to an amazing restaurant called Book Binders. Of course, she could barely eat because the amount of adrenaline pumping through her body made it almost impossible to swallow. Not to mention, she kept picturing how each morsel of food would look once it was lodged in her teeth.

"So how long have you played the piano?" Jacob asked while smoothing the napkin on his lap.

"Well, let's put it this way. I can't remember not playing the piano," Haley laughed slightly.

"And what about your sister? Does she play as well?"

At that, Haley laughed harder. "Oh no, Samantha never took to an instrument. I did offer to teach her many times, but that girl can be a bit stubborn. There are remnants of her five-year-old personality running through her core." This time Jacob laughed.

"I'd like to hear you play sometime," Jacob said, but Haley was beginning to notice that his eyes shifted around the restaurant at each pause in the conversation. When he wasn't talking, a quiet sadness settled in his eyes. Maybe, just maybe, if she dug a little bit, Jacob would let her in, let her know what caused the darkness in his eyes.

"Do you play an instrument?" Haley asked.

"No, I was more of the athlete in school. Football mostly." Again, he glanced around the restaurant. "Did you go to many games way back when."

"Probably not as many as Samantha, but I enjoyed watching. So were you the stud quarterback?"

"No, wide receiver."

"Were you good?"

"I did all right. Not worthy of a scholarship, but then it wasn't what I was really going for either." Jacob paused for a moment. "So what were Samantha's hobbies if they weren't music?"

Haley shifted in her seat a bit, uncomfortable with the interest, once again, in her sister. "I'm sure you could guess. Cheerleader. Boys. Staying in just a bit of trouble. She's calmed down a lot since then, of course, but there's always that little spark ready to ignite."

Again Jacob laughed but this time Haley felt chills creep down her back. She should have known then, but she painted the picture of the reality she wanted to see. Haley then turned the conversation to work knowing it would not involve Samantha.

Then they went to a show at the Altria Theater. She left her hand available for the taking, but Jacob didn't take it. He remained a gentleman, opening doors, touching the small of her back to lead her in before him, walking her to her door at the end of the night. They stood under the porch light. Jacob asked what she thought of it, and she politely replied, "Well, it was interesting." He laughed just a bit before looking around, switching the weight of his body from leg to leg, noticeably uncomfortable. Yet still, Haley's heart raced as she hoped beyond hope that he would kiss her.

It was awkward for only a moment until he leaned down and their lips touched. Haley felt the softness of his lips swim throughout her body, and she savored every bit of it until she felt him move away. Slowly, she opened her eyes and looked into his. It was the first moment she saw something there that made her terrified that the sadness in his eyes reflected her.

Chapter 10

Samantha

Samantha knew the moment she had won. It was at a Starbucks, of all places. She hardly ever went there, especially alone, but she was craving quiet people-watching and an overpriced coffee. She brought her computer with her but had no intention of actually using it. It just seemed like part of the outfit of the Starbucks customer. No one would wonder about her sitting alone in a corner if she occasionally glanced down at a screen, making it appear she had a purpose. She was happy to find two empty chairs in a quiet corner but was also prepared, if necessary, to sit uncomfortably close to another patron, forcing them to drink their coffee just a bit faster if need be.

In came the regular guests; girls in colorful scarves, men in smart reading glasses, moms with strollers taking up too much room and chatting a bit too loudly about some trivial playgroup matter. She put her feet up on the adjacent chair trying to look needy of all the space next to her to assure herself there would not be a crying toddler moving in on her quiet retreat.

It had been two months since she had met Jacob at her parents' house. From what she knew, Haley had been out with him no less than four times since that evening. She felt her body tense at the idea. Each date was sealing their fate just a bit more. One date was a lunch. Not much commitment there. She had been on many lunch dates that never went anywhere. Then Jacob asked Haley to dinner. Their first real date. Samantha had to admit this was a bit more concerning. It was an upscale place too. Book Binders and a show. Samantha knew it was a date Haley must have loved, and the idea of her walking out with her arm wrapped around his was a bit sickening, to be honest. Did he walk her to the door and kiss her goodnight? She pushed the idea out of her mind. From what she gathered from her parents, the next couple of dates were dinners as well.

She was staring into nothingness wondering how to stop the relationship from escalating when a hand waved in front of her face.

"Hey, Samantha."

It was him. She had been slouching, spread out like a teenager on the family couch, eyes cast into an imbecile gawkiness, and this was how he saw her for the second time. If her smile was supposed to entrance him for months to come, then what would this do?

"What are you in such deep thought about? I was starting to question whether I remembered your face correctly."

"Oh, I was...It's great to see you again. Would you like to join me?"

"Well, I don't know. Where would you put your feet if I sat in the chair?"

"I'm sorry. I don't usually take up so much space. I was just trying to ward off the mommy train...not that I don't like kids. Well, you know, sometimes if they're not related you just don't want to…"

Jacob held up his hand to end her suffering. "I get it, really I do. So I can join you?"

"Yes, please." He took a seat on the now-available chair.

"I was wondering when I would run into you again. I guess you know I've seen Haley a few times since the party." *Four time*s, Samantha thought bitterly.

"Yea, she mentioned it to me. It seems like she had a nice time, from what she said."

"Yes, we did. Haley's a very pleasant person." He paused like he was trying to think of what he should say next. "Your dad is very proud of her. He was quite insistent that I meet her." He smiled, as if recalling an amusing conversation.

"Yes, they are proud of their Haley."

"Do I sense a little sibling rivalry going on?"

"Oh no! Haley is a great sister, really. It's just they expect certain things from her and certain things from me, and that's all there is with them. Haley's path and mine. She's going to impress the world with her talent and brains and marry a gentleman and make everyone proud."

Jacob watched her with an amused smile, and she realized how immature she must sound.

Instead of calling her out on it he just asked, "And what are their plans for you?"

"That's the thing. I don't think they have any. I will live with them, making mediocre money, until I am picked up by some handsome guy looking for a trophy wife." She realized how trophy wife must have sounded and quickly tried to cover her vanity. "Not that I think I'm a trophy wife by any means..."

"I get it."

"Do you?"

"Yes, I do. You want to be more than the little sister getting by with her looks."

Samantha lowered her eyes to her cold coffee cup, embarrassed by being seen so clearly.

"Don't be insulted when I say you would make someone a beautiful trophy wife, but I don't see you as someone that wants to be admired on a shelf her whole life."

"Exactly, but I haven't found my thing yet either."

"You will." They found themselves smiling at each other until the look became uncomfortable.

"Well, listen, I should get going, but I'm going to be giving this some thought." As he continued to speak, he wrote his number on a napkin. "Why don't you text me what your degree is in, your interests, and hobbies and I'll help you find your thing."

"Really?"

"Really. See you soon, Samantha."

"See you soon, Jacob."

Samantha watched as he made his way out the door and across the parking lot to his car. How did he, a mere stranger, expose her most vulnerable feelings just by sitting next to her, feelings she seldom shared with her closest friends? All the significant phrases from their conversation ran through her mind: beautiful trophy wife, giving her future some thought, seeing her soon. She found herself clutching the napkin to her chest praying that soon would come fast.

The following week Haley was downstairs having coffee with their mother when Samantha woke up. It was already nine o'clock when she poured her first cup and went to join them at the table.

"Morning, Sam." Her mother's usual natural energy was missing from her greeting.

"I just don't know what happened. Things were going amazingly well, and now he seems so cold. I mean he's still nice, but it's just a bit too polite."

"Did you sleep with him?" Samantha surprised herself with her question and apparently her family as well, by their look.

"No, Samantha, I didn't sleep with him. Why would you ask that?"

Samantha scrambled for an answer other than it would kill her to know that her sister had slept with the man she couldn't get out of her mind. "Well, sometimes they get what they want and…"

"Samantha!" her mother scolded.

"I seriously doubt he's the type of guy to do that, Samantha. Not to mention he works for our father, and it would be a bad career move," Haley scolded.

"Sorry, it was just a thought." She smiled into her coffee with only a slight pang of grief for her sister. "Why don't you try going on a date with someone else and see if that gets his attention?"

"I'm done with men right now. Plus, there's still the slight chance this is all in my head, and I don't want to mess it up if it is. I really like him."

Haley's mother rubbed her hand that had deserted its coffee cup. "Oh honey, I'm so sorry," Liz mumbled while shaking her head.

Samantha felt a bit angry with herself. Haley really wasn't a bad person, no matter how much easier it would be for Samantha to twist a lifetime of memories to make it appear that way. How could she let a man come between them? But it wasn't just any man. It was Jacob Truax, the man she couldn't stop thinking about, and it wasn't just about beating her sister anymore. She had a feeling about him, a feeling that was intoxicating enough for her to be just a bit more selfish than she knew was right, a feeling that he could be the one she could share a lifetime of memories with. Wasn't that feeling worth fighting for?

It was the feeling that allowed herself only hours later to text him. "My degree: business. My interests: everything. My hobbies: reading, running, anything active." Safe answers, she thought. She did have a degree in business that her father had recommended. Being interested in everything made her sound fascinated with life while assuring she wouldn't leave out his interests, and including reading without mentioning *People* magazine while getting a pedicure was also well thought out. According to her text, she had real potential.

There was about a twenty-minute pause before receiving his reply. "So you're a well-read business woman that likes to stay active and involved in many things. Sounds like someone ready to tackle the world and look good doing it."

Samantha smiled to herself, realizing he had already made her a better person than she ever thought she was capable of being. "If active means boating, maybe we could discuss this more this weekend. I've been meaning to get my boat out, but didn't have a good shipmate to take with me," Jacob suggested.

Samantha boldly replied, "It's a date."

It would be months of letting one relationship fizzle while another grew before Jacob approached Samantha's father and let him know his feelings. With a torn heart, John accepted the pain one daughter would feel so that his other daughter could feel some joy. Jacob called Samantha that weekend and, for a while, the closer they became the farther apart she grew from her sister until they reached a new level of sisterhood that would forever be slightly below friendship.

Chapter 11

Haley

Was Haley surprised to hear from Samantha the day of the accident? She had to sadly admit that yes, she was. It was a truth that tore through her because Samantha had once been the most important person in her life. Haley would have done anything for her. There was a time that Samantha would bounce behind her like a shadow, wanting to take in everything. Haley could remember mornings when, still in their nightgowns, Samantha would scoot next to her on the piano bench and quietly listen to everything Haley would play.

Samantha started to change, though. The older they became, the more distant Samantha grew, and up to that point in her life, the sting of her sister tossing their friendship to the side was the most hurtful experience she had yet to encounter.

In the beginning, when Samantha omitted Haley on her shopping excursions, Haley worked harder at keeping their friendship intact. Still, Samantha wanted distance. Haley had even wanted to attend the same college. Even if she had to go to a college that would accept Samantha, giving up an opportunity to go to a tougher school, Haley would have done it. But when Haley mentioned it to Samantha, she was met with a less than excited response.

Her whole life, Haley felt as if she should keep her talents under cover, never leaving an A test grade hanging on the refrigerator door, minimizing awards and offers, even saying no to opportunities if she felt it would drive them farther apart. Nothing mattered. Samantha was determined to shove Haley out of her life.

Haley wanted to tell Samantha, and in some way or another she felt she had, how amazing she was and how envious she was of her as well. Samantha had an eye for things, just as their mother did. She always knew the latest trends, and may even set some of them herself. She made friends so easily and knew just how to make everyone feel important. People just wanted to be near her. The world would comment first on her beauty, but Haley saw so many strengths. If only Samantha didn't hate Haley for the ones she had.

Maybe it was why Haley found her own small betrayals a little less hard on her consciousness. After all, in many ways, Samantha was the one that set the tone for what their adult relationship would be.

After Haley hung up the phone on the day of Jacob's accident, she found herself racing through the flower shop, literally almost shooing an elderly woman out the door. Her name was Edna and she came in once a week to refresh the flowers she would leave on her table. Sometimes, Haley wondered if she came in for the flowers or the conversation.

Haley enjoyed her, but then she found that most people had some endearing quality if one looked hard enough to find it. It pained Haley to see the surprised expression on Edna's face as she locked the door behind her this one time without offering her so much as a goodbye.

When she reached the hospital, she noticed that Samantha was an emotional mess, yet her blue eyes sparkled as usual, but now it was due to the tears. When Samantha had to leave to get the children, Haley considered leaving as well, but there were so few moments when she was able to see him alone. She had never believed in muses before she met Jacob. Muses, Greek goddesses that bestowed inspiration. It was clear that Jacob wasn't a Greek goddess, but he made her life have a melody, an energy that nothing had ever done before.

She loved him the first time she met him, or at least her inexperienced self believed she did, and dreaded the fact that her life would most likely be bound by those feelings. An emptiness would follow her through each relationship, each experience. Every memory would be tainted by the fact she wouldn't feel that way again, that no other man could make her feel so alive just by being near her.

Haley's husband, Bradley, had entered her life at the perfect moment. She met him buying flowers at his shop, and every week from that day forward she was given a bouquet worthy of a reception. He charmed her with his romantic gestures, wooed her with his intelligence, made her feel like a princess by giving her endless compliments and support. And lastly, he bored her to tears. Literal tears. How many nights had she let one tear after the other drift softly down her cheeks as Bradley lay sleeping next to her? More than she could count?

Each morning, Haley would wake ready to laugh a little too loudly, focus on the completely mundane, and pretend she wasn't freezing inside begging to be near the one person who had ever made her feel warm.

At times, Haley would wonder if Jacob had drifted off to some place far away, if her pain would have eventually subsided, but something told her that once a person met their muse they would be blessed or cursed for the rest of their lives. Apparently, her melody would never contain enough magic to compete with the beauty of her sister.

Chapter 12

———————————————

Jacob

Uncomfortable. That was, unfortunately, the first word he could think of when he thought of his wedding day. Samantha's father would always be a gentleman, but for so many years there was an air of disappointment. The wedding was no exception. The stiff handshake followed by, "Welcome to the family," held so many unsaid thoughts. In time, Jacob believed it would all work itself out. He loved Samantha. Her parents would just have to understand.

Jacob had tried to talk to Haley before the wedding. He wanted forgiveness for what, for not being able to love her, for causing a hole to form in their family? He knew that she was helping the florist with the arrangements. He told himself everyone would understand his wanting to stop by to see how the reception set up was coming along even though he knew of no other man who would have cared enough to go look. At first, he just stood in the doorway watching the two of them fluffing the flowers on different tables and standing back to analyze their work.

Haley had lost weight. Her small frame looked so breakable, her arms twigs, as she stood with her hands on her hips, a lock of brown hair drifting in front of her face momentarily before she pulled it behind her ear. Only by accident, did she meet his eyes for an instant, when Bradley saw Jacob in the doorway and asked, "So what do you think?"

"It's beautiful," Jacob responded without releasing her gaze. And then she was gone.

Haley walked over to Bradley and began talking in a volume too low to hear. The sadness in her eyes disappeared as she laughed quietly and brushed arms with Bradley. For just a moment, Jacob wondered if he could have loved her. He watched Bradley's eyes focus on only her, watching her as she glided to the next table, and prayed that Haley could someday find happiness, that someday she wouldn't need to fake her soft giggle when she looked into Bradley's eyes. But something told Jacob even then that Haley would be acting for a very long time. Without another word, he drifted away from the door.

At the wedding, Haley robotically went through the motions of the maid of honor, never again making eye contact with Jacob. She smiled politely at everyone and held her chin high, but Jacob would swear he physically felt her pain when she passed anywhere near him. What was he supposed to do? Force a love that wasn't there or be with her and always desire the younger sister until many years down the line when the denial crumbled, destroying everyone in its path? He did the right thing. He was honest. In time, everyone would see it was good.

Jacob noticed Haley drinking more heavily than he had ever seen. He prayed she would get through the speeches without embarrassing herself. A large part of him felt so protective of her. She was beautiful in a different way—smart, talented. Someone would love her, maybe already did. She deserved someone who would care for her deeply.

The speeches drew near. He barely listened to the best man, his college roommate, as he showed his rarely sentimental side. His attention was on Haley downing another glass of champagne. He could see Samantha watching her as well. After everyone had toasted, Haley stood and, with effort, said, "I'm not very good at speeches, so I'm going to do something I am good at." She then stumbled to the piano, glass still in hand, spilling as she went. By the time she had clumsily adjusted the mike, she had everyone's full, yet sympathetic, attention. She started by saying, "I want to sing my baby sister a song." Every word was slightly slurred, and hushed voices whispered words she wouldn't hear. "This one is by John Legend.'Things Don't Have to Change.' Right, baby sister?" Jacob glanced at Samantha and saw her mouth the word, "Right," as her eyes filled with tears.

Haley's beautiful voice could still be made out through the drunkenness, and Jacob listened in devastation as she began. Haunting words about family, and remembering, and changes rang out across the reception hall leaving everyone feeling a chill that would last the rest of the evening.

She would finish the song somberly before stumbling to the parking lot on Bradley's arm. It was several minutes before Jacob could meet eyes with Samantha. Both of them suffering, both knowing they had destroyed someone they cared for so deeply.

***

Through the years, he watched them drift apart. He watched as family functions became more awkward. He watched as Haley entered a marriage with Bradley that was mundane at best. It was a relationship suicide attempt, giving up on any hope of happiness and finalizing it with a vow to go through life as a dull and lifeless creature. As the years passed, he hoped a child would give her the love she was missing, but no child came. Her caring attitude, one of her best qualities, became colored with bitterness as she drifted into a background of nothingness. Jacob imagined Haley as a spiritless body approaching middle-age.

On Jacob and Samantha's fifth anniversary, he visited their floral shop to get Samantha flowers. Choosing between being loyal to a family business and saving Haley from any more pain was not easy, but he decided to support their business. It was this decision that started the many conversations and texts that would secretly bind him to Haley.

He stepped into the shop and saw her behind the counter adjusting some flowers, a black-and-white face amidst the vibrant colors.

When she turned to see who had entered, he saw something on her face that gave him power. It was addicting to watch her face light up, to hear energy come from a dying soul, to know he was the cause of it. In the beginning, he loved watching the hope and excitement, seeing the glow of a young girl emerge from behind the fine lines of age. Didn't he owe her that? He knew it would go nowhere, but she was a candle that deserved a flame even if it was a small one. It was on that day, Jacob knew he would always answer her texts and phone calls, even if Samantha could never know.

Chapter 13

——— ——— ——— ——— ——— ——— ——— ———

Samantha

After leaving the hospital, Samantha drove home down her road, which was lined with fully blossomed pear trees. On other days, she noticed how the trees seemed to create a child's imaginary world of popcorn and dreams. The petals drifted through the air, leaving in their trail a less-than-fairytale-like smell. Nonetheless, she found it beautiful. She pulled into her driveway noticing the well-manicured lawn, the trimmed bushes, the hyacinths peeking their heads up through the soil to check for spring. Had she noticed how beautiful it was the day before when Jacob spent his Sunday cutting paths through the thickening spring grass?

The children would walk home in the afternoon, since time was not as much of an essence. She always met them at the corner, minimizing the time they were out of an adult's sight, even if they were unaware of her protectiveness. She finished picking up the breakfast dishes that had been left behind after the phone call and went to wash her tear-streaked face before reapplying the makeup she hoped would cover so much. Who would know? She hoped people would be respectful enough not to say anything to her about the subject, but there were always the ones, like Suzanne Walker, who would pry into everyone's business by trying to be sympathetic. Samantha would avoid her at all cost.

When she reached the corner, she stood a safe distance from the crowd, sunglasses covering the puffiness around her eyes that her make-up could not conceal. She saw Sydney first, walking with her friends like the queen of the crowd, commanding their attention with her charismatic conversation.

Ryan cut through the grass behind them to catch up but was quickly corrected by the crossing guard and had to backtrack to the sidewalk. His stomping could not go unnoticed by even the less observant parent, but just in case, the tossed, then kicked, lunchbox, would let everyone know he did not agree with the sidewalk rule. Somehow, while Samantha stood watching her "easy" child rebel, she did not hear the approaching footsteps.

"Hi, Samantha. How's everything going?" Suzanne chimed with a knowing look.

Go screw yourself, was all Samantha could think to say for the first few seconds, but she did not give Suzanne the gratification of letting the words leave her mouth. "Fine. How's everything with you?"

"Oh you know, typical day, laundry, the gym, more laundry." Suzanne allowed for a small pause before continuing. "Are you sure everything is okay? I mean...it's just that I was watching..."

"Excuse me, Suzanne. I'm kind of in a hurry to get the kids home today." Sydney continued to walk past Samantha with hardly a sideways glance. "Ryan, let's pick up the pace, honey."

With a burst of energy, Ryan took the final distance in strides and ended with a less-than-graceful jump, landing dangerously close to Samantha's foot. A desperate agitation began to creep into her crazed mind until his tiny hand grabbed onto hers. It amazed her how much that innocent hand could calm her.

Stepping into her home and shutting away the outside world was the first step towards the denial phase. She would try to create an environment for both her and her children to live in for as long as they would need. With the smile she had somehow pasted on her face, she asked Sydney and Ryan if they would like their favorite snack and started pulling out the celery, peanut butter, and raisins while not actually listening for their answer.

"Can I put the ants on the log?" Ryan eagerly asked.

"I can put my own ants on, Ryan. I don't want your dirty hands all over my raisins," Sydney retorted.

"My hands aren't dirty!" Ryan yelled as he simultaneously glanced down questionably at them before wiping them off on his jeans.

"How about you both wash your hands, and then you can both put your own ants on your own logs," Samantha suggested.

Ryan was off and running, smacking the pillow off the couch on the way while making a sound from Star Wars or from whatever battle scene that was going on in his head at the time. Samantha numbly watched without the energy to be amused or angry, two emotions that typically took turns arising from almost identical situations.

As they sat down at the table, Samantha quieted their squabble with only the unexpected concern emanating from her voice.

"Kids, I have some bad news to share."

Ryan stared at Samantha imploringly, a small drop of sticky peanut butter hanging off his lip, while Sydney pushed her glasses up on her nose. Sydney, being the old soul, as she was, looked as if she had just entered a somber board meeting and was ready to start taking notes.

"Your daddy has been in a car accident, but he's going to be okay."

"Oh man, he's going to be so mad he wrecked his car. That sucks…"

Sydney scolded, "Ryan, it's not about the car!"

Ryan gasped. " Is Daddy hurt? Where is he now?"

"Well, like I said, Daddy is going to be okay, but yes, Daddy did get a little hurt."

Ryan's face fell into a pale shock, a shock of a young boy realizing a superhero can bruise.

"Can we see him?" Sydney asked. A tear began to trickle down Sydney's cheek, and Ryan started to squirm in his chair as if he might need to take on another couch cushion.

"Not tonight. He's very tired and is resting at the hospital where they can give him medicines to feel better. But I promise you will see him soon."

Sydney, in rare form, came over and wrapped her arms around her mother's shoulder and slid herself onto her lap.

Be strong, Samantha reminded herself, *be strong.*

"There's more I need to tell you." Samantha continued.

Sydney raised her head and studied her mother's eyes, so young and still aware that she might not get the answers she desired.

"It was raining so hard this morning, remember? It's what caused the man to hit Daddy, but before that, the policemen are saying that Daddy accidentally hit a woman while she tried to cross the street, and she was very hurt." Her voice began to crack. She took a big swallow of water to calm the sob trying to surface.

Samantha begged the universe to let her stop there, but she knew they would hear about it at school. They had to hear from her first. How could she word it? How could she be honest without blaming the man they loved? It was all too impossible

"Unfortunately, some people think it may have been your daddy's fault. But you both saw how hard it was raining this morning. Daddy couldn't see her."

She decided not to mention the texting accusation. She didn't even really know if that had anything to do with it.

"Daddy, is very, very sad. He would never hurt anybody. We all know that, but..." But what? A million buts and no answers as to why.

"Is Daddy in trouble?" Sydney looked as if she could crumble at any moment.

"I'm not sure, Sydney. People will have to look at the accident very closely before they can decide. We just have to be strong right now. Are you strong? Ryan, let me see your muscle."

Ryan pumped his arm with much less enthusiasm than usual. Samantha imitated him with the best show of strength she could muster.

"So how about you, Sydney? Can I see your muscle?"

Sydney raised her limp arm before sliding off her mother's lap. Samantha gave her backside a light tap and said, "How 'bout we get done that annoying homework of yours, order a pizza and a movie and stay up a bit too late tonight. We can all sleep in tomorrow and play a little hooky."

Ryan jumped out of his chair and motioned an emphatic "Yes!" with his arm.

They both grabbed their backpacks and disappeared into their rooms, leaving Samantha to stare mindlessly at the half-eaten ants on a log strewn across the table. She wondered how long she could get away with staying curled up on the couch with a child tucked under each arm, protecting them from a world that wanted to destroy the man they adored. How long before the world came knocking at their door demanding they look it straight in the eye just so it could knock them all down?

After two days in the hospital, Jacob was cleared to finish his recovery at home. Sydney and Ryan cautiously stepped into the room, not knowing what they would find. Their father embraced both of them, letting his face cringe with both emotional and physical pain as he tried his best smile. Only when they were safely tucked in his arms did he let the darkness behind his smile surface.

"Oh Daddy, I'm so glad you're feeling better," Sydney almost cried. Ryan squirmed out of the hug and bounced up on the side of the bed.

"Easy, Ryan. Your daddy still has some healing to do," Samantha gently reminded him.

"This place smells funny." Ryan said while scrunching his nose.

"Ryan!" Sydney reprimanded him for no other reason than to correct him.

"Well, it does. It smells like sick people," Ryan replied.

"That's because people are sick here, brainless," Sydney snorted.

"Okay, that's enough. Let's just get your daddy home before we insult the whole hospital."

Excited talk about school filled the car on the way home, what so-and-so said in the cafeteria, the A Sydney got on her math test, and how fast Ryan ran the track in gym. When that excitement dwindled, Samantha announced it would be taco night for dinner. It was Ryan's favorite, so Jacob always echoed his excitement. When the conversation found pace again, Samantha stared at the road ahead in silence, letting their voices fill the uncomfortable distance forming between Jacob and herself.

It wasn't until many hours later that they were able to settle into their bed and, for the first time, approach the subject while in the security of their blankets. Face to face, holding their pillows and searching each other's eyes, Samantha began. "What's going to happen? What's the next step?"

"The police had blood drawn at the hospital. I guess they have to rule out drugs and alcohol even though there wasn't any evidence of any at the time of the accident. From what they told me, they'll be in touch with me in a couple of weeks after all the results come back."

"Well, you weren't drinking. What else are they waiting for?"

"They'll look at the phone records and the blackbox on the airbag."

"Blackbox? I didn't even know they existed."

"They're called event data recorders, I guess. I didn't know about them either."

"What will it tell them?"

"When they cross-check it with my phone records they'll see I had just received a text right before the airbag went off." They let the ugly truth settle between them even before the words were spoken. "I'm so sorry." Jacob paused before continuing. "Samantha, your dad texted to see if I was going to be on time for the meeting. I was just deciding what to respond. I might have typed three words tops." A tear trickled down his cheek. "I remember feeling a bump. I would have stopped. I swear, I would have stopped if I knew."

"I know, Jacob. We just have to convince them." Samantha rolled over, unable to allow him to see her tears, and moved as close to him as she could. She felt his arms reach around her, and she held them to make sure he wouldn't move. They both quietly cried, together and alone at the same time, as they let sleep creep in to ease the pain.

***

The rest of the week they spent trying to make everything as normal as possible for Sydney and Ryan. They couldn't stop the rumors from circulating around the school about their daddy going to jail. Samantha had tried to prepare herself for the moment when they would be forced to address it. Sydney dropped her backpack and ran to her father after only two days in the classroom.

"Daddy, Kaitlin said you're going to jail because the woman you hit died, and they said you just drove away. Are you really going to jail?"

She looked feverish as she searched his face for answers. He came down to his knees and took hold of her arms. Ryan stood with one hand still holding a strap of his bag, his mouth open, unable to make sense of what he was hearing.

"Listen, Sydney, I promise you I would have stopped if I knew I had hit her. I didn't see her. I didn't know."

"So you are going to jail," Sydney began to earnestly cry.

He tried to regain his composure as he wrapped his arms around her. "No one knows anything for sure, but I promise you that whatever happens, everything will be okay. If I end up having to spend some time in jail just think of it as a long business trip, and I promise you I will come back home as soon as possible."

"But Daddy..." There was nothing left to say. She crumbled in her father's arms, and Ryan quietly joined them in their huddle.

Ryan looked up from the embrace as a new thought came to him. "But Daddy, aren't there murderers in jail? Are they going to hurt you?"

"There are many different kinds of prisons, kids," Samantha quickly added. "The really bad people go to a big jail, and the good people that make mistakes go to a little prison where they are safe." Samantha knew this was a half-truth, but it was one she needed to believe as well. "Plus, nothing is for sure yet. We just have to be strong for each other right now, and maybe Daddy won't have to go anywhere."

"Do you think that will happen, Daddy? Do you think you will get to stay home?" Sydney pleaded.

"I hope so, Sydney. How about I help you get through your homework and take a break from worrying about all that." Sydney had never needed help with her homework, but Samantha knew she would be soaking in every moment she could with him even if it meant faking neediness. Sydney managed to get out a shaky "okay" and began digging through her backpack until she remembered what it was she was digging for.

Nighttime approached without permission once again. The need for closeness the night before had transformed into an impossible need for distance. Mood swings Samantha would become accustomed to throughout the months to come. Their king-sized bed became an ocean with an impossible distance between them. He needed her, and she knew it, but instead of reaching out across the sea of pain she stared into the darkening space of her room. With new insight, Samantha studied everything as if it had not been right in front of her every day, each piece of furniture holding a piece of a tender past and an unsure future. Even the bedroom set was a marker of success, a step in their lives together.

For so many years, too many, they had slept on their eclectic set that had been pieced together through time, his dresser attempting to accent her bed frame. She told herself for years that it was special because it was a piece of both of them had brought together. When he finally settled into his management position, they celebrated. She thought of the two of them, ten years younger, going from mattress to mattress like children, sneaking in giggling pillow talk whenever they thought they were alone. Where would she be sleeping when this was all over? Would she still have this home? This bed? Could she handle being alone? Then a wave of other thoughts crashed into her mind. What awful nightmare of a bed would Jacob be sleeping in, alone, or worse, with a dangerous criminal in the bed next to him?

Samantha rolled over and stared at Jacob's back, watching the rise and fall of his breaths.

"I love you, Jacob," she whispered into the night, but he was already fast asleep.

Chapter 14

━━ ━━ ━━ ━━ ━━ ━━ ━━ ━━ ━━

Samantha

The second weekend Jacob was home from the hospital, Haley called to ask if she and her husband, Bradley, could bring dinner over. The idea of not cooking and not having to sit in the stress-filled air without distraction sounded refreshing, so Samantha accepted her offer. The doorbell rang promptly at six o'clock, and they opened it as a family, all so eager for the interruption of their reality. Haley stood next to Bradley, she with a beautiful potted bouquet of hyacinths, and he with a steaming hot dish of something yet to be discovered.

Kisses were given on cheeks as the gifts kept them from embracing. They made their way to the kitchen. The light that showered through the many kitchen windows danced along the countertops, making the hyacinths even more cheerful. Both children crawled up on the bar stools to stick their noses into the bouquet that exuded the sweet scents of spring and hope.

"What beautiful flowers, Haley. I've always loved hyacinths." Samantha now found the time to wrap her arm awkwardly around her sister.

"One of the nice perks of owning a flower shop, I can always get my hand on a last-minute gift." She smiled at her sister as she returned the embrace. "These actually hold some meaning. They are meant to tell you that I'll be praying for you. They can also mean sincerity and constancy, but we'll stick with I'll pray for you."

Samantha felt a surprising urge to break down but instead choked out a whispered thank you. "So what is the meal that smells so wonderful?"

"That, my sister, is a very garlicky chicken casserole," Haley replied while removing the lid.

"Let me guess—we're warding off evil spirits," Samantha replied.

"Actually no, garlic symbolizes courage and strength, but it makes for a very unappealing bouquet. That's why I decided to hide it in a casserole," answered Haley.

Sincerely touched by Haley's ability to put old feelings aside, Samantha again uttered a beaten thank you and gravitated towards the wine they had breathing on the counter. "Malbec good with you?"

"Malbec is great with me."

The evening spun magic in an otherwise dark existence. After dinner, Haley even shared a few songs on their keyboard, not the grand piano she was used to, but no one in their home had proven worthy of investing in anything larger. After dinner, Samantha took Ryan and Sydney upstairs to prepare them for bed, leaving the other adults to clean up the remaining dinner dishes. She held each child a minute longer than usual and kissed both their eyes goodnight the way she had for years.

Sydney still allowed her this moment even though she occasionally rolled her eyes and acted annoyed; Samantha suspected she secretly liked their ritual.

She came down the stairs and found Jacob and Haley alone in the kitchen talking quietly while drying dishes. Samantha paused, trying to hear what conversation they shared when no one was listening, but the words were not audible.

She could see the consoling look on Haley's face and watched as she set the glass in its proper place and let her hand find Jacob's shoulder to gently rub away the pain.

It surprised her when Jacob met her rub with a quick hug, leaving Samantha feeling like an intruder in her own home with her own family. She wanted to run back up the stairs and pretend she had not been witness to their moment, but Bradley came up behind her.

"Are you waiting until they have it all cleaned before you go in?" Bradley chimed.

Samantha turned quickly, embarrassed to face him, struggling to find the right words to hide her thoughts. "Well, I see you managed to wander off at a convenient moment yourself." She smiled lightly at him, but could not help watching as Haley let a little distance grow between her and Jacob.

"Touché," Bradley said.

"Would you like me to get some cards out?" Samantha offered.

"Well, I'm not ready to run off yet. There's still wine in the bottle," Haley replied eagerly.

I'm sure you're not, Samantha thought as she headed for the game closet.

The four adults sat around the table boy, girl, boy, girl making Jacob the centerpiece between Haley and Samantha. Haley suggested the game Bullshit. Each time Jacob played his cards, Haley would scream, "Bullshit," smiling at Jacob like a teenager in love, playfully flirting. Didn't Bradley see it? Didn't Jacob see it?

At one point, Samantha held all four Jacks when the turn to lay Jacks fell on Jacob. She studied his face as he laid his card saying "one Jack." She knew it was a lie, yet the words left his lips so easily. When she called BS on him, a slight smirk formed at the corners of his mouth as he casually picked up the stack of cards knowing he had been caught. Haley laughed loudly, pushing Jacob's shoulder gently while calling out, "Caught." Samantha wanted to laugh with her, but somewhere deep inside a sourness was growing. It wasn't funny, BS was never funny.

Samantha clung to her wine glass like a life preserver every time Haley found another opportunity to touch Jacob.

The games continued until the wine took them from warm and relaxed to fuzzy and exhausted. It was Haley that suggested they stay the night since they had all drunk too much to get behind the wheel. A slightly uncomfortable agreement was uttered, and the guest room prepared. With groggy heads, they all fell into a drunken, restless sleep.

As often happened to Samantha, she woke up around three o'clock to the wine insomnia that allowed a million thoughts to pass through her mind. One of them was the thoughtfulness of the flowers that lit up her kitchen. She got up and poured herself a tall glass of water. Due to the inability to rest, she decided to research the meaning of the hyacinth on her own. All that her sister had said was true, but there was more to the hyacinth than a message of prayer.

According to legend, the hyacinth got its name from a young Greek boy named Hyakinthos. Apparently, the sun god Apollo and the god of the west wind, Zephyr, adored Hyakinthos and would often compete for his attention. That is until the day that Apollo was teaching Hyakinthos how to throw a discus. This action put Zephyr into a jealous rage, forcing her to blow the discus back so hard that it struck Hyakinthos in the head and killed him. A flower grew from his blood, and Apollo named it hyacinth in honor of him.

Samantha stared at the screen wondering if her sister had any idea that she had given her a flower that sprung from such jealousy it could only lead to disaster. She shut off the computer and went back to a bed that would offer no sleep.

Chapter 15

Samantha

On Monday, Jacob and Samantha met the lawyer her father had graciously selected. Samantha stared out over the small Richmond city horizon, as Jacob paid twenty-five-thousand-dollar flat-rate, as if not seeing the transaction would make it less real.

Mr. Sinclair then explained what they should expect in the weeks and months leading up to the trial. First would be the arraignment, or bond hearing, where the judge would set bond. This would happen within seventy-hours of arrest. Next would be preliminary hearing within thirty days of the arrest. This would be a sort of mini trial where the judge would decide if there was enough evidence for the case to move on to the circuit court, and then the trial, which he expected would have to happen. Mr. Sinclair went on to explain that he had a right to a speedy trial, meaning that Jacob's trial must happen within six months unless they waived that right. On Mr. Sinclair's urging, Jacob would waive his right, giving more time for Mr. Sinclair to build Jacob's case. He would also be pleading not guilty.

The conversation made Samantha feel ill.

First, waiving his right to a speedy trial made her feel it was admitting it would be a tough trial or even worse, that Mr. Sinclair thought he would be found guilty and therefore was just biding time for Jacob. Admittedly, Samantha could not presume such things in matters she didn't understand, but she couldn't stop her thoughts from barreling through her mind.

She also had to trust Mr. Sinclair when he said Jacob should plead not guilty even if it could hurt him in the end. If he pled guilty, he would get about five years in prison, but if he went to trial and lost, it could be eight to ten years. Her mind circled back to the first thought. If he was saying waive your right to a speedy trial, then it must mean he thought Jacob should have more time with his family while he was allowed. She had to trust their lawyer. He understood it so much better than either of them.

She forced herself to sit back quietly and let them make the decisions. Samantha felt that sinking feeling like the one she remembered from sitting in the back row of her college statistics class. She should listen, she should understand, but instead it was foreign gibberish, leaving her dreading the exam.

It was Jacob's idea to stop at the Strawberry Hill Cafe on the way home. It had been one of their favorite stops whenever they were near the Fan District, and Samantha knew he must be wanting to take in all he could in the short time allowed. They walked hand in hand down the quiet, tree-lined streets. She felt a tranquility to the area that not many places equaled, quiet in the middle of a still-active and sought-after area. She tried to push everything else out of her mind and focus on the feel of Jacob's hand and the warm breeze that encircled them.

During lunch, she could not resist bringing up Haley's name and studying his face like a detective looking for signs indicating regret or guilt. Even though she felt silly, the hyacinth had put her on edge.

"Wasn't it sweet that Haley and Bradley brought dinner over," Samantha asked while straightening the napkin on her lap.

"Sure. Could you pass the ketchup?" Jacob asked with an outstretched hand.

Samantha found the ketchup and slid it to him without ever letting her eyes wander from him.

"Bradley's a bit of a... I don't know how to put it. I guess he's just flat. Don't you think?" Jacob asked.

"He seems to make her happy," Samantha desperately offered.

"You think? I never get that impression from either of them. They just seem stiff together." Jacob took a large bite of his burger, forcing the abundant amount of ketchup to run onto his hand. He grabbed for a napkin to clean himself. He always used too many condiments, and it always ended up oozing grotesquely. Samantha had always found this to be yet another pet peeve Jacob never bothered to correct. She once again found that his stubbornness forced a bitterness to simmer within her.

"She never complains to me," Samantha said, swallowing her irritation.

"Would she? I mean you two have been nothing more than cordial to each other ever since I've known you. I'm not sure she would confide in you." Jacob put the saturated napkin to the side and reached for another. Samantha glared at it as if it were the very epitome of the problems between them.

"And what kind of person do you see Haley with if it's not Bradley?" She folded her hands on the table and waited for his answer.

Jacob paused, Samantha was sure to pretend to think even though she believed it was something he had already thought about many times before. Hadn't they even discussed it before? She could remember nights when they had "what if" conversations. What would their relationships be like if Jacob and Samantha could have found the perfect man for her and forced their paths to cross? What if, in some way, they could have given her the relationship she was dreaming of since the day Jacob left Haley for Samantha? What if they could stop feeling so guilty?

Jacob stopped eating. "I don't know. I just always had the impression that she had more to her than that. What happened to her music, her career?"

"Maybe it's just because they never ended up with children," Samantha offered.

Jacob appeared to think for a moment while dipping a fry in his ketchup. "That's probably it. It's a shame. She would be a great mom."

Every compliment cut Samantha, making her feel like an immature teenager. She hated herself for it, especially since she agreed. Haley would have been an amazing mother.

"Aren't you going to eat?" he asked.

Samantha had not even noticed that her plate lay untouched. The day's events had left her stomach in a knot, and she feared any food could be violently rejected.

"I think I'll just have mine boxed. I'm really not in the mood to eat."

Jacob stopped eating mid-fry and pushed his meal away, as if he was suddenly aware once again of the pain he had caused. He stared at his wife and Samantha could see the struggle on his face as he appeared to contemplate the correct words. A heaviness clouded his face as he began searching the restaurant for their waitress and waving her over as soon as she was spotted. "Let's get out of here," he urged.

"Sounds great."

The next week passed colorless and distorted. Each day Jacob and Samantha walked the kids to school, giving only the casual wave to the other parents. Each day they prayed that the police car, the one that would surely come as soon as they felt they had enough evidence to formally arrest him, would choose to do so before their children returned home. They begged the heavens that Sydney and Ryan wouldn't be witness to the arrest. The heavens listened.

The police pulled in front of their house on a Thursday, and the whole hellish process began.

Jacob grabbed hold of his wife and held her shaking body, trying to hold back the sobs that wanted to surface. The doorbell ended their embrace. Samantha invited them in with a hand gesture and watched as if she were reaching the top of a giant roller-coaster. She was about to lose all control of everything that was going to happen in her life.

"Jacob Truax, you are under arrest for vehicular manslaughter. You have the right to remain silent," the officer stated coldly.

Samantha's head began to swim. Unknowingly, she leaned back against the wall and continued to watch in horror as the reality of the situation took hold.

"Anything you say or do may be used against you in a court of law," he continued.

They began slipping the handcuffs on him, and Samantha gazed out the window, thankful that no one was around to witness Jacob's nightmare. In the background, the words continued to be rambled off by officers who had no idea what a good man they were restraining. Cuffing the arms that should be embracing their children and touching her face the way he always did before he kissed her. She stopped watching but heard Jacob once again say, "I'm sorry, Samantha," before the door closed behind them. They walked down their driveway. Each step making her husband shrink to a mere fragment of his former self until he disappeared behind the police car door. She watched them drive away and then sat for an immeasurable amount of time trying to decide how to move forward.

Chapter 16

————————————————

Haley

She should call her sister. Samantha may even be wondering why she had not called since the other night had been so pleasant, the four of them together. Haley quickly grabbed the phone and dialed the number before she could change her mind. The phone began to ring, and her mind drifted, as it had all morning, to every moment she had spent with Jacob—every two-second conversation that she would analyze for hours afterward, every expression she tried to freeze in her mind as if they held a secret for her to uncover.

One part of her saw the truth, which was that Jacob was only a friendly brother-in-law. It was Haley's other desperate half that could be more convincing, though. The other half saw a smile meant just for her, felt the half hug she begged the stars meant that he was holding something back and not just appeasing her. He could have loved her. Somewhere deep in her heart, she knew he would have loved her. Every emptiness she felt would be nonexistent if it weren't for Samantha's stepping in too soon, before she had time to completely hold his heart.

She thought back to the moment in the hospital when Samantha left them alone. Haley touched his warm, strong hand to reassure him she would be there, but he only turned toward the window and asked to be alone. She told herself that it was not against her. He didn't even want Samantha there. Haley had slid out of the door like a rejected child and saw Samantha rounding the corner. She let Samantha get some distance. There was no reason for Samantha to know how quickly she followed behind.

How could it be that she felt so much electricity from a man that felt nothing back? It couldn't be. If scientifically she was drawn to him like a flower to the sun, didn't it make sense that he felt it too, but she pushed the thought from her mind.

Did he ever think about their first kiss? They had gone to dinner at Book Binders and then for a show. She couldn't remember the show because it had been boring, but a small price to pay for his company.

They had walked hand in hand. He did hold her hand right? Haley remembered him holding her hand. She remembered him laughing, a laugh that rang through the night air like music. He must have been having a good time. They stared at each other only moments until he softly drew her face to his. He had to have felt it. Haley remembered it perfectly. She was sure of it. She wanted to scream to the universe. How could he not have felt it!

Her world had changed, and the future appeared. She floated into the house with visions of memories yet to be formed, children, dates, holidays, vacations. Everything made sense. But even as she fought with fate, there was a nagging feeling inside of her that there were signs she was choosing to forget, would continue to choose to forget. Memories had a way of shifting and reforming, but how could she give up the moments in her mind that were so addictive. She had to keep coming back to them, yet each time they became more sweet, more overpowering.

For a short time, a painfully short time, the happiness continued, and then one night as they were walking to her door a quiet fell upon them. "Do you want to come in?" she asked with the most seductive expression she was capable of and was met with a half-smile and a, "Maybe next time."

"Are you sure?"

"Yes, I'm sure. Sorry, Haley." He turned back toward the car, and she saw that even his half smile had already faded before his face was turned from her. She wondered what was on his mind, what thought was distracting him from what she tried desperately to tell him was a sure thing. She pushed his distracted mood to the back of her mind and told herself that time would only make the moment more special. But in a few short months, she found out who was causing his distracted mood, and Haley's world collapsed around her.

She was brought back to reality as the sound of the answering machine kicked on. Probably better. She placed the phone back in the holder and busied herself with the flowers that had not fit into a bouquet to her liking. After studying it for a moment, wondering about the best way to organize them, she opened the garbage and tossed them.

Chapter 17

Samantha

Samantha stood in front of her full-length mirror trying to button her blouse with hands that refused to obey her commands. Her shaking fingers struggled with each minute task until the last one was fastened, and she looked up at her blotchy face. Again this outfit did not seem right, but as she glanced over at the pile of rejected garments thrown onto her bed, she knew nothing would be. Mindlessly, she made her way to her bathroom sink where she clumsily pulled out her chair and knocked her makeup case onto the floor. It was hopeless.

The phone began to ring incessantly, like a nagging background noise that would not go away. She ignored it until it quieted.

The judge had been given all of the facts about Jacob and his case. Today at the arraignment, Jacob would be given his bond amount and enter his plea of not guilty. They were told to expect it to be up to one hundred thousand dollars. This was an amount Jacob and Samantha could not just pull out of their bank account. Samantha's father offered to help financially, but they all knew this was an amount too large to ask for and Jacob and Samantha, in one of their many late night discussions, had agreed to keep her parents out of the financial end as much as possible.

What Samantha didn't know was that since she could not pay the amount in cash, she needed to see a bail agent who would write a security bond, but it also meant that the agent would keep the bail bond premium—and in their case, the amount could be ten thousand dollars. After that, she would be able to bring Jacob back home to their family to await his trial. Ten thousand dollars—it wouldn't destroy them, but it would hurt. Just the thought of it made bile rise in her throat. She pushed it out of her mind. She had to think of Jacob. She couldn't be angry right now.

The doorbell rang, and Samantha hurried down the stairs with shoes in hand. Her mother stood with the same blotchy face on the doorstep. They didn't need to speak. Samantha let herself get lost in her embrace for a moment and take in the smells of her mother, always graciously pampered and sprinkled with Aqua Di Gioia.

"You're here early," Samantha said as she slowly released her arms.

"I know. I thought I would make up a special snack for the kids. Think they'll like banana nut muffins? They're just going to be from the box, I'm afraid."

"They'll love them, and they'll love having you here. This is taking a lot out of them. I can see the stress on their faces." She felt the unwelcome pounding of tears at the back of her eyes. "Thanks for watching them today. It's good to know they'll be with you."

"I'm happy to come. You know that, right?" Liz stared at her daughter as if searching for the right words. "You will get through this, Samantha. Your family is here for you. We'll do whatever we need to for you." Liz held Samantha's hands as she declared her loyalty.

Samantha looked away as she mumbled, "I know." Although she didn't know that they would make it through it. What did that even mean anyway? That in ten years she would still be living. *Oh look, I made it through it. I didn't jump off a bridge.* Every consoling remark made her angry but she knew, in people's defense, there weren't any correct words.

Samantha reached the courthouse faster than she had wanted. As she crossed the street, she saw her father nervously fixing his tie and standing next to Mr. Sinclair, the man she would be entrusting her future to in the coming months. As she approached, she saw them both stand a bit taller, all fidgeting put to an end for the time. A hand reached out to her that she had no choice but to grab.

"Hello, Mrs. Truax. It's nice to see you again."

"Hello. You can just call me Samantha. Please just call me Samantha." Samantha found herself wiping her hand on her skirt after releasing his hand, not quite sure what she was wiping off.

Her father took the first available moment to take her in his arms, where she allowed herself a moment of reprieve.

"Are we ready?" Mr. Sinclair politely interrupted.

Samantha straightened her blouse and tried to hold herself tall and proud. "I guess I have to be, right?" Her numb legs carried her up the courthouse stairs, through the sterile hallway, and finally to the seat behind where Mr. Sinclair would be seated. She sat studying the courtroom and its alien atmosphere. She lost herself in the woodwork and scents that she tried to befriend. They would save her, not destroy her. They had to save her.

The courtroom bustled with people in uniforms and suits and worried faces. The judge sat quietly at the bench awaiting the next defendant to stand before him. She scanned each wrinkle on his face, trying to detect a mood, but it was a face she presumed had sat serious for so long it would be impossible to interpret. Samantha heard the courtroom doors bang shut, as if someone was in too much of a hurry to allow them to quietly settle back in place. Haley, flustered and out of place, scanned the seats for her sister. They made eye contact but did not exchange smiles. She then slipped into the seat next to Samantha without a word.

From a side entrance, she saw her husband being led into the courtroom. Samantha prepared herself the best she could to see Jacob, trying desperately to find the look of a strong, proud person he could count on. She thought she could imitate the person she wanted to be, until he stepped into her presence. They had taken her husband, a man of class and honor, and dressed him in an orange jumpsuit and shackles. Samantha almost cried out, but with everything in her being she forced herself to be silent. She felt her father's strong hand take hers and with the small gesture, Samantha let some of the misery subside. She would get through this. They would take Jacob home shortly.

Samantha knew somewhere on the other side of the room sat Ava Johnson's husband and probably other family members as well. She could hear occasional sniffles echoing in the courtroom, making them harder to ignore, but she raised her chin, took a deep breath and stared forward, trying desperately to avoid making any eye contact with any bitter or terrified family members before her, Jacob included. It would feel too personal.

Before she realized it, the nightmare was coming to a close. She expected to hear the bond amount, and prepared herself to deal with it. She stared at the judge, willing him to say a number smaller than she had prepared herself for, and instead she heard choppy phrases with words jumping from them like snake bites. "Flight risk... accruing time...revoked bond." Samantha could feel the blood rushing from her face and her knees going weak. Haley reached for her hand and, for a moment, Samantha wondered if she was offering support or seeking it. She knew the realization was setting in for both of them that Jacob would not be coming home for a long time.

The courtroom began to clear of the handful of people there for Jacob's case. They slid through the benches in an unsaid order, leaving the most relevant people to face each other as they tried to exit. Samantha tried to keep her eyes on the ground, but she could feel Ava's husband watching her. When she looked up she was met with beautiful, bluish-gray eyes that had the same pull she felt when looking at an Alaskan Husky, such beauty and danger. She somehow knew the danger only existed because of the accident, and it was only intended for her and her family. In his eyes, she had no right to be alive. No one had ever hated her. No one had ever looked at her the way he had looked at her. Samantha desperately wanted to show him that she was a good person. She needed to wash the anger away in order for her to remember how to breathe.

His look would follow her down the hallway and into the quiet room where Mr. Sinclair tried to explain the unexplainable. Some judges might see people with money as a flight risk, especially Jacob, since Jacob's father lives in Canada. He may also feel that the chances for Jacob to be sentenced to some amount of time are high enough that it may be beneficial for him to start serving the time now.

"I know this is unexpected for all of us. I would have warned you had I thought this would happen, but truly Samantha this may not, in the long run, be the worst thing." Mr. Sinclair offered.

"How can you say that? My children think their father is coming home today. How can I tell them they can't see him?" Samantha let herself sink into her father's comforting arms and sobbed through the rest of what Mr. Sinclair tried to explain to her.

"If it didn't happen this way, you would be at home fearing it was coming for six months to a year. He would have an ankle bracelet and restrictions. It wouldn't be living, or at least not the kind of living you want. You heard them talk about the evidence. People are angry about this topic right now. There is a chance he will get something. By the time the trial is over, he will have some of the time already served. It's a chance for your life to start over more quickly. Think of it that way, Samantha. This can be behind you maybe a year faster this way."

It would be days of soaking it in and explaining the benefits to other people before Samantha could begin to believe that anything good had come out of the court appearance, but as with many things, slowly the brain sees things the way it must in order to survive.

Chapter 18

Judge Murphy

Another case of texting and driving crossed Judge Murphy's desk, forcing a feeling of regret to rise in his chest. He was a young judge, only forty, who had come into this position with rave reviews and accolades from his peers, only to have one of his first cases get more publicity and criticism than he was prepared for in his beginning career as a judge.

Too many emotions were warring inside him. He taken a pay cut to change positions from his law practice to being a judge. And now he hated the position he was in judging texting and driving cases. He hated them more for what it had done to his career than for the actual act of texting. If he had to be honest, he had sent a quick one himself when he thought the conditions were right. But that was before.

He thought ow of Jessica Allen—a name he would never forget. She had been beautiful, full of life, according to everyone that had anything to say about her. Everyone seemed to have comments about her. Having graduated in June with stellar grades, she had now enrolled in Virginia Tech to continue classes in the fall. To make extra money she took a waitressing job and was driving home from Bottoms Up when the man who hit her was texting to his pregnant wife as he returned from work.

Although Judge Murphy had sworn to be unbiased in sentencing, he knew only the facts counted, this case was proving difficult. Just a little over a year before the accident, the accused had been arrested on DUI charges. He had just had his license restored. These wee the major facts. But he felt he had to weigh other factors. The accused was now leading a respectable life. And as his pregnant wife stood by with their young child in her arms while tears stained her face, the judge could not help relating to them. He couldn't help but see the destruction jail time would bring them.

When he handed down the sentence of a revoked license and community service, the courtroom burst into something close to an uproar. The fact was it could go either way. Killing poor Jessica while texting would not have sent him to jail without the previous DUI charge. He chose to handle it separately. There could come a time Virginia would opt to make it an imprisonable offense, but, unfortunately for the victim's family, it was not where the law stood, and he did what he felt was best.

Then the ripples started to spread through the town. The voice of the young accident victim was echoed through her multitude of followers, and they were loud. They appeared in papers and local news segments. Judge Murphy's name was everywhere. No one thought of the family he felt he had saved because no one thought they should have been, or, at least, those people were silent.

When Jacob Truax entered the courtroom, Judge Murphy felt it starting over. He saw Jacob's beautiful wife, the tears, the anguish. On the other side of the courtroom was the face of a young father, two young children he heard, equally anguished. The young father's eyes were begging for justice just as Jessica's parents' eyes had pleaded a short time before. Every day the world became less tolerant. Every day another family demanded that something change. This time he had to show he understood what the world expected from him. They expected change. They expected maximum sentences. If the jury found Jacob guilty, he would give the community what they demanded. Jacob would pay.

Chapter 19

Samantha

On Friday, Haley showed up unexpectedly with her pajamas and wine after tucking the kids into bed. The wine began to flow easily, as did the conversation. Memories long forgotten were brought to the surface of the choppy waters, and somehow the waters began to calm. They were good memories—of apple-picking at Carter's Mountain, eating apple donuts and drinking hot chocolate before they would run to pick out the pumpkins.

Samantha didn't mention how she would always make sure she chose second to make sure she ended up with the one that was just slightly bigger than Haley's, but somehow Haley knew.

Haley began laughing at her memory before choosing to share. By the time she got it out, they were both laughing so hard that tears formed in their eyes. They could both still picture the infamous pumpkin. It was dirty and lopsided, but it was the biggest one Samantha could find. She knew that whatever pumpkin Haley chose, it could not top hers. All this she thought was going on in her mind, never imagining her competitiveness was so evident.

Samantha, with a grin too large for her tiny face, bent to pick it up. After only two steps, she tripped over all the other pumpkins, leaving her slightly bruised and embarrassed. She looked down at her trophy. The stem lay next to the lumpy body no longer attached. Then she ran into her father's arms and hid the tears that streamed down her cheeks.

Haley recalled through her laughter, "I knew you were trying to find a pumpkin big enough to make it impossible for me to beat you. Unfortunately, Dad felt so bad for you that he broke his rule and helped you carry it. You did insist on carrying the stem."

Samantha became quiet for a moment, as the memory changed form in her mind. How silly it all was when she looked back at her feelings, her constant desire to beat a sister who played a completely different game. For one insanely freeing moment, she saw everything from the outside and the memories of a competitive childhood lost their power giving way to something she had not allowed herself to feel for too long.

"More wine?" she offered, not wanting the moment to end.

"Oh, are you trying to see if you can outdrink me now? Keep it coming, Sis."

Samantha opened another cabernet knowing she would regret it in the morning. Somehow this bottle brought a new feeling to the air, and the conversation began to turn.

"How are you doing, Samantha? I want to be there for you. I want you to talk to me. Are you and the kids okay?" Jacob had been in jail for over a week. The preliminary hearing would take place in the upcoming weeks. She was still praying it would be worked out there, and Jacob could come home, but Jacob's lawyer wasn't optimistic.

"We'll get through this." She looked around her simple yet beautiful living room again and felt thankful for the everyday stuff that could so easily disappear. Haley got up from her chair and came to sit by Samantha. With only a slight bit of hesitation, she wrapped her arms around Samantha making her feel frail and strong at the same time.

"I know you will, Samantha. Things always seem to end up working out for you. Just be patient." They decided to find something light-hearted on television and get lost in their thoughts before retiring to their beds.

Samantha lay staring at Jacob's empty side, longing desperately to reach over and feel him there, to touch his lips, to slide together the way they had a million times. Instead, she could only whisper into the darkness, "Goodnight, Jacob," and hope somehow he heard her.

When she woke in the morning, Haley was already gone, which she found to be a welcome surprise even though the house was despairingly quiet. She needed the quiet to ponder her misery, to study every crevice of her life.

Chapter 20

Samantha

Samantha became an empty shell, drifting aimlessly through her days, dreading each problem that would spring up like a weed in a neglected lawn. She dreaded each bill-demanding payment, unwilling to acknowledge paychecks were no longer existent. She dreaded each question her children would ask, afraid of the answers she would need to give them.

Her mind began to reel over the possibilities. They had a small savings, but if Jacob went to jail, it could be for ten years, for all she knew. How long could that money last? Panic welled up inside her. It had only been a month, and she could see everything spiraling.

Samantha could feel herself breathing, but she couldn't get air. What would she do? She had never had a well-paying job. Even so, how could she change the children's lives by working now? Right when they needed her, she would not be there for them when they came home from school, for holidays, for summer? The future was crashing down on her.

What job could she even find after so many years at home? How could she lose the house the children needed for a sense of stability? She found there were so many things to do, so many things to think about, that she was frozen in place doing nothing.

She could visit Jacob on Saturdays in a large visiting room that reminded her of a cafeteria. The first visit was beyond awkward. She forgave herself for the lack of words and emotions she was able to share. She stared around at all the people, aliens on their new planet, speaking in whispers, making promises and plans for the unknown futures. When she finally met Jacob's eyes, she found him studying her. She imagined it was to see if she would accept the new him and his foreign family.

She grasped at a raspy voice that tried to escape and forced it to cooperate, to sound smooth and natural. "How are you doing?"

"I'll be fine, Samantha." His eyes begged her to be the same. "How are the kids?"

Samantha tried not to feel guilty for leaving the kids with her mom. She had to experience it beforehand so she could prepare them for what they would see. But once Samantha saw the inside of the jail, she wasn't sure there was any way to prepare them. She just had to trust that they were more resilient than she believed, that they would all learn how to survive in their new world.

"They're holding up. Lots of questions, as you can expect. I try to answer them." Her voice began to crack, and Jacob wrapped her in his arms. She attempted to take in his scent as she buried her face in his chest, but even that was different. Now they had correctional officers ready to break them up as if they were two promiscuous teenagers.

"It's going to be all right. I promise. I'll make it up to all of you somehow. It's just going to take time," Jacob insisted.

"I know. We can do this. Day by day, we can get through it." She straightened herself and wiped the one tear that betrayed her. "I need to get going. I'm meeting Mom for lunch." She surprised herself with the lie.

"Will you bring the kids next time?"

Samantha glanced around the room again and wondered quickly at each person's offense. "Maybe, but I promise to bring them soon."

With understanding and defeated eyes, he could only reply, "Okay."

The next week he tried to hide his disappointment when he entered the visiting room, and the following week it was just too difficult to do. She knew it was time to expose her children to his dark world. When she told them the next Friday night that they would be seeing their father the following day, they sprang from the table and hugged her with so much enthusiasm she questioned her hesitation.

They were up before her on Saturday morning wearing their Sunday best. "What time can we leave, Mommy?" Ryan screamed as he jumped onto her bed with a running leap. Samantha felt as if she had just closed her eyes. Her sleep had been impossibly restless.

"Slow down, honey! I need to wake up first," Samantha said through a yawn.

"You are awake, Mommy. Look at your eyes," Ryan said.

"I meant my brain has to wake up."

"I'll make you coffee while you shower," Sydney chimed.

"Great idea. Now give me some privacy to get ready, and I'll be down as quickly as I can." Samantha slowly let her feet find the floor.

Together they ran down the hallway toward the stairs. She could hear Ryan rambling, "I can't believe we get to see Daddy today. I'm going to draw him a picture for his room."

"Me, too."

Samantha smiled at their sweet idea and hoped Sydney had not forgotten her promise of making her coffee. She let the cold water drip over her, challenging her to be able to take on anything, to let her children's enthusiasm chase away the sick pain she felt inside of her whenever she thought of them at the jail. They deserved her enthusiasm, and they would have it today.

As they approached their destination, their little voices became less and less audible until silence overcame the backseat. By the time they had walked up to the door of the jail, their precious pictures were dampened by their tiny palms, creased forever with their fear. They each grabbed one of Samantha's hands tightly as they entered the visiting room and only let go when they saw their father begin to walk toward them. Samantha disappeared to them then, and the entire visit was about the kids and their father. She observed quietly, watching through a fence made of love and something bordering hatred or at least an anger she had never felt toward her husband, emotions that were bitterly painful when experienced together.

Jacob smoothed out their pictures on the table in front of him. Ryan's was a cowboy riding a horse that resembled a dog at best. Sydney's was a bouquet of unidentifiable flowers.

"When will you be home, Daddy?" Ryan asked. It didn't matter that Samantha had gone over the process a million times with him. He had to hear it from his father.

Samantha could see Jacob taking the moment to find an even voice. He watched his hands as they smoothed out the cowboy. "So who's the cowboy? You or me?" Samantha knew his attempt at diversion would not work.

"That one is me, but I'll draw you next time. But, Daddy, when will you be home?"

"It may take a bit Ryan. The lawyer needs time to go over everything and get his case ready and then the judge needs time to hear the case."

"Is it scary here?" Ryan asked but Sydney looked on so attentively it was as if the question had been hers.

"It's a lot like camping. The bed isn't too comfy. The food isn't too tasty. The toilet, well, let's just say there's no place like home," Jacob tried to smile but it was weak and unbelievable. "There are strange sounds in the night that sometimes wake me up," Jacob began to drift when he spoke these words and Samantha found herself there with him in that cold lonely bed hearing the despairing groans of lost souls. "But every morning I wake up just fine. Just like camping. Remember the time the raccoon was in our cooler? It was scary in the night, but it was kind of cool to see his little footprints all over our campsite."

"He ate our hotdogs," Ryan exclaimed at the memory.

"Yes, he did didn't he."

"Will people take our pictures while you sleep?" Ryan asked. Still Sydney just watched with an expression that showed she could break at any moment.

"No one will take your pictures," Jacob assured them.

"Do you promise?"

"I promise. I'll hang them right over my bed. I'm on the bottom bunk so it's like a fort. I'll keep good watch over them."

Ryan smiled and fell into his father's arms. Sydney followed. Samantha knew they were crying, and she knew that she would lose it in front of them if it lasted much longer.

"We need to get going kids," Samantha announced. To her surprise, they didn't even argue. They gave Jacob a few more moments and then turned, beaten and exhausted. Samantha went in to hug Jacob goodbye as well. Their arms awkwardly bumped trying to find the fit that was once so natural. They both tried to laugh it off, but Samantha knew they both felt it.

The way home was nearly silent and when Samantha glanced in the rearview mirror she found they were both sound asleep. As soon as they pulled into the driveway, though, Ryan jolted out of the car and ran for the mailbox. The letters would be there. They were there every day that the mail came. Jacob had been great about that.

They would each save their letter until they were curled up in their beds at night, a ritual that Samantha began to savor as well. She tried to push the idea out of her mind that one of the many guards may have read her letter before she did, and when she put her pen to paper, she tried desperately to write naturally to her husband of many years knowing that someone might also be reading her letter to Jacob. But no matter how hard she tried, a face appeared, judging her words, her relationship, her very being, pushing her farther and farther away from the marriage she took for granted.

Chapter 21

━━ ━━ ━━ ━━ ━━ ━━ ━━ ━━

Samantha

Samantha got the kids to school wearing her yoga pants and ponytail, looking like all the other moms eager to get to their morning gym class. Just one more thing she had taken for granted, meeting friends for conditioning followed by a caramel macchiato at Starbucks where they would share the latest interesting stories. But that wasn't the plan for the day, not for her anyway, even though she was quite sure there would still be Starbucks and gossip going on for others.

Keeping her head down as she had learned to do, she escaped all conversation. Instead of jumping into her car, she opened the garage door and stared into its darkness as if it were an enemy deserving of being conquered. This wasn't her place. At least, it had never been.

It had been weeks since the lawn had been mowed and she knew the letter from the HOA was probably being addressed at that very moment if it were not already in the mail.

Jacob kept the garage tidy. The lawn mower sat parked in its spot and, fortunately, full of gas.

Samantha saw the gas can next to it. She could have handled filling it, she was sure. After wheeling it out to the driveway, she surprised herself by starting it on the third try. Pride welled up inside of her momentarily, until she saw Suzanne making her way toward her with her walking partner. Lucky for them, they would soon have a new topic of conversation to spice up their morning stroll. Samantha quickly put in her earbuds so they wouldn't try to get her attention.

Apparently, there were several issues with not mowing a lawn for weeks, the first being that the bag filled with clippings at an unbelievable rate. After trying to carry the oversized bag to the garbage, Samantha found it would be much easier to bring the garbage can to her. The heat bore down on her as she reached, time and again, into the bag to pull out the clippings that refused to be dumped. Each time her hands came out a darker hue of green. The grass was becoming embedded under her nails, and she sniffled back the cry that wanted to emerge as a bee decided to hover around her sweat-covered hair.

Then she had an incredible thought. Why not just leave the bag off the mower? Proudly, she began again. The mower was lighter and much easier to manipulate. A small skip in her step took over until she turned the machine to go back down the next path. The clippings lay across the lawn like a hay in a farmer's field. She put the bag back on the mower and went back over her work. Once a week she would do this. Never again would she wait.

She had watched Jacob a million times as he used the weed whacker on the edges of the lawn. How hard could it be? It had to be easier than mowing, Samantha thought. That was until she saw the damage she so quickly inflicted on the mailbox. The clean line that Jacob so easily created along the edge of their yard no longer existed. All she could do was stare out at the very first yard she had ever mowed, her hands tingling from the vibrations of the machines she had used, and felt an angry pride at her forced accomplishment and a forgiveness for her mishaps.

It was at that moment her mother decided to pull in front of the house. She stepped out of her car with her hair styled to a tee, her white blouse dressed up with a dangling necklace, and a Panera bag in her hand. Mrs. Gorman walked toward Samantha without a word until she stood beside her daughter staring out at the yard.

"Samantha, my dear, you amaze me."

"All these years, and all it took was me mowing the lawn?"

They smiled at each other. Liz put her arm around Samantha's shoulder momentarily before removing it to wipe off the debris. Samantha admired her mother a moment. So ready to pull up her sleeves and get dirty one moment and so easily transformed into a picture of class the next.

"I brought lunch."

"You could not say a nicer thing to me right now." Samantha looked down at her green hands dripping with a few determined blades of grass. "Give me thirty minutes."

Within the hour, Samantha and her mother found themselves sitting at her kitchen table, Samantha's nails still showing evidence of her morning adventure. Her mother took Samantha's hands in hers and studied her nails with a soft smile on her face.

"I am proud of you, how you're holding up, how you're keeping it together, but didn't I teach you to wear gardening gloves when you do yard work?"

Samantha laughed with a hint of cry behind it. "I believe you did, Mom. But then I was always a bit of a slow learner, wasn't I? But as for holding up, I'm not quite sure I am. Some minutes I feel like I'm just going to crumble."

"Of course you do, Samantha. None of us were created to be perfect. Sure, some people hide it better than others or you're judging them at one of their nearly perfect moments, but I assure you that no one is, and no one expects you to be either."

"Well, that's relieving, because my sanity is a minute-by-minute reality at the moment." Samantha took a large bite of her sandwich and reached for her drink.

"Your dad and I really want to help, where we can anyway. Unfortunately, we don't have as much money as it may appear on the outside. But we have money."

"Mom, Jacob and I have discussed this. We don't want to ask for anything from family. We'll figure it out. We have savings, and Jacob mentioned stocks we can sell."

"Just know that we are here, and a warning, your father will be having a similar conversation with you soon, I'm sure." Mrs. Gorman took a drink and then continued. "I have a proposition for you."

"A proposition?" She swallowed down her mouthful with another gulp. "You have me curious."

"I'm reaching an age where I would like to slow down a bit."

"Yea, right. I can't imagine you ever slowing down."

"I didn't say quit, just slow down. I was thinking maybe you would like to partner with me with my interior decorating business. I know it's small, but maybe with your help we could actually make it take off."

Samantha put down her sandwich and stared at her mother as if she had just lit a candle in a lighthouse a million miles away. "Really, you think I would be good at that?"

"You would be incredible at it. I used to watch you whenver I took you to the nursing home to visit the elderly. You would drift off, away from Haley and me, and I would find you rearranging pillows or the flower arrangements in the lounge areas. It was a little gesture, but I saw myself in you, finding your peace in making things pretty. It's a good gift. Not everyone has your eye for things."

"Funny, it's not how I remember our visits." Samantha glanced out at her mowing job. "Maybe."

"I hope you consider it. I would love to work with you. Not to mention, Jacob won't see it as a handout. It will be some well-earned money."

For just a moment, Samantha let a vision of a future with some direction creep in, but the waves of the unknown quickly swept over them making the vision unrecognizable.

Chapter 22

_____

Jacob

Jacob watched as his mashed potatoes were slopped onto his tray. Camping, he almost laughed out loud in the middle of the mess hall. He had heard the stories of what happens in prisons. Camping, seriously? Well, then, weren't the men in the movie _Deliverance_ camping? Would insanity help? Maybe if he just laughed everywhere he went, people would keep their distance. So far, so good, though, besides his fears, his inability to sleep, to rest his mind. He was always on alert.

Jacob's eyes were beginning to sag. At times, he felt as if he didn't have cheekbones to hold them up they could actually slide down his face. The fight between staying alert and needing sleep was becoming too much. Insanity? Maybe he was insane.

On the outside, Jacob remained calm, speaking only to his cellmate when he couldn't avoid it. Short simple answers. He wouldn't let this place become a part of him. But on the inside, something was changing. One minute he was so angry. Then next he found himself deeply depressed, something he had never truly experienced. His favorite times were the blank moments when his mind went to a place that may not even exist, a place of nothingness. If only he could stay there.

His whole life he had wanted to prove himself better than the small town he had come from, to prove himself worthy of a father who had moved on to a new and improved family after his mom died. He worked three jobs to get through college, bus boy, scrubbing pots and pans, and his favorite, a bouncer. The entertainment never ended. He could never quite understand the draw that people had toward drinking until they became the slush puddle that his fellow bouncers and he would drag to the door, ideally before they became a human vomit fountain.

There was nothing like walking through a jail mess hall line, watching tasteless mashed potatoes being slopped on your plate, to humble a person. Hell, the man in the back washing the pots and pans was suddenly his superior. When was the next class reunion? He couldn't remember. Just like he couldn't remember what was so wrong with his small town simplicity. He had not only dropped to the bottom of his ladder, but his ladder was being swallowed by a muck he had never known in his life. Or maybe he was never meant to climb that high in the first place.

Meeting Samantha was the first time in his life he saw the finish line. The job was great, the promise of advancement was incredible, but it wasn't until he saw Samantha that he knew what he was really seeking. There weren't words, just a feeling of completion, a voice in his head saying run this way, and once a person sees the finish line why would they divert their paths or let a hurdle get in their way? That was Haley. A hurdle always trying to trip him up, trying to divert him.

The next woman, another face of stone, hairnet hiding any free part of her personality, scooped out a spoon of peas. Jacob knew they were from one of those giant cans. The coloring was off and they were dimpled. What was wrong with him? He was angry with everyone. Himself, Haley, the man he couldn't see in the back washing the dishes.

Every few days he received a letter. And then the visits started. At first, he wanted to tell her to stop coming, but as the distance between Samantha and him grew, he began to think of her as a lifeline. Haley was able to be a spy on the outside, to tell him how his family was really doing. Yes, Samantha came and spoke, but he needed more. He needed to hear from someone he trusted to tell him the cold hard truth when things got too hard for Samantha to share them. He couldn't turn her away. Once again, he couldn't turn her away.

Chapter 23

Samantha

Samantha's mind was always drifting to other places, or sometimes just nothingness. She could almost picture the black shadow of depression following her every move, a shadow she almost found comical in the commercials for some medication she never envisioned needing. Now she wondered. Life was a weight bearing down on her.

When Sydney and Ryan were babies, she remembered staring at their sweet faces and letting everything drift away except for them and that moment. If only staring hard enough could have frozen them in that place forever. As they grew, she would catch herself again, staring as they told a story, letting herself be so wrapped up in their voices and mannerisms that nothing else mattered. Maybe it was human nature to need to leave that place, or maybe it was just her or her life now, but she could not remember the last time she let herself get lost in their world. She would say the right words, or, at least she hoped she did, and pretend to listen, but her mind was on the next chore, the next problem, or just on the moment she could finally rest for the day.

After her mother spoke with her about offering money, Samantha became fixated on the stress of their finances. Jacob had mentioned that they had stocks, but Samantha had allowed herself to be removed from the investments. In just the short time of living with no paycheck, she could already see the future. The savings account would soon begin shrinking at an incredible pace, and there would be no fix in sight.

She couldn't avoid the conversation with Jacob any longer. Samantha had her mother ride with them to the prison so that after the kids finished with their visit, she could have some time alone to plan their future. She was hoping for a business-like conversation and that she would leave with clear steps to take in this unchartered water.

"Okay, kids, give your dad hugs goodbye. Mommy needs some time to speak to him," Samantha said.

"Why can't we stay? We'll be quiet," Ryan begged.

"Samantha, I'm sure they'll be fine," Jacob argued.

"I think it would be best if we had a minute to discuss some things privately." Samantha did not want the kids worried about money on top of everything else.

"Mom, please take the kids to the car."

"Samantha, I see the kids once a week. Please, let them stay."

Samantha stared at him, willing the rational man she knew to resurface. "We need to discuss money, Jacob. I don't think the kids need to be hearing about all of that."

Before taking Ryan into his arms, Jacob glared at Samantha accusingly for just a moment. She wanted to scream, "This is your fault, not mine!" For the kids' sake, she held it in and watched as they said their goodbyes. Once Sydney and Ryan did their final wave from the door, Jacob and Samantha turned to each other.

"Things are getting tight, Jacob."

"What are you talking about? It's fine. It's only been a little over a month." Maybe that was true but the future had forced its way into the present.

"I think I need to find a job, but I'm too overwhelmed to think of another thing. I'm trying to keep up with everything inside the house and out. I had to weed whack yesterday, Jacob. I don't even know how to weed whack. I gouged everything." Samantha began to cry hard and let it all pour out, no longer caring if it made him feel guilty.

"Other women mow lawns and skip manicures, Samantha. You can do this. It doesn't have to be the best-looking lawn in the neighborhood."

"Skip manicures! Are you kidding me! That is the last thing on my mind, Jacob. I'm just trying to make you understand."

"Understand? Are you kidding me? Do you understand what this is like?" Jacob lifted his arm to point out the sterile visiting room they were sitting in but all Samantha could see was Jacob. Black circles were prominent under his eyes. His skin ashen. Yet, more pressing than her concern was how hurt and angry she felt. Her tears subsided to the rage building inside of her. She didn't want to hear any more *I'm sorries*, but his total lack of sympathy floored her. "I can't believe you just said that to me. Skip manicures? Do you really think that is my big concern?"

"Relax. It just came out wrong. What I'm saying is you're a strong woman, and I know this is new to you, but you can do it. I'll owe you a lifetime of manicures when I get out of here."

"If you say manicure one more time, I swear I'm going to hit you right across the face. I don't care about manicures. I care about paying the bills, keeping the house, not letting everything fall apart. Keeping the kids happy. How am I supposed to work and keep up with everything at the house? I need answers. I need this to not all be on me."

It was the first time she dared to fight with him, to not worry about his feelings and say every ugly thought that crept in when she lay in bed at night worried about everything and it felt wonderful and terrible all at once. Jacob put his head in his hands and rubbed his forehead. She noticed a few gray hairs springing up, and even those made her despise him more and it made her sick. This wasn't them. They didn't fight. They hated fighting, but that's all she wanted to do at that moment, to let release all the stress he had created with his negligence.

"Don't work yet." Jacob said more calmly. "Remember, we have stocks we can sell to get us through this. After the trial, we can decide what needs to be done, but for now just keep it as normal as possible for the kids. And who knows? Maybe we will have it all worked out in the preliminary hearing." He paused, hoping the sense of hope would spread. It didn't. "Why don't you hire one of the neighborhood boys to do the yard work? We can afford that, I'm sure. The trial should be in a few more months, six at most. Just keep things as normal as possible."

Jacob stood, and for the first time, he was the one to call an end to the visit by walking to a correctional officer without saying goodbye. Samantha sat, deserted, until she could stop spinning. He had no right to be angry. She was the one who got to be angry, not him.

The ride home, her mother distracted the kids with conversation somehow knowing Samantha had no words. What was happening to them? Jacob looked so tired, more tired than she had ever seen him. She wanted to take back the whole conversation, to reword it. The yard was nothing. She would mow a million yards for her family. Why did she mention it? Why did she bring that guilt to him, a man that loved to take care of her? All she wanted was direction, to not feel so alone.

Several days later, Samantha finally received a letter from Jacob along with the letters to the children. It was the first time he had missed a day since he was imprisoned. She didn't wait until bedtime to read it. Instead, she slipped off to her room and locked the door, afraid of what the letter might say.

Samantha,

I'm not going to say the two words I'm so tired of thinking. They are meaningless, like pebbles in the ocean. They just become lost. The past fifteen years I have had the pleasure of taking care of you. I was a man. I was in control, not of you but for you. You just got to be who you are, the Samantha I fell in love with, and that was all I wanted or needed from you. I wanted to bring you a paycheck and give you a beautiful home, to mow the grass and send you for your manicures. I loved your smile when you showed off your pampered hands.

I have never felt more imprisoned than I did at your last visit, seeing you struggle and not being able to do anything about it. Watching your glowing face darkened by tears and your beautiful hands callused and unkempt. I would rather have my hands tied behind my back and be beaten than to watch my family suffer. All I can do is watch. All because of a ten-second decision at best, I will be punished for years or maybe a lifetime. Maybe this will change everything.

I wasn't angry with you, but I know that's how I seemed. I think we both know that the situation has made us both forget who we are at times and that deep down our fight had nothing to do with manicures. But I am so angry, angry beyond words with life, with fate. Please be patient and strong. You are the love of my life. Forgive me and I will do everything I can to make it right.

Yours forever,
Jacob

Samantha held the letter and unbelievably found more tears to let fall. What were the right words to make him know they would be all right, to honestly believe they would make it? That night she lay in bed and tried her best to find them.

Jacob,

I'm glad you are sick of saying I'm sorry. Not because they are pebbles in the ocean, and not because they didn't need to be said, but because they don't belong in our ocean any longer. Our waters have always run deeper than just the ability to forgive each other. What we need to say, what we need to remember is that we love each other today and always and that is all we have to focus on right now. The rest will work itself out.

As for my pampered hands, I know that you think more of me than just being a girl that needs manicures to be happy. I seem to recall a text that you sent me many years ago that said I was a well-read, business-minded woman that wanted to take on the world. Well, it's time to get my hands dirty my dear. I'm strong enough even if I have my weak moments. Have faith in my abilities. We will get through this.

Forever yours,
Samantha

She read the letter several times, wishing she felt as strong as the girl she created. One thing she learned was that she could not share her concerns with Jacob anymore. No matter how angry and petrified she was, one thing would always be true. She loved him and if lying made him hurt less, then it was something she was capable of doing.

Chapter 24

Samantha

Samantha's mother graciously picked up Sydney and Ryan to take them to the zoo. Samantha would be meeting her father for lunch to discuss finances. She chose Europa's, where she planned on eating as many tapas as she could comfortably fit and having at least two glasses of the best chardonnay they had, knowing her father would pick up the tab.

Samantha knew she would need to down the first glass quickly to ease her nerves. Yes, this was her adoring father, but she somehow felt as if she was going to an interview that was way over her head. She knew little about their finances beyond the monthly bills she was in charge of, always leaving the investments to Jacob. It made sense since that was his field, but now she cursed herself for her lack of interest.

Her father met her at the entrance and kissed her on the cheek. "How are you doing, my dear?"

"I'm doing okay, considering," Samantha replied while avoiding his eyes.

A hostess guided them to a seat by the window, and they remained quiet until she drifted back to the entrance.

"You can talk to us, you know. You haven't asked for much of anything, and I'm proud of you for that, but it's okay to ask, too." Her father studied her and Samantha suddenly became aware of every movement, every facial expression.

"Good, because you're treating today." Her father let out a relieved laugh.

"Oh Samantha, I wish I could make this go away," he said, reaching for her hand.

"Me too, Dad, me too."

"So what's the plan?" he asked.

"Jacob wants me to stay home with the kids until after the trial, and then we'll talk about options. Jacob wanted to know if you could sell some of our stocks for us to help me with bills. I don't have the account numbers on hand, but I can get them to you tonight."

"Easy enough. As for account numbers, I'll have access to all that anyway. Did Jacob mention anything specific?"

"No. It was kind of an uncomfortable visit," Samantha said while wiping her hands on her skirt. They had suddenly began to sweat.

"Yes, Haley mentioned." He cut his words short knowing he had said too much.

"Excuse me? How would Haley know?" Samantha asked, no longer concerned with her expression.

"I think he was pretty upset after your last visit, so when Haley saw him Sunday, he spoke of it." He looked across the table at Samantha's face and knew what thoughts were racing through her mind. "Samantha, we have all visited him. He needs everyone's support right now." Samantha could only stare, bewildered. "Listen, Samantha, it should make you happy that he has people around him right now."

"I just would've thought I would know that she was visiting him. It feels a bit secretive if you ask me. And why are they discussing our conversations? I just don't…"

"Samantha, he needs people right now. Think of Jacob."

Her wine came just in time and she drank half of it before setting it back on the table. Why was it so easy to become a child in front of one's parents no matter the age? She stared stone-faced out the window as she tried to regain her composure, embarrassed she had lost it.

"Samantha, he married you. Remember that and act like a grown woman and not a child with some kind of unresolved childhood rivalry. You are both adults." John's face was stern. The face he would often use to let them know the conversation was over.

She took a deep breath. "Let's get back to the finances. I worked out a budget." With that, she pulled out a sheet of paper neatly accounting each expense. "I have here what Jacob and I believe I will need in savings to get us by for six months. We started to get things worked out, but we thought he would come home on bond and we could work out the rest of the details. What I need from you is to help me with the selling of enough stocks to get us what I need for six months. By then, the trial will hopefully be finished, and either Jacob will be home, or I will be looking for work."

John took the sheet, happy for the change in topic. "I'll check into the stocks and get this set. In the meantime, your mom and I insist on paying for lawn care services to take some pressure off you." Samantha wanted to speak, but he put his hand up. "I will respect your decision not to ask for other money for now, but a father needs to know he is taking care of his children. I insist about the lawn care at least."

"Dad, you don't need to. I've been doing fine with it." Samantha wondered if her father saw the tears begin to form, betraying her words.

"It's already set up. You have enough to worry about."

Samantha looked down at her short, unpolished nails and uttered, "Thank you." She knew he was right. She would have enough to worry about beyond the yard.

The following week, Samantha decided she would invite Haley to ride with them and have lunch afterward. She knew it was, in reality, her way of letting Haley know she wasn't getting away with anything, and as an added perk, Samantha would look like a kind, confident sister. Haley graciously accepted. The childish pleasure she received by walking in the visiting area with Haley by her side was a bonus.

Samantha saw Jacob rise from his seat and wipe his hands on his legs. She was sure his palms had started to sweat at the sight of Haley and her approaching together. Even though he tried to hide his tension, the tightness in his voice gave him away.

"This is a surprise, seeing you both here."

"Yes, I thought it might be," Samantha responded while trying to keep the sarcasm out of her voice.

He hugged them both with what appeared equal familiarity and took a seat. "So what's the special occasion that I get the two of you in one visit?" Once again a statement that Samantha felt equalized them.

"We're making a day of it and grabbing lunch afterward," Samantha answered innocently.

After their embrace, they sat stiffly and let an awkward moment of silence pass between them. Samantha could see Jacob squirm ever so slightly in his seat, and she let the silence drag on allowing him to feel the discomfort.

Haley glanced at Samantha expectantly, but Samantha stayed silent letting Haley begin. "So Jacob, how are you doing." Haley asked.

"All right." Jacob's eyes shifted from Haley to Samantha. "How's life on the outside?"

Samantha strongly suspected he was trying to get the weight of the conversation off himself.

"Well, the wedding season is keeping me very busy…" Haley rambled on as Jacob locked eyes with Samantha's hardened eyes.

"I got your letter." Haley stopped talking when she realized no one was actually listening to her. Samantha stayed quiet and let Jacob study her. "I hope that means we're good."

"Of course, what would have changed that?" Samantha let her solid stare answer the questions. Haley sat squeezing her hands together on her lap as if waiting for the conversation to turn to her openly, but knowing it would not.

"I hope nothing would change that," Jacob answered.

"Me, too." And Samantha honestly hoped beyond imagine that she saw the waters she swam in clearly, that there was no dangerous intruder threatening the bond they had taken years to form, but then Haley spoke.

"Is there anything you need for me, or any of us, to bring next time?"

Again, Jacob's eyes found Samantha's. "I'll let Samantha know. I have faith she'll be there for me."

Samantha tried to give him a small smile, but only managed a hint of one.

They continued to talk about mundane things, or rather, they listened to Haley ramble nervously between Samantha and Jacob's short exchanges. Somewhere in the middle of the cold stares, something intimate began to form between them, and as Haley told yet another story, boring them to tears, Samantha's smile became a bit more genuine, and she felt both Jacob and herself soften.

Samantha decided that she should be planning some summer activities, something to share so she would never sound as uninteresting as her sister was sounding at that moment.

When the three of them stood to hug goodbye, Samantha did what she had not felt comfortable doing in a crowded room of strangers patrolled by correctional officers: she kissed Jacob and let her lips linger on his for as many moments as she could. She knew why the idea had seemed so appealing, but what surprised her was how badly she missed his touch. When they parted, their eyes held each other, speaking volumes of the unfulfilled desire between them. Somehow she wished she had never awakened the demon she forgot existed.

Chapter 25

Samantha

On Monday, Samantha woke up rejuvenated with her plan of having a life again. She packed lunches and readied Sydney and Ryan for an outing. Within a short time, they pulled into Maymont Park and set off on their wildlife adventure. First, they passed the pigs and goats and other domestic farm animals. The young goats danced wildly around the barnyard, and without knowing, the three of them were all genuinely laughing, amused at the freeness of the innocent creatures.

They traveled down the hilly meadows through the fields of fenced-in deer, past a wild cat, a fox, and two black bears that kindly did a walk-by for their amusement. Then they hiked to the far back corner to find the Japanese Garden, which allowed them the escape they all needed. The simple beauty of flowers and landscape design transported them to a carefree world she wanted to stay in forever.

The three of them gingerly skipped across the stone pathway to an island in the pond, and she listened as they delighted in spotting the large carp swimming in their serene world. She smiled, knowing on the next visit she would have something to share with Jacob and prayed the experience would bring him joy and not sadness. Samantha envisioned how the kids would relive their adventure with excitement in their voices, somehow assuring Jacob things were okay and Samantha was still giving them a good life despite everything.

They had been fortunate to be mostly alone on their journey, but as Ryan pointed out yet another carp swimming toward the only path onto their island, Samantha noticed a father and two children hopping toward them across the stones. She first felt annoyed due to the intrusion, and then she saw who it was. Her hands went numb, and she felt the tiny hairs on her neck begin to rise. They were trapped. How many times had he seen her? Only once, she believed. Maybe he wouldn't recognize her in casual clothes and large sunhat.

He carried a little girl with curly brown hair and held the tiny hand of a boy she knew to be three, as he eagerly took on the stepping stones. He hadn't looked up yet, cautiously guiding his children, his being the only hands left to do so. They were beautiful, all of them. He had wavy brown hair like his daughter, and the boy must have taken after his mother, having blond hair cut short and neat.

"Sophie, look at the fish," the man exclaimed. Sophie excitedly replied with a word that Samantha was sure was meant to be fish as the boy lost his footing and almost fell into the pond. His father's strong arm easily reached out to save him from his fate. Samantha was so entranced in watching them approach she didn't feel Ryan's arm tugging on her own.

"Mommy, I have to pee!" Samantha snapped to as his family reached their untouchable island.

"Really?" Samantha looked around at the woods trying to remember where she could find the closest bathroom. If memory served her, it was quite a distance and she began to accept that they would be settling for a bush when no one was looking. "Okay. Let's go." There was no way around it. She would have to cut through them.

"Excuse us." Samantha half whispered.

"Connor, move to the side and let the family through."

Their eyes met for a brief second as she mumbled, "Thank you," and rushed across the stones. It was too hard to tell if he recognized her. If he did, would he know she shared his pain in many ways? Did he know she was, at least for now, acting as a single parent too, struggling every day with her loss and her challenges? If he did, would he know how lonely she was and how desperately she wished they could all go back to before the crash? Would he care?

Why did Samantha feel the need to research his family? It was like a polar opposite family existing in the same realm. Two forces that were rotating around each other in a community not that terribly large. Two forces that had no business coexisting. They needed to understand each other because, for some reason, their existence had become dependent on each other. Good versus evil. Victim versus criminal. They were forever bound together in an indestructible bond, and she had to understand them, to know them, to somehow accept them in her new reality.

They lived in the West End, and the deceased wife, Ava, once worked at a bank on Broad Street. She was only a couple of blocks away from her destination on that fateful day. Had she not decided to run for a quick cup of coffee, had Mother Nature not decided to release the floodgates on her way back to the office, had she been paying better attention, all their lives would be different. Samantha would not be frozen in time between the needy eyes of her husband and the haunting, unforgiving eyes of Ava's husband. She learned quickly that his name was Seth. Samantha rolled his name around her tongue hoping somehow to change it from a jagged pebble into a harmless pearl. She could not.

It was easy enough to find their neighborhood and easy enough as well to drive by their home. It wasn't the largest house, but it was well kept and quaint. Flowerbeds had an array of colors. Samantha could picture Ava's blond hair pulled back into a ponytail as she carefully planted each one.

A whole scene unfolded before her, a scene where Seth stood admiring Ava's work, before gently pulling the loose hair away from her face and kissing her forehead as she turned to look into his eyes. Maybe their son played around the yard. Their little girl maybe sat in her bouncy chair admiring her mother before she even understood what she was doing. Did Seth think of her every time he passed by those flowerbeds to enter their home? Did her arrangements bring him peace or only make him hate Jacob and everyone related to him even more?

Samantha noticed their home was walking distance to the neighborhood pool. Glancing at her watch, she found she had plenty of time to just pull in and check it out, promising she would only stay a moment. She parked under a large tree and watched as the neighborhood children pulled up on their bikes. Her mind could not help but picture him there with the two of them. What were their names? Connor and Sophie. She remembered their names from the park, and if she tried hard enough, could still hear his voice uttering them.

What conversations did the mothers have around the pool as they watched the young father trying to be a single parent? How many of the women that passed by, struggling with toddlers and pool bags, were once her friends? How many of them were missing her? How many of them hated Jacob and his family, hated her? These women that in another situation could have been her friends.

Samantha knew she needed to leave. Admittedly, she was acting bizarre, hiding in her car behind big sunglasses and the shade of a tree, but she felt no need to explain her actions. Forces she had no ability to understand insisted that she pause in time to live in Ava's shoes for even just a short time, to see the world her family had destroyed.

Maybe it was honoring her in some way, to say, *I'm sorry*, to say, *I see what we have taken from your family and you*. Maybe Samantha was just punishing herself even if Ava was somewhere at peace and completely unaware that Samantha sat in a hot car, forced to be a stalker searching for peace in a strange world.

Samantha knew it was almost time to grab the kids from camp, conveniently located at the YMCA near his home and just enough time to pick up the dinner necessities at the local grocery store. They were out of chicken nuggets and applesauce, and since she had gone at least four days without serving them, she felt it was time to put them back on the menu. She grazed along the aisles looking for an adult food that interested her, but she didn't feel the excitement for cooking for herself or her children when there were so few dinner foods they liked. Dinner once again would be picking some leftovers off their plates as she cleaned up.

She found the wine aisle and settled on at least an adult beverage to wash down her nuggets. All of a sudden, dinner seemed more appealing. Smoking Loon Chardonnay she was sure paired nicely with chicken. As she pushed her cart around the corner, another cart rounded the corner at the same time. Avoiding a collision with a giggling child, she met eyes with a man in what could only be a cosmic joke. Or maybe when a person stalks someone and shops in the grocery store by their house, chance meetings happen.

"Excuse me. I'm sorry." Then there was quiet. Maybe two seconds, or was it hours? "Do I know you?"

"I don't think so." She quickly tried to get around him. Had she secretly wished for this encounter? Maybe she didn't need to answer that question.

"You look so familiar for some…" His sentence stopped there and his face changed from polite male shopper that almost collided with her to a stone-faced hardened man.

She begged with her eyes, *See me, not my husband. I didn't do this.*

"Excuse me." He moved from her so quickly that he took a piece of her with him, and she suddenly felt desperate to get it back. Too desperate.

"I'm sorry." Her voice surprised her. He turned toward her, and her heart stopped. Fear and hope leaped inside of her. Panicked, she waited for the words she could almost see forming on his lips. Daring herself, she looked into his eyes, eyes that held the same ever-present moisture of threatening tears that hers held. Forever passed, or so it seemed, before he turned and left her alone. Maybe it was a shared pain, but she was left feeling as if she knew him; she needed to know him. Somewhere deep in his eyes was the cure for her pain and, she hoped, that maybe somewhere within her he could find a cure for his.

Later, she would mindlessly eat a few chicken nuggets, less mindlessly drink her chardonnay, tuck her kids in without much-needed tenderness, and nurse the rest of the bottle alone until the tears brought her sleep. To her knowledge, no one had ever hated her before, and it cut deeper than she could have imagined. She had to fix it. She had to mend the wound.

Chapter 26

Samantha

The day of the preliminary hearing, Samantha woke hopeful. Maybe she had no reason to, but it felt exhilarating to believe in miracles for even one day. She prayed out loud. She begged the heavens for a miracle her family desperately needed. Let there not be enough evidence. Let Jacob come home more quickly.

Once again, she had to watch as the guards led Jacob into the courtroom wearing handcuffs and a jumpsuit. With effort, she placed herself somewhere else, in a faraway emptiness where nothing could touch her, and she watched silently as the first witness, Alexa Rogers, took the stand. This was a woman Samantha had never seen before. She sat in the witness chair with an unnaturally straight posture and pursed lips—ready, Samantha was sure, to help pass judgment against Jacob. She was right.

"Could you please tell us what you witnessed the day of the accident?" the judge asked.

"Yes, well, I first noticed him because he was driving erratically and almost caused me to rear-end him."

Samantha came out of her numbness as a feeling of overwhelming and slightly violent protectiveness washed over her. *What is this woman talking about?* she thought. Jacob doesn't drive erratically, and if he almost caused her to rear-end him, then why didn't she keep some distance? Samantha shifted in her seat trying to shake the urge to strangle the woman.

"Please explain what you mean by erratic driving." Seth's lawyer, Mr. Davis, urged.

"He slammed on the brakes, which almost caused me to run into him and for the man behind me to hit me. I didn't want to follow him anymore because of this, so I pulled up next to him, and that's when I noticed he was texting."

"What exactly did you see?" Mr. Davis asked.

"He had his hands right up on the steering wheel like so," she motioned with her hands how she claimed to see it, "so it was very obvious what he was doing. Then the light turned green, and he sped up very quickly considering the rainy conditions. By the next light, I was just slightly behind him. At this point, I was watching him because I was worried he might be dangerous on the road, and I could see him look down at something again—probably the phone because that's the direction he placed it. I saw the light turning yellow and then red, but he never even put on his brakes."

She stopped to catch her breath. "That's when it happened. He wasn't even looking. He just ran into her as she was preparing to cross the road. I stopped immediately to try to help her. But he did not." She wiped a tear from her eye as she accusingly glared at Jacob. "There was nothing I could do. Then I heard the crash farther up the road, and I knew it would be him."

Samantha could hear the crying on the other side of the courtroom and stared ahead at the woman she now despised. How did she paint such an inhuman, ugly picture of the man she loved? Jacob sat with his head in his hands. She wanted to hold him. She needed him to hold her.

After a few more exchanges, Alexa Rogers took a seat in the courtroom, and they called for Officer Talbot. The enormous man sauntered slowly to the front of the courtroom. His job was to recount the details of the accident to the judge. There were only a couple of people to share the evidence that would help the judge decide if it was enough to go to trial.

The stoic figure began factually describing the eyewitness's account, the weather, the running of the stop sign, the texting, the truck hitting Jacob.

Judge Murphy focused in on the texting part of the accident. "Did the texting records show evidence of texts being sent and received at that time?"

"Yes, two texts came in, and two texts went out in the timeframe of the accident. One of the texts came from his boss and another text was from a woman, Haley Bishop. Jacob responded, 'I'll call you later.'"

Samantha could feel the color leave her cheeks. She stared at the back of her husband's head knowing he, too, was feeling some strong emotions. Fear would be one. Why had he lied to her? Why was he texting Haley? If it was nothing, why hadn't he mentioned it? He tried to cover it up. Nothing felt real. For the first time since it started, she was happy he would be returning to the jail cell and not to their bed. She was at the same moment a jilted woman who wanted to scream the most hateful things, but she was also the seven-year-old girl who knew she never really had anything to offer, anything to make Jacob love her more than Haley.

Nothing else mattered. He had lied. How many lies were there? She felt tiny and crumpled. She couldn't hold herself upright no matter how hard she tried. She was limp from the inside out. Samantha didn't bother to brush away the tears anymore in an effort to appear strong because she wasn't. The end of the hearing was closing in, and she could feel it. Everyone could feel it. It wasn't going to come to a miraculous end today, and she no longer knew what to pray for anyway. Jacob was lying. This whole nightmare began by his texting Haley. Did she know it when she brought the hyacinth? When she hugged her on the couch after their night of wine and bonding? She felt more alone than she had ever been before.

Something diverted her eyes. Was it a movement or an animal instinct? She wasn't sure, but when she glanced over toward Seth, he was staring at her with something besides hatred in his eyes. He didn't look away, and neither did she, allowing so many feelings to pass between them. It was sympathy and concern, maybe curiosity as well, and she would do anything for more of it. Somehow she needed to make him verbalize his gaze, to take her in his arms like a wounded child and tell her that he forgave her.

Maybe it was impossible, but who else could give her the forgiveness she so needed just because she was married to Jacob? Jacob, a man who had somehow made her a criminal as well. Jacob, who she was now wondering if she knew at all. Who else could make her feel whole again? She finally looked down at the tissue she clung to in her lap, letting the moment pass.

The hallways emptied after the hearing ended for the day, and she said her goodbyes to her parents before entering the restroom. They knew better than to address the text issue with her. Maybe they had known all along. Maybe they encouraged it.

She slowly washed her hands, feeling in no rush to get anywhere. Standing in a public bathroom by herself was about as good as it was going to get for the day, and she welcomed the quiet before seeing her kids again. As she opened the bathroom door, she saw him there leaning against the wall. Why was he there? Only him standing there waiting, but why? She looked up and down the hallway again to prove it to herself, and no one was in sight. Making herself as tall as possible, she prepared to walk by him, but he began walking beside her.

"Could you stop walking, please?" Seth asked.

Samantha slowed and turned toward him, torn between the desire to freeze or flee.

"I'm sorry I walked away from you at the grocery store. It's just that…" Seth shifted from foot to foot glancing around the hall for the words to continue, "I didn't know how to respond."

"You don't have to apologize. How do either of us know how to respond? How to behave?"

Quiet fell between them for a moment, more peaceful than awkward.

"I know this may seem like the strangest question in the world, but would you like to grab a cup of coffee with me?"

"Wow!" she stuttered. "I really wasn't…" She looked up and down the hallways again, desperately wanting someone to appear and also secretly praying they didn't. "I really wasn't expecting you to ask me that."

"I know. I know. I'm sorry. It's just that I thought maybe it might help in some way. You know, to talk to someone else going through it. Never mind, it was a crazy thought."

He began to walk away.

"Wait." She looked down at her shoes that refused to take her away from him and then met his gaze. "I think you're right."

With a slight understanding nod, he murmured, "Okay."

Hesitantly, they walked a short way before he said, "I know there's a Starbucks a few blocks down the street."

"Okay."

More silences and then, "Did I see you at Maymont a few weeks ago?"

"Yes." She glanced up at him to judge his reaction. There wasn't one.

"So you have two children, too." Seth asked.

"Yes, Sydney and Ryan. Sydney is ten, and Ryan is eight."

"How are they doing with all of this?" Samantha stared at him a moment until he glanced back at her due to the silence. "I'm sorry, should we not be talking about this?"

"No, it's fine. It's better than fine. It's been hard for them, and I have to admit I've been so distracted that I'm not giving them as much attention as they deserve. How about your children?" Samantha asked, scared to hear the answer.

"Probably the same as yours, but mine are a bit younger. Sophie cried for…" He paused to catch his breath before continuing. "She cried for Ava a lot in the beginning, but now sometimes she just seems fussy. Maybe it's just me, and she always had her fussy moments that I never noticed. Maybe it was because Ava dealt with them. I just have to deal with them alone now." Seth's hands were in his pockets like a dejected child.

Samantha felt her words catch, and she swallowed painfully before saying, "I'm sorry."

They allowed the silence to settle between them and for the conversation to form slowly as they approached the coffee shop.

"You know the hard thing is that neither of my children will remember their mother. Connor may have a vague memory at best. They were her world, and they won't even know who she was." Samantha could hear his voice crack. It was such a personal sound to hear a man's voice crack that she felt an immediate intimacy. It would have felt natural to reach out and embrace him, but she also knew better. The shame too deep for words held her back.

"I don't even know what to say. I wish we could reverse time, and everything were different. I wish my kids wouldn't grow up visiting their father in a prison." It was her lame attempt to relate, but Seth cut her off.

"I'm sorry, Samantha. It is Samantha, right?"

"Yes," she replied aware she had crossed a line. Like the feeling when you have half drifted into a dream you weren't aware you were having until you woke from it, a magic had lifted.

"It was good to meet you, but I have to pass on that coffee. Maybe another day I'll be able to talk to you about it more easily," Seth spoke his last words quickly.

He turned and walked away, staring at the sidewalk as if he did not trust the ground to be there for him with each step. Samantha sat at the outside table and watched until he was safely out of her path before turning back. It was the tiniest taste of forgiveness that left her craving more of it, more of his companionship, more of him.

Chapter 27

——— ——— ——— ——— ——— ——— ——— ———

Samantha

Samantha set her coffee cup down on the want-ads and watched as drips of coffee slid down her mug and blurred the writing on the page. Blankly, she looked away and found the bird feeder that sat outside the kitchen window. An angry cardinal bounced around the openings looking for a lingering seed. It was yet one more task to add to the to-do list.

The phone began to ring. Since the hearing, her parents had called several times. Not Haley. She didn't dare. Up to this point, she had ignored the rings, but she had to face the uncomfortable conversation. She figured she could just listen to whatever bull they wanted to say, mumble a few things they would barely understand, and put an end to their calls for a bit. She reached the phone on the fourth ring.

"Hello." Samantha said curtly.

Silence.

More impatiently, "Hello."

"Hey. Hello, this is Seth Johnson. Is this Samantha?"

Nervous adrenaline shot through her and she stumbled, trying to find simple words.

"Yes, hello, Seth."

"I hope you don't mind me calling."

"No, not at all. In fact, I'm glad you did."

"Good. I just wanted to apologize again for the other day. I just…"

"You really don't have to apologize or explain. I know this is making us both a bit crazy." She was hoping he heard how she grouped them together, that he would remember she was suffering, too.

"Yes, it is." Silence "Do you think you would be up for that coffee? Maybe someplace a bit out of the way."

"I think that would be great."

Seth told her the name of the diner, and Samantha raced upstairs to get ready. He had become the only sliver of hope in her mind. Samantha knew she couldn't control what the outcome of the courts would be, but there was the other end of the conviction, the one that involved the outside world, the world she and her children would need to survive in after the trial ended. Seth represented mercy in that world, and she ran toward it, starving for a piece of it.

Many thoughts crossed her mind as she threw on a casual yet attractive sundress, sprayed herself with an ample dose of Elizabeth Arden, and applied her lengthening mascara. Samantha thought back to an article she had read in *Psychology Today*. It caught her eye because it was titled, "I'm Successful Because I'm Beautiful"—How We

Discriminate. According to the article, people are just nicer to more attractive people mainly because there is a desire to be liked by attractive people. Maybe not fair, but Samantha added a bit more mascara in hopes that people also forgave attractive people more easily as well. By the time the first cup of coffee was downed, Seth would find it impossible to hate her.

Within an hour, Samantha found herself walking into a dimly lit diner and searching the few occupied tables for a man that should be the enemy. It was uncomfortable at first as she slid herself into the booth seat across the table from him. Only a moment had passed before he began the conversation.

"Thank you for coming, Samantha." His voice was warm and smooth. Samantha couldn't help but think of the spiraling eyes of the cartoon snakes that put their victim into a trance. Seth's eyes were such a warm blue they made a person want to dive into them to see what lurked beneath. They captivated her and intimidated her at the same time. How many people had gone out of their way to make him like them just because of his eyes? Samantha suspected many.

"Thank you for asking me," she responded.

The heat coming from her face and neck were her evidence that she looked as nervous as she felt. She hadn't blushed in forever. She knew she needed to calm herself. Samantha felt she was representing her family, saving them from his judgement. The thought of Jacob would inspire her until the unwelcome image of Haley attached itself to him. Still, she was here for her family, she reminded herself.

The waitress came, and Seth ordered eggs over-easy, rye bread, and home fries. Samantha, coffee.

"Are you sure you don't want to eat? My treat," Seth offered.

"I'm positive. I had breakfast at home." She lied to defend the butterflies in her stomach that would have rejected the smallest morsel. Samantha was finding that not only did attractive people make people want acceptance, it also made them nervous. It was an unwelcome feeling.

They sat silently for a moment after the waitress turned away and then Seth let out an almost inaudible laugh. "I know this is uncomfortable. I just really felt like it could help us both."

"Agreed," Samantha smiled.

"How about we start simple?"

"Perfect. You first," Samantha said.

"That seems fair." Seth paused and thought for a moment. "Well, I live in Glen Allen, but you may have known that from seeing me in the grocery store. So you must live around there too?"

Samantha panicked thinking about stalking the pool before she remembered she had a perfectly good reason for being there.

"I live somewhat nearby, but my kids go to the camps at that YMCA. That's why I was over there." Did she say that with too much conviction? "It's a nice area."

"Yes, Ava and I, sorry I hope that's not uncomfortable." He stopped himself before finishing the thought.

"I don't think we can avoid uncomfortable."

"I suppose you're right. Ava and I really liked the schools and the pool. My son loved the pool."

"It looks like a great community center," Samantha said mid sip, almost choking when she realized her mistake.

"You've seen the pool?"

"Um, well, sometimes if I get to the camp early, I'll drive around to pass time."

Seth just nodded an a 'makes sense' kind of nod. "Anyway, does your neighborhood have a pool?"

Before long the conversation seemed effortless and time raced by too quickly. What started as feeling a bit like an interview, ended up feeling, if possible, like a friendship. After two hours, they knew each other's elementary schools through colleges, jobs, hobbies, the number of siblings each had, and many other miscellaneous details that they clung to like lifeboats, each one offering a piece of themselves that the other needed. He must have felt it too, the need to understand the enemy. The need to somehow befriend who they feared most, so they could take away their power to kill.

When Samantha picked the kids up at the bus stop, there was a lightness in her step that had been missing, an energy, a hope that was breathing life into her dying soul. That night, for almost just a moment, she forgot how angry she was at Jacob as she climbed into bed with his newest letter. After the first paragraph, she tucked it into her nightstand drawer, not ready to hear his explanations.

Chapter 28

Haley

The visits were becoming easier. Haley was happy that Samantha knew about them. It was better that way she told herself over again even though a piece of her wondered. Each time she dressed brightly, hoping to bring cheer into his depressing world, and she believed she did. Sometimes it was just a lift of his eyebrow or the slightest smile that showed his thankfulness to see her, but she would take it. She would take whatever she could get.

Today she wore her white capris and a lavender top. The top two buttons were left undone leaving only the slight taste of what lay below. She sprayed a few extras sprays of Chloe on her neck and wrist and even though she would never be truly happy with the face that smiled back at her in the mirror, she knew today was as good as it gets.

There was a new officer working the check-in desk. When she walked up to him, she noticed that he actually looked her up and down. Whatever was going on in his mind mattered to her for one reason only—it was a gauge of how Jacob would view her. It always came back to the same pathetic truth. If the world saw her as anything worthwhile, attractive, talented, kind; then maybe that meant Jacob would as well.

"Good morning," Haley said cheerfully.

"Good morning," the officer responded with a small smile, like someone surprised by the burst of positive energy she brought in with her.

"I'm here to see Jacob Truax," Haley announced.

"And are you Mrs. Truax?"

Haley felt the guilty blush come over her as a hint of laughter escaped. "Oh no, I'm his sister-in-law. We're a tight family. I like to, well, you know, keep his spirits up." She felt herself beginning to ramble and decided it was best to be quiet.

Once she was checked in, she proceeded to the visiting area where she waited for Jacob to arrive. It was taking an unbearable amount of time and her mind begin to drift to places it didn't want to go. Haley thought about Bradley back at the flower shop, covering for her. He knew where she was going and allowed her the freedom she needed. Two worlds, so different from each other, the warmth of the flower shop with its bright colors and smells that made any day amazing, versus the cold, sterile and somewhat terrifying room in which she sat. And she chose the cold and sterile.

She thought of Bradley, so devoted and in love with her. And then there was Jacob—the man that had rejected her so easily, tossed her to the side, gently and slowly, but nevertheless, he did dispose of her. Bradley who had filled her apartment with flowers, made her favorite dinner, slow danced in her living room with her and then dropped to one knee to ask for her hand in marriage. Jacob who watched Samantha with such adoration Haley wanted to smack him. Jacob who risked his job just to get away from her. Jacob who was the father of her niece and nephew. And whom was she choosing to shop at Victoria Secrets for? The man that never cared what lay beneath.

Jacob had a seat in the chair next to her. He mumbled something she couldn't decipher.

For just a moment, before the adrenaline had a chance to take over, she hated herself. She hated herself as it crept through her veins making her heart race just a little bit faster. She hated herself for the urge to take his hand in hers and the unmistakable knowledge that, right or wrong, she loved him and she had no idea how to stop.

"How are you doing?" Haley asked.

"Fabulous," Jacob mumbled.

Haley watched as the muscles in his jaw tightened. This wasn't Jacob. His gentle demeanor was buried, but that was fine. Haley wanted to know this Jacob as well.

"Have you seen Samantha and the kids this week?" he asked.

"No, it's been busy at the…"

"Are you seeing them soon? Maybe you could take the kids for Samantha for a bit. She's been pretty stressed."

"Yah, I could do that. I'll talk to her."

"Great." His answers were quick and short like someone that had overdosed on caffeine. His skin looked ashen. His eyes darted around, yet they seemed as if they could fall into a deep sleep at any moment. What was he searching for? What was he scared of? "I hadn't told her."

"Told her what?"

"That it was you. It was you that texted me before the accident."

Haley felt herself shrivel in her chair, like a child in trouble. "So? It wasn't inappropriate."

"It was still you, Haley. Why did you have to text right then? I should have told her. She shouldn't have found out in the courtroom."

There wasn't an answer and she knew it. Why does anything happen when it shouldn't? She refused to take blame. Haley looked around again, feeling as if she could be sick. She didn't do this. How was she to know when he was driving or not driving? She wasn't the one that read a text while behind the wheel.

"Are you okay, Jacob. Are you sleeping?" Now Haley did dare to reach for his hand which he quickly jerked away.

"Are you kidding me? Sleeping? Are you seriously asking that?" His voice was bitter and frightening. Maybe she didn't care to know this side of Jacob.

"I'm sorry, Jacob, I'm just worried. I'm just really worried." Haley could feel the tears begin to form, and they both let silence take hold for a moment.

"I'm sorry, Haley. No, I'm not sleeping. How do you sleep with a criminal in the bed next to you?

I don't even know for sure what he's here for. How am I supposed to sleep?"

Jacob laid his head on the table, resting on his arms, and for a moment he became so quiet that she wondered if he had dozed off right in front of her. For several minutes, she let him rest quietly while she studied the room and its inhabitants. She hated all of them, whether she had a right to or not. At the far end, she could see the correctional officer beginning to look at them as if their time might be coming to an end.

"Jacob," she whispered, "do you ever think about that night, the night before…?"

Jacob's head shot up. "No, Haley, I don't. And neither should you." Then he stood and left her again.

Chapter 29

Jacob

Jacob lay on his cot, staring at the pictures his children had created. He tried desperately to envision their tiny hands wrapped around each crayon, Sydney pushing her glasses further up the bridge of her nose as she intently designed her masterpiece, Ryan with mindless sounds shooting from his mouth as he broke crayon after crayon with his intense art.

He tried to smile at the image, but the emptiness was too deep. He was losing them. What would Samantha be thinking? He tried to explain, but the truth felt imprisoned with him. He needed to be alone with his wife. Not just for a visitation, but for days, days that would allow the truth to set in for her. He loved her beyond anything, but why would she believe him? Why would she care? Especially if she knew everything. There were too many things he would like to take back.

The pictures began to blur and sleep became too difficult to resist any longer. Jacob thought of Haley, of what she said, and let his mind drift there for a moment. So much in his life clung to strands of reality, strands that were now becoming frayed. What torment could sleep bring that was worse than his waking hours? Images began to form, flashes from his subconscious, and then he would startle awake. Rain, headlights, Samantha, Haley standing in the doorway, until he stopped being startled and the images lost their control, and then finally, Jacob slept.

Chapter 30

___ ___ ___ ___ ___ ___ ___ ___ ___

Samantha

Samantha walked into the house after dropping off Sydney and Ryan. The sound of the phone ringing split the silent atmosphere.

"Hello."

"Hello again." His voice was already familiar and addicting. He had become the solution to her pain. If he could forgive them, could understand them, to like them, did it really matter about the Suzanne's in the world and the whispers that seemed to follow her in her sleep?

"Hey, Seth."

"I just wanted to tell you how good it felt to talk yesterday. It just felt like it lifted some of the weight off my shoulders, if that makes any sense."

"It makes perfect sense."

"I would be willing to meet again if you wanted to," Seth offered cautiously.

Samantha hesitated but only for a moment. "I'd like that." But she knew it was more than liking it, she needed it. Her family needed it. This friendship could save them all.

"Just not today. I have an appointment." Samantha did not offer that she was going to see Jacob.

"Well then, how about Monday?"

"Monday it is. You pick the place." Samantha replied.

"Sounds great. I'll text you later."

"Perfect. Bye, Seth."

"Bye, Samantha." Why did it sound so exhilarating to hear her name come from his mouth? She hung up and practically skipped up the stairs to prepare for her meeting with Jacob. She dreaded the conversation, so instead she focused on Monday, a day of sunshine in the middle of her hurricane.

Her feelings of excitement faded more with each mile she drove. By the time she entered the jail, she felt as if she were attending the funeral of her past life. The cold cafeteria-style visiting rom held too many emotions from so many types of people—people she had easily looked down upon in another life. She had dressed nicely but not too nicely. She learned from the last visit that the gawking eyes were more frightening than complimentary. The great equalizing orange jumpsuits were only set apart by the quality of visitor they received.

Across the room, she saw a woman with a gold tooth eagerly grabbing at her inmate under the table. Not far from them, a tattooed biker chick held tightly to her rugged partner's face as she mauled him with her tongue. Samantha knew the rules. They were allowed a quick kiss at the beginning and the end of their visit. They were also permitted to hold hands. She glanced at the correctional officers that appeared distracted with other things. Maybe it was the human part of them that understood the undeniable and scientifically proven need for touch.

She looked at Jacob, and his eyes read everything she was thinking. If they were to touch, to kiss beyond the kiss of a greeting, to embrace, they would fall into a class of lowly desperate criminals. How long could she last? If they were to hold off, they might be waiting for years. Even through the baby years, they had not lost their desire to be intimate. She was not one of those women who didn't want to be touched or felt too tired at the end of the day. In fact, she may have craved him more, or at least craved the way he made her feel beautiful as he let his fingers trace her ever-changing body. Changes she could accept as long as he still desired her.

They would only hug and give a quick kiss to resist the fall from grace. She hated him and loved him. She wanted to hit him and get lost in him all at once. Seeing his face, a face that had amazed her from the first moment, made the guilt well inside of her. She considered mentioning her coffee with Seth but then she remembered the conversation that needed to happen, and his handsome features transformed in front of her to deceptive traps. She was sure he read the change on her face.

"So would you like to start talking?" she asked.

"Samantha, it was nothing, really. I would have told you, but that's what a little thing it was in my mind."

"You remembered the text from my dad. You could tell me about that. What was so different?"

"I don't know. Maybe because I knew it would bother you, and I didn't want to upset you. I'm sorry. I should have mentioned it."

"Yes, Jacob, you should have." Silence slipped in as they confrontationally stared at each other.

"Is there anything else you should be telling me?"

"No, Samantha, I swear. It's just that sometimes she texts me about stock tips. I only answer her to be polite. It's not like I really need her tips, but she is family. I'm not going to be rude."

Samantha's anger began to shift. Why the hell would Haley feel the need to text him anything? She didn't even text her sister. "Whatever, Jacob, it's the least of our worries right now, I guess. Just be honest with me for God's sake. The last thing we need right now is to start lying to each other." Again, she considered telling him about her conversation with Seth, but something held her back. Maybe it was because she wasn't sure if the conversations were a good thing or a bad thing, and she knew Jacob would feel the same.

Samantha couldn't be angry anymore. It was too exhausting. She took his hand and watched as their hands slipped perfectly together. The warmth of his skin screamed out to her. She needed more. She needed him. They would end their visit with a long embrace, leaving both of them longing for the other.

She left the jail feeling an emptiness that was impossible to fill. Her choices had come down to groping each other under a table or walking away empty after each visit. The tears began to roll down her cheeks as she fumbled for the ignition. She lay her head on the steering wheel and begged for answers from a universe that held them tightly to its breast. For reasons she didn't understand, maybe didn't want to believe, she thought about Seth, and how he looked at her as she spoke about all the menial topics they discussed. It was a momentary thought, so quick she could tell herself it didn't happen.

By the time she reached her home, she had only a couple of hours before camp ended. She needed to run. The air was thick and insanely hot and humid. Each breath she took, she felt the air try to drown her with its moisture. Samantha turned on her music and found her running playlist. Eminem started shouting out "Shake That." Morally, it was everything she wanted to keep from her children, but she secretly desired the way it allowed her to get lost in a world so far from her own. She felt the heat of the pavement reaching up to drag her down with it as Eminem insisted that some ho shake her ass.

As her feet began angrily pounding the pavement to each inappropriate beat, she concentrated on the feeling of her still-young muscles getting lost in a mindless pattern. After four miles, the heat won out, and she placed her hands on her hips as she tried to catch her breath.

Samantha entered her house but still had an angry energy that wouldn't leave her body, so she went into the air-conditioned living room, found her favorite station, and let the dark music fill the air. She found her weights and began every arm exercise she could remember. Each muscle burned, and still Samantha found herself seeking something else that would make her feel like she had just given life the fight of its life. She wondered how bizarre a punching bag would look hanging from her living room ceiling. The desperate urge to beat the shit out of something overpowered her. She would have to remember to check out the gym times for the next kickboxing class.

After what seemed like hours, Samantha finally tired. She carried her exhausted body into the shower and let the cold water trickle down her body, washing away the salty sweat. After toweling off, Samantha found her favorite lotion and began the ritual of slathering her toned skin from head to toe. She felt her slender waist and hip bones that stuck out just enough.

A sickening loneliness seeped from somewhere deep inside her. Who would touch her now? Whose hand would graze her hips? Whose arms would pull her close? Whose body would she melt into while they fell into a familiar and comforting sleep? The next time someone touched her, would she still feel young and toned? Would her breasts still stop them in their tracks, or would she nervously remove her bra hoping they didn't disappoint?

These were her years. Fit after the childbearing weight faded into the background, ready to be intimate with the man she loved through it all. How many years would it be? Could she wait that long? The answer was surfacing inside her like an unfamiliar sea creature. No, she feared, no she could not.

Chapter 31

Samantha

After Jacob and Samantha decided to move forward with their relationship, everything happened so quickly. There was the day on the boat, the first kiss, the first touch, the first *I love you's*. And then there was one week, maybe two, of unexplained silence. Samantha remembered how her heart sank farther every day that passed that Jacob didn't call.

Surprisingly, the silence was not broken by Jacob. She would always remember the strange air in the kitchen when she came down the stairs for her late Saturday breakfast. Her father was sitting with his coffee looking out the window. Instead of his usual, "Good morning, sunshine," she was met with a formal tone.

"Come sit with me, Samantha."

"Is something wrong?" Samantha cautiously crossed the kitchen and took the chair across from him.

"Do you have something you want to talk to me about?"

Samantha's mind raced through the past events in her life and could only settle on one thing that would concern her father.

"Maybe."

"You've crushed your sister," her father said. Samantha hung her head, not wanting to see the disappointment.

"I wasn't trying to hurt Haley."

"Are you sure of that?" her father asked.

"Dad, I love him, and he loves me."

"So I hear."

Where? How? Samantha wondered, but he must have read her mind. "Jacob came to me."

Jacob told Samantha he was eventually going to speak to her father, but he didn't tell her he had done it. Maybe that was why he had been so distant.

"I told him to at least be man enough to tell Haley himself. She feels very betrayed. I thought our family was better than that."

"I wasn't trying to hurt Haley." Samantha insisted again. "He makes me happy, Dad. Doesn't that matter to you?" Samantha said emphatically.

"Have you ever stopped to think that it's not just about what makes you happy? I want to believe that taking from Haley isn't what…" He cut himself off. His private thoughts about his daughter would remain his own.

He stood to leave and Samantha stared out the window. Before he could leave the room, Samantha turned to him and demanded, "Why wouldn't you have thought to introduce me? Why didn't you think I would have been good enough for him?"

Her father looked at her disapprovingly. "It's always a competition, isn't it, Samantha?" He turned and left the room.

Samantha grabbed her keys and drove until there was nowhere to go but Jacob's apartment. She let a million thoughts wreak havoc in her mind on her way there. What did her parents expect of her? Of course, it was a competition. Did they expect her to live on the sidelines cheering on Haley as her sister showed the world the gifts God had graced her with?

Jacob answered the door, but she didn't sense any excitement. He was distant. Was she losing him too? What had taken place between him and her father, between him and Haley?

"I've missed you." Samantha began.

"I've missed you too," he responded without looking up.

"What's wrong? Please talk to me."

Instead, he took her in his arms and kissed her with an intensity he had not shown before. Jacob began guiding her toward his bedroom. A shirt shed here and a shoe shed there, and with each loss Samantha felt what she was gaining.

A part of her wanted to slow things down so that she could focus on each moment his hand grazed a part of her body for the first time, but the final act began a finish line and they raced toward it. He spent the rest of Saturday showing her how much he had missed her, and when she woke curled up in his sheets Sunday morning, there was no doubt in her mind which sister held Jacob's heart.

Jacob

Jacob woke up with his arms around Samantha knowing then that she was the only one he wanted to hold for the rest of his life. He had never felt that way before, not with his long term high school, college girlfriend that fueled passion with childish antics, nor with the few quick romances that were mistakes he immediately understood, and definitely not with Haley. He knew it right away, but he always had a hard time breaking hearts. Some would say it was a strength, dragging things on just to avoid the heartbreak, but he knew it was a weakness.

It was all done, all the mistakes, all the misery of mismatched love. He had found the one. He softly kissed Samantha's bare shoulder as she slept and slipped his arm out from underneath her. He would wake her with a hot cup of coffee in bed. As he went to step out of bed, his foot landed on something hard. Looking down, he saw it was a bracelet and every drunken hazy moment came back. What had he done?

Chapter 32

Samantha

Monday came quickly. Samantha once again ripped through her closet for just the right outfit. What does a person wear to befriend her husband's enemy, to make him care for his family just enough not to go for the kill? She settled with a casual skirt, white sleeveless top and sandals. Friendly, attractive, but not too attractive.

Again, they went to the same out of the way restaurant. Samantha had prepared herself for a bit of awkwardness since they had discussed everything possible on their last encounter. What else could be left to talk about without getting too close to the case?

Seth walked in five minutes behind her in jeans and a t-shirt. He was undeniably attractive. His skin was a golden tan, and his arms were the arms of a man that used them for a living, not a weight lifter, just the tone, natural build. Samantha was quite sure Ava had been proud to be seen by his side.

She caught herself observing a bit too closely and realized that Seth was not the type of man that a woman should meet for coffee in normal situations, but this wasn't a normal situation and this man had to like her. She was her family's only hope of forgiveness—first her, then her children. Eventually, he would even begin to forgive Jacob, or at least not hate him. Jacob would understand when she finally found the right time to tell him about their meetings.

"Sorry, I'm a bit late. I know it's not polite to keep a lady waiting," Seth said.

"No problem. I've only been her a few minutes."

The waitress pretty much followed him to the table and was off to grab his coffee before he had picked up the menu. Samantha could not help but notice that he still wore his wedding ring. Something about seeing it made her feel safe.

Seth's phone chimed and he glanced down with a smile. Before speaking, he turned the phone toward Samantha with a look of pure adoration on his face. There they were, his two beautiful children smiling from the phone. It was hard for Samantha not to find something not cute about any child, but truly, Seth's kids were remarkable. And then it happened. They started talking again about kids, and parks, and museums. One conversation would interrupt and spill into another. It was so free and easy that it should have also been uncomfortable, but it wasn't.

Did Seth want her to like him too? Was that for some reason important to him as well? Samantha couldn't understand why it would be, but how could she not like him. In a different situation, another universe, she may have even liked him a great deal. But not in this one. In this one, she fought for her family. And because of that she agreed, as they said their goodbyes, to have coffee again.

Chapter 33

Haley

It was one of the largest weddings Bradley and Haley had ever been asked to provide for, and Bradley had lost a bit of his calm demeanor.

"Haley, we have hours left, and you still don't have the last arrangements finished," Bradley nearly shouted.

"I'm working on it, Bradley. I had a few issues," Haley nearly shouted back. Issues like she couldn't focus. Issues like she had used the wrong flowers for five arrangements before she realized her mistake.

She could see him shaking his head and knew it wasn't just the wedding that was wearing on him. For days now, he had reached out to her only to be turned away. She couldn't think about being intimate with him right now, but how long could she have a headache for really? Lately, when Bradley touched her arm the way he would when he thought things might go his way, she actually flinched. The thought of lying with him, of letting their bodies move together as they should, was exhausting. It wasn't like she never had feelings for

Bradley. At one point, she loved him. She knew she did. It's just that there are so many different ways a person can love another person.

Haley felt Bradley's arms reach around her from behind and his lips softly kiss her neck.

"I'm sorry, Haley. I didn't mean to be so short with you. Can I help you with them?"

Haley closed her eyes and only for a moment pictured someone else behind her besides Bradley and maybe in that moment when she let her body ease into his just slightly, he felt the desire from her that he had been needing to feel. She turned, keeping her eyes closed and lay her head on his chest.

"I'm sorry too."

Bradley held her tightly, and listened to her breathe the words, "I love you," and she sounded just like she meant it because, with her eyes closed, when she couldn't tell who she was finding comfort with, she did.

Chapter 34

—— —— —— —— —— —— —— ——

Samantha

Samantha's neighborhood would often have neighborhood events and Samantha had successfully avoided all of them since the accident. But when Sydney and Ryan saw the blow-up houses and water slides being inflated, she knew that it was inevitable. Ryan's face had been plastered to the window staring down the street at the cul-de-sac all morning. After all, these were the kids they had adjusted to facing during the school year. They were ready to move on. Samantha came up behind Ryan and ran her fingers through his hair as she loved to do. She herself was petrified to face everyone.

"Can we go yet?" Ryan begged.

"They're still blowing them up, Ryan. We can wait a few minutes." Samantha answered.

"But they have popsicles and all the other kids are probably eating them already."

Samantha had to admit, there were many kids running around clinging to the little frozen tubes she also bought in bulk all summer long.

"My friends are already down there," Sydney chimed in.

"Fine, get your shoes on."

Sydney and Ryan cheered and ran for the closet while Samantha tried to swallow the acid rising in her throat. Surely, they were all adults. People would be polite.

They headed down the road, Sydney and Ryan several feet ahead, bounding toward their friends and sweets as if they had been deprived for years.

Generally, someone would be heading toward her with a smile and beverage, but instead she only saw awkward glances that always ended with the person searching for someone to make that secret unspoken conversation with. The one that went a lot like, "Do you see what I see?" "Oh my God, I can't believe she's here."

Maybe she should head back and grab some wine. Maybe she should just grab the kids and head back. No, she couldn't do that to them. She watched as the chain reaction of nudging elbows spread like wildfire through the group of people that just months ago she called friends. Maybe they were more acquaintances now that she really thought about it, but how many so-called friends unveiled themselves that way in times of tragedy.

There was Sheila holding her one-year-old on her hip. Hadn't Samantha brought them a lasagna when her husband was home taking care of the siblings on his own? And Jordan, how many times had Samantha rushed over to let their dogs out to avoid accidents when Jordan and her husband were running late? Trisha, right before this happened, they had met to start a neighborhood

Bunco group. Samantha wondered if game nights had begun and her name had conveniently been left off the email list. But worst of all, there was Suzanne who stood in the middle of everything, the metaphorical spoon stirring the pot.

Did people really not think Samantha could hear the whispers and see the sideways glances? She found a shady spot off to the side and put her hands in her pockets mainly because she couldn't figure out what to do with them and looked out over the crowd.

Jacob had brought her to this shameful moment, and an irrational bitterness rose within her. She was so alone in the world, and the one person willing to talk to her was the one person who shouldn't want to. Maybe if they knew that Seth had befriended her, she would once again find her place in a world Jacob had taken away from her. Seth was the answer to the problem Jacob had created.

Maybe that's why when Seth asked her to join him for a movie at the Byrd theater she said yes. The theater was small, and she felt confident that no one would see them. They settled in side by side. Seth had bought a large bag of popcorn to share and a couple of drinks. Did it feel like a date? Yes, she had to admit. But she thought back to how cruel the rest of the world was being and Samantha didn't care. She didn't care when their hands accidentally brushed as they went for a handful of popcorn. She didn't care when their shoulders casually touched when he leaned in to comment on the movie. And she only slightly cared when later they found themselves side by side on bar stools and she was ordering her third wine.

It felt beyond good to laugh at stupid things as she let herself lean into him at whatever funny comment he made. He encouraged a fourth glass but Samantha knew that at three and half she would begin to lose control of her choices. Three was it. Seth reached for the door handle of his car, momentarily putting them face to face. Three glasses, she had control at three. She resisted looking up. She couldn't be lost in the blue eyes that mesmerized her even when she was sober.

He began pulling out and Samantha tried to push her last feelings away as she stared straight ahead.

"Can I ask you something?" Seth started.

"Sure."

"So you don't talk very much about your sister, about your relationship now. Are you close? Wasn't it your sister that texted Jacob?"

Samantha's three glasses of wine began swirling inside of her making her more nauseated than she should have been.

"How did you know that it was my sister?"

"Well, the case is kind of big thing in my life at the moment," he said with a hint of sarcasm. "When I heard the name in court, I did a little investigating."

Samantha felt immediately violated but then she thought of herself hiding under the tree at his pool and decided not to become confrontational. Who was she to judge?

"She is my sister. I don't know how to describe us. We are close." She looked for words for a moment. "What do they say about siblings sometimes— best of friends, worst of enemies?"

"I get it. I guess. So is she close with Jacob? I mean my brother didn't text Ava."

"Can we let this go? Maybe another time."

Seth was quiet for a moment. "It's all forgotten, but just know, I'm a really good listener."

"Good to know. I may need one." They smiled at each other quickly before Seth gave his attention back to the road. When they reached her house Seth walked to her door and gave her a lingering hug, and just like the small brush of his hand in the theater, Samantha was absolutely sure she enjoyed it.

Chapter 35

———— ———— ———— ———— ———— ———— ———— ————

Jacob

Something's changing. Jacob could feel it like an animal feels an approaching storm. When he went in to kiss Samantha hello, he was met with the slightest brush of her lips. She told him she felt on display and it made her uncomfortable. What was she waiting for?

Ryan had so much to say and Jacob was sure Samantha was happy to have an excuse to be quiet. Ryan sat on her lap as he rambled on and she rubbed his hair. Every now and then their eyes would meet over his head and she would smile a sad distant smile. When Ryan finally seemed to taper off, Sydney jumped in, too cool to have the energy of her brother. When he asked Samantha questions, the answers were cold and distant like a child telling their parents about their day at school.

"How's the yard service working out?"

"Great. It's nice not having to worry about it."

"Maybe I'll have to keep them when I get out. Free up some time for family."

"That would be nice." Again, the smile with nothing behind it.

He tried several more painful attempts but could not find his wife behind the wall she was building. Jacob hated himself more with each passing moment. How could he keep someone as beautiful as Samantha when he had been stripped of everything that made him who he was, that made him a husband? Sadly, he knew that he couldn't. The survival of their marriage lay completely in her hands, a hand that barely held on to him when he reached out to her.

"I love all of you so much," Jacob nearly whispered, his voice cracking.

"We love you too," she replied.

And then she gathered up the kids and left.

Chapter 36

Samantha

Samantha's parents invited everyone over for a Sunday brunch. She entered the house and passed each door frame as if it were a museum of her past. The place where she first spotted Jacob, the sister who thought she held him first watching from the kitchen, the table where her father had placed her as under a microscope. She couldn't help thinking of Seth. It seemed every day the idea of him consumed more and more of her time.

Why did he have to be that kind of person, that made you want to slide just a bit closer to him because something inside of you clung to his energy the way a starving person gravitated to the scent of a waffle cone? Every part of her knew that the irresistible treat was bad for her, that there were healthier choices, but right across from her sat a waffle cone, and she was growing impossibly hungry. She thought of how his eyes had met hers as they said goodbye on her doorstep and wondered if he had seen her hunger. Seth's eyes, the same eyes that had frightened her in the courtroom, now haunted her. Ava must have loved his eyes.

Would her family see it on her? It was only a friendship, yet somehow there was something else, a guilty pleasure that she was sure blanketed her like a cloak, making her unworthy of her family's presence. But hadn't she always felt that she was a bit unworthy of their presence?

She had not spoken to Haley in weeks, and she was sure Haley dreaded this visit as much as she did. The women busied themselves in the kitchen while Mr. Gorman took the grandkids outside to play a haphazard game of kickball. Samantha's mother put her in charge of the salad. She chopped vegetables and listened to her mother make small talk with Haley, something about floral arrangements for an upcoming wedding that Samantha couldn't care less about. She heard her father calling her mother's name from outside.

"Come outside and see these two athletes," he called.

So typical of them, Samantha thought. They probably had it planned the night before how they would get the two of them to stand awkwardly alone together.

"I'm coming." Mrs. Gorman wiped her hands on the kitchen towel and headed out the back door. Samantha watched as she stood on the deck and adoringly clapped at Ryan's perfectly placed kick.

"So, how are you doing?" Haley asked. Samantha held in the burst of emotion that wanted to erupt from her.

"As expected, I suppose." She kept her attention bouncing between the window and the job at hand.

"I've been wanting to talk to you about, well, you know, about the text," Haley said. Samantha hoped Haley was nervous as hell broaching the subject.

"What's there to say?"

"I'm sorry, for starters."

"What exactly are you sorry for, Haley? Is it putting my husband in jail or is it something bigger than that?"

"Samantha!"

"Samantha, what? What do you want me to say? I called you that morning after the accident. You couldn't mention that you had just been communicating with him? Don't tell me it was nothing so you forgot. I really don't want to hear it. It's been months, and you never brought it up. It makes me wonder why."

"Samantha, what do you think? Do you seriously believe I would be doing something behind your back with your husband? What kind of sister do you think I am?"

Samantha stopped to look at Haley.

"I don't know right now. Why wouldn't you mention that you were going to see him at the jail? Why do I keep hearing things from other people and not from you?"

"I'm sorry, Samantha. I am, but I promise you nothing is happening between us."

"You know what, Haley, I believe you that nothing is happening between the two of you, but I don't think it's because you don't want it to."

"Samantha, I'm your sister. Do you really think I would do that to you?" If her words didn't make Samantha guess her double meaning, the look on her face daring her to continue assured it.

"What are you really trying to say, Haley? You weren't married at the time. You were barely dating," Samantha argued. "It's different you know, dating and married."

"You'll make the rules bend for you. Or totally forget some pretty universal ones, like sisterhood and loyalty. I'm used to that by now. I've even learned a bit from you over the years."

Samantha put down the knife and studied her sister. "What have you learned, Haley? What have you done?"

"Looks like I'm finished with the chicken salad. I think I'll join them outside. I need some fresh air."

Samantha would pick at her food and listen to the conversations like an outsider the rest of the afternoon. Who were these people? Who was she? All of the constants in her life were slipping away and leaving her with something, something she was not sure was a beginning or an end.

Chapter 37

Samantha

How many times had she met with Seth? She pretended she needed to count them, but she knew. There were seven times now that they had slipped out to have an hour-long cup of coffee or to grab a bite to eat. And then there was the movie. She knew so much about him, far more than she should. He owned a lawn care business and seldom placed himself on any actual jobs anymore unless he wanted to. He liked football, mostly Virginia Tech, fall, chili, and beer, but not too much beer.

Each fact inched her closer to a cliff, and she begged herself to back away. It was impossible. She felt caught in a current heading her straight toward a waterfall. Every time a branch reached out across the choppy waters to save her, she let it pass by her. There was something about him that she needed so badly. Her thoughts became clouded by desire. He energized her, and she knew without him she would be dying inside. The gloom of her real life would take over. There would be nothing to look forward to, nothing to ignite her when she felt lifeless, nothing to get her up in the mornings. Another branch would pass her by today, maybe a call from a rare friend, an invitation from her mother, an idea for an unmade special treat for her children. Not one of those things brought her the happiness she needed because not one of them included Seth.

She scrambled back from dropping off Sydney and Ryan and prayed the phone would ring again. It was only moments until the sound echoed through her kitchen, making her heart ache like a teenager in love for the first time. How could she give it up? The feeling was amazingly empowering.

"Hello," Samantha chimed.

"I'm sick of coffee and movies."

"What?" Her heart sank.

"I was thinking after we talked the other day about how you said you were a runner."

"Well, actually I said I like to run. Calling me an actual runner may be insulting to the true athletes out there."

"Let me be the judge of that. I know this path. It's a little bit away, up near Carter's Mountain, but if we leave now, we can have time for a run and lunch, and we will be back before the school day ends."

"I'm putting on my shoes."

"I'll be outside your house in fifteen."

She put down the phone ecstatic as she ignored the sound of the raging waterfall looming in front of her.

For the first time, she slipped into his car. Another step to a familiarity that screamed danger. It would have been so easy to lean over and kiss him hello. Why, she begged, did it seem like such a natural reaction?

"Well, you look like a runner." She felt his eyes skim over her body.

"That's the most important part," she said with a smile.

The drive to Charlottesville passed quickly. It was amazing how many things they could find to talk about without ever mentioning Jacob and Ava. She could feel the two of them in the silences when the conversation edged too closely to the border, but they both knew to divert the topic quickly.

It was cool as they began their slow jog along the wooded trail, and she could tell they were both happy for the peace that nature brought them. They playfully raced up the rugged hills, pushing past each other trying to take the lead, and found themselves winded at a small overlook on the trail. They stopped, speechless, as they looked at the beauty of the mountains and stood side by side taking it in.

Even though Samantha felt an overpowering desire to reach out to Seth, she was still surprised when she felt his hand slip around hers. For only moments as she caught her breath, they stared straight ahead and then she felt him looking at her. Samantha begged herself not to look back at him because she knew her temptation would be too powerful, too impossible to resist. She turned toward him anyway.

He reached up and brushed his hand down the side of her cheek.

"You're very beautiful, Samantha."

She made her eyes stare at the ground beneath her. "Seth, I can't do this."

"Then don't. Just let me. Close your eyes, Samantha."

Without permission, she felt her eyes slowly close, and the soft touch of Seth's lips brushed against her own. She heard the other runners coming down the path. They were a branch she should grab; she needed to grab. She turned away and began to run; the sound of Seth's feet on the gravel kept a slow pace behind her.

She focused on the narrow trail formed through years of travelers. As with life, there was a clear path in front of her. Yes, it had ruts and hills and jagged rocks willing her to stagger over them, obstacles that promised scars that would forever remind the passerby of their presence. But it was a path. The one she was meant to stay on. She hated herself more with every step she took. She thought about the feel of Seth's hand gently touching her cheek, but every time the image came to mind it was chased away by now-painful memories, memories that used to be sweet but were now tainted by Seth's touch.

***

Jacob, his young face full of promise and expectation, hope and happiness, stood at the helm of his boat. It was one of their first real adventures together. Even though they had discussed going out on Jacob's boat, from the beginning something, guilt, kept holding them back. They had spoken on the phone plenty, found a quiet bar for a drink several times, but neither of them had been comfortable enough to cross the line. Haley still weighed heavy on both of them. After several weeks, Samantha finally found herself floating down the James and watching him in awe, already in love, or at least, she thought, still unaware of how much more she was capable of loving a person.

Jacob looked over at her and saw her watching him. He was so confident, so beautiful. He motioned for her to join him at the wheel and she stood in front of him as he guided her. She felt his fingers trace her arm. Like a child, she found she giggled at his touch. He turned her toward him. She remembered how her nervous laugh had stopped when she met his eyes. They were a mysterious hazel, changing with the colors around him, and always deep with thought. Lost in the moment and in everything she saw in his gaze, she would have done anything for him. She felt his hand brush her cheek. Competing with her sister was the farthest thing from her mind. She rose onto her bare tiptoes and kissed him softly on the lips. When she pulled away, she watched as his eyes slowly reopened and a small smile curled his lips. He was beautiful, and she knew then and maybe even before then that he loved her as well. It was one of the moments she prayed she would never forget. Samantha would have never guessed it would take another man's touch to remind her.

Seth would apologize on the ride home, leaving room for uncomfortable conversation, and silence. Silences where Samantha's mind took her back to the kitchen with Haley. What was it that Haley tried to tell her between her empty words? What was it really that Samantha was trying to save? A marriage to a man she sometimes feared she half knew?

The Charlottesville getaway was followed by days when the phone would not ring.

Chapter 38

Samantha

Jacob's letters continued to come daily. Sometimes, she clung to his words, trying to believe they could be enough. Sometimes, she despised them for trying to be. It made her sick how distant she had been to him the last time she saw him. She repeated the words in his letters in her mind while she completed her cleaning and while she pushed the cart through the grocery store. They followed her through homework and dinners.

There was a destination ahead of her, one that involved Jacob. She could see it in the distance gleaming in the darkness. She was determined to make it be enough. At first, she was able to force his words to light up her days but after only a couple weeks they were but a nightlight she struggled to see. The darkness once again threatened to smother it, the not knowing, the not trusting no matter how hard she tried, and she started to see the other light in the darkness calling to her. She began, slowly at first, taking glances, letting her mind drift when the house became quiet or when she lay in bed alone. And then finally she gave in to her temptations and texted him.

"How was your week?" Samantha tried to find the safest words possible to test the rocky waters. Within thirty seconds, there was a response.

"It just got better."

A smile crept across her face without permission. The phone rang as she tried to think of how to respond.

"Hi," was all she could utter.

"It's great to hear your voice."

"Sorry, it's just that…"

"Samantha, you don't have to apologize. I'm the one that needs to say I'm sorry. It's just that," he paused, "I'm just really surprised how much I enjoy being near you. I need to be near you."

Samantha sat with her head resting in her hands as she prayed for the right words. Her favorite flannel pajamas offered security as she sat cross-legged in the kitchen chair.

"I wish I could say I don't feel the same way." She paused wishing she could put down the phone and run. "I'm not this person. I've never been unfaithful. I don't want to be that person."

"I know, Samantha. I can tell that about you. I'm not the kind of man that thought he could feel so strongly for someone so soon after losing my wife. You must think I'm pretty heartless."

"Maybe I would if I weren't the one you developed feelings for, if I weren't the one married to a man going through hell while I'm sneaking around."

"Do you want me to stop calling?" Seth asked.

"I wish I could say yes, but I can't. You're the best thing I have going for me right now. How can I give that up? You're the only one I can talk to right now."

"Then please don't." They listened to the silence settle between them as they accepted their fate. "So what is it that's weighing on you?"

"How do you know something's weighing on me?"

"I'm starting to be able to read you pretty well."

Samantha smiled to herself loving his familiarity, yet hating herself at the same time for allowing it.

"I had a weird interaction with my sister the other day."

"Continue."

"I guess I should start by telling you that Jacob dated Haley before he was dating me. Well, I guess I need to also mention they were dating when Jacob and I first got involved. She has never gotten over it and I always sense she still has feelings for him."

"Wow, I didn't see that coming."

"I know I sound terrible, but they were just dating and I really believe it would have never worked out. Anyway, we were talking about the text and she said she learned some things from me. Do you think something could be going on between them."

Unbearable silence followed the question.

"Seth," Samantha begged.

"Sorry, I'm thinking how to put this. The expression, where there is smoke there is fire comes to mind. Samantha, I don't mean to upset you, but I find that a very odd thing to say if there is nothing except a few innocent texts."

Samantha started to cry openly.

"Oh my God, Samantha, I'm so sorry. I didn't mean to upset you, it's just…I was just giving my honest opinion." Samantha continued to sniffle into the phone unable to find words. "I'm coming over."

"No, please, I just need to be alone right now."

"I understand, but I need to see you soon." More silence and then Seth said exactly what Samantha needed to hear. "Samantha, do you think you could go somewhere with me this weekend?"

"Overnight?"

"Or maybe two. You need it, Samantha. You deserve it."

"I have to think about it, Seth. Where would we go?" Panic and excitement welled up inside of her at the same time. "What if someone saw us? Where would I say I was going?"

"I think people would understand if you just needed to get away. We'll get a cabin in the mountains. No one will see us. We'll stay in to eat and only step out for an occasional hike. Please think about it, Samantha. We need this. You need this."

Samantha thought about Haley's texts, about the visits to the jail, about the fact that Jacob had destroyed their lives, about what seemed at the moment the ugly truth of the marriage she no longer had faith in and before Jacob's next letter had time to arrive, she was arranging a grandparent weekend for the children and packing her bag.

They pulled in the driveway of the picturesque mountain cabin. The fall leaves framed the purposely rustic exterior. On the inside, a stone fireplace reached to the ceiling, and the door to the only bedroom lay invitingly open. Samantha turned to look at Seth. A little stubble showed on his otherwise perfect face, and she wanted desperately to drop her bags and go to him right then. How did it feel so perfect, so meant to be?

They unloaded the car and unpacked the groceries with the familiarity of an aged couple. Samantha laughed as she set the six bottles of wine on the counter.

"Seriously, how long are we staying?"

"If you'll notice, my dear, I brought chardonnay, malbec, cabernet, merlot, and some other things because I am still enjoying the pleasure of learning everything about you, and I have yet to discover your wine of choice." She could not help but smile as she glanced back over the selection.

"Very thoughtful."

She felt calmly happy as she glanced around the kitchen. What memories would these walls hold by the end of the weekend? He came behind her to set the French bread on the counter near the wine. She leaned against the counter watching as he came within inches of her. Their faces nearly touching, both of them wearing soft smiles of possibilities.

Every part of her was alive. He turned to put the steaks in the fridge, and then rubbed his hands together as he took inventory of the completed task.

"Now what?" he asked.

"Let's check out the trails you were telling me about. I'll need to work up an appetite for the steak dinner you have planned."

"Great idea. You want to change first?" he asked.

Samantha grabbed her bag and closed the bedroom door behind her. She found herself staring at the queen bed. Would they share it tonight or would he offer to sleep on the couch? Would she tell him not to? She came out, allowing Seth to go in to change next. Was he looking at the pillows and comforter and picturing them wrapped together in them? She hoped he was.

They headed down the closest trail and within minutes she felt his hand slip around hers. She didn't stop him. So naturally, they walked along trails taking in all that nature had to offer. The paths could never be long enough. She could have walked forever with him, but as the sun began to set she longed for the next part of their evening.

The trail ended back near the cabin, and she was sure their pace quickened when they saw it. Seth told her to shower while he prepared dinner. She slipped into the warm water and wondered if he was picturing her, the way she was sure she would be picturing him. Only a few persistent moments forced Jacob to enter into her mind, but his image was shoved out quickly, allowing her anger and distrust to fuel her decisions. It wasn't her fault she was nestled away in a cabin with a man she was quickly falling in love with.

She slipped into her comfy skinny jeans and a long sleeved t-shirt. She glanced at herself in the mirror, attractive and casual. Perfect. When she opened the door to the living area, she smelled the mushrooms and butter warming on the stovetop and heard the crackling fire already roaring. His back was to her, busy cutting bread. Her red wine awaited her. Seth heard her and turned to her with a smile. Knowingly, he had her wine glass in her hand before she could even reach for it, again letting himself become dangerously close to her.

"Your wine, beautiful."

"Well, thank you."

"I'm going to shower, and then I'll throw the steaks on the grill. Everything else is ready."

"Wow. I'm impressed."

"As you should be. Enjoy your wine, and I'll be right back."

Seth was amazingly fast, but somehow she still managed to drink her first glass and pour her second before he returned. She had to slow down. She wanted to remember everything. His wavy brown hair was still damp when he returned. He wore jeans and a t-shirt, just tight enough to show the well-defined muscles beneath it. Seth smiled at her as he stepped outside to start the grill. When he came back in, he noticed her almost empty wine glass, and then spied the quickly emptying bottle beside her.

"I thought maybe I should have a water next," Samantha said with a guilty grin.

"It's your weekend, Samantha. Do whatever you want."

She surprised herself by reaching up to run her fingers through his cold, damp hair. Her hand, a foreign entity, moved easily, and she watched it before looking into eyes that studied her, testing how far to go. Apparently, he thought he saw hesitation because he turned toward the counter for the steak.

"Do you want to come outside with me while I grill? You better grab your jacket because it's gotten quite chilly out there."

With a water and jacket in hand, she followed him to the grill. He was right. It could easily snow. She threw on her extra layer and wrapped her arms around herself. With her back to him, she stared out at a sky overflowing with stars. Where had all those stars been? They didn't shine on her that way in Richmond. Once the steaks were grilling, Seth wrapped his arms around her from behind, and they silently gazed at the marvel of the universe together. Happiness overflowed inside of her. She didn't know at the time that the eye of a hurricane could bring such abundant peace. After all, she didn't realize she was sitting in such a path of destruction.

After dinner had been cleaned up, they settled in front of the fireplace. Samantha curled her legs underneath her on the soft leather couch so that she could watch him as he spoke. What was he talking about? It didn't even matter. Apparently, he realized it as well and became silent. Again his eyes searched hers and, this time, they saw what they wanted. He leaned in, and their lips met softly at first and then more confidently, becoming ever more eager. From the first touch, she knew nothing would change the direction of the night, and they began making memories they hoped the walls would never share.

Chapter 39

―――――――――

Samantha

The front door opened, and Ryan and Sydney raced in to see their mother. The sound of their voices, the feel of their arms wrapped around her began squeezing out the memories that had floated her, undeserved, into her family's home. It was a perfect weekend that, at the time, she allowed to be guilt free. She lived in another universe where she could be another person, free of obligation and commitment, but the reality of her children and the love she had for them transformed the memories into something much darker. She didn't want the two to mix. She desperately needed both worlds.

After the children had run off to put their bags away, Samantha's mother came up and gave her a motherly embrace.

"So how was your weekend?"

"It was just what I needed, a little nature, a little silence. You know, time to think and get things into perspective."

"You've never been one to just want to run off on your own like that."

"I've never been married to a man in jail either, have I?"

Her mother's eyes studied her. "I guess you have a point."

Samantha busied herself in the kitchen, feeling like a teenager caught in the act. How did mothers always know?

"Samantha, is there anything you want to talk about?"

"No, Mom. I just needed to get away from everything for a bit. Thanks so much for watching the kids. It really helped."

"I'm always here for you, you know. I may have never been in your same shoes, but you may be surprised how many shoes can pinch a foot in the same way. We don't all need the same experiences to understand." Samantha looked at her mother as if she had never seen her before. Was it possible that her perfect mother had her secrets?

"Thanks, Mom. But today can we just leave it as it is?"

"Definitely." She smiled softly at her daughter. "Well, I'm going to get going, but you know how to reach me. Anytime, Samantha, I'm always here for you." Samantha's eyes began to sting. She gave her mom a quick embrace and choked back her emotion.

"Thanks again. Tell Dad I said hi, okay?"

Her kids raced down the stairs in time to walk their grandmother to her car. Samantha waved from the porch. She spent the afternoon trying desperately to focus on their sweet voices as they recounted the weekend's events, and she was more successful than she thought possible. But once she had them tucked in for the night and the wine was poured, everything changed. She flicked on the switch to the all too easy gas fireplace and let the sweet weekend memories come forcefully back.

She went insanely from smiling to crying, to hating herself, to loving Seth. She could imagine the crackle of the wood-burning fire that Seth had ignited. It became the backdrop to the many quiet moments and many conversations that haunted her.

There were possibilities for them. They were both sure of it. Somehow over the weekend they had taken on every hurdle before them and stood together in the imaginary future, hand in hand. There would be a new home where they would create new memories. Of course, the children would blend eventually. People would understand if they were patient with exposing their relationship so they wouldn't seem unfairly premature with their feelings. They would have to cover for a bit, move secretly, meet while the children were in school. It was possible.

In his arms, warm on the inside from one of the many varieties of wine, there was nothing she wanted more. She couldn't imagine a last time with him, a last time his warm lips would linger on hers, a last time his hands would explore her body, a last time she would be allowed to run her hands along his. The future with Seth was the only one she could imagine. All their possibilities made her feel alive where everything else felt like death. How could she give up a small pulse of her existence?

But now she sat in their living room. The living room that she had decorated while pretending Jacob had a choice. She could remember his smile as she threw all the paint samples on the kitchen table and awaited his opinion. When only silence met her questions, she looked up at him and found him staring at her. She felt beautiful in his eyes. He always made her feel that way, as if no one else mattered. Samantha pulled her hair behind her ear and innocently said, "What?"

His smile grew. "I want the one you want."

"Perfect answer." She smiled as she pulled all the samples into a pile. "You won't be disappointed."

"I never am." God, how she loved him. How did she keep forgetting? Haley, that's how she kept forgetting.

The wine began to sour on her palate. Lifeless, she flicked off the imitation fireplace and headed to her cold, deserted marriage bed.

Chapter 40

——— ——— ——— ——— ——— ——— ——— ———

Samantha

She couldn't stop their secret encounters any more easily than she could stop her breathing. She could pretend, but eventually her body would demand one more touch just as it would demand one more breath. Seth had discovered a little dive near the city. Literally, it was much like a dark cave, yet famous for its subs. "It was actually on some TV show," he told her. They found a table toward the back where they could barely be spotted. All the guilt faded away, and teenage-like giddiness once again replaced it.

Even in the dim lighting, his eyes drew her to him. They sat the way only lovers do, on one side of the table leaving no room between them. She felt his hand slide teasingly up her thigh, and she melted into him forgetting a world existed around them. His words encircled her, and she easily leaned in to steal a kiss, being braver in public than she had ever allowed. He watched her as she pulled away as if he was trying to judge her actions. She knew he was wondering if it meant her decisions were final. She had chosen him.

He leaned in again as if testing his theory, not sensing the bits of doubt that still vibrated through her soul. She smiled softly when he pulled away and then stared down at the untouched sub in front of her. The food on her plate would never satiate her appetite.

The door of the restaurant opened, letting an offensive light into their darkness. At first, it was only a silhouette that beamed in the doorway, and then a familiar face found her in her corner. They locked eyes before her father turned and left the restaurant. She was sure no breath escaped from her for several tortured moments. Seth's hand wrapped around her now-limp hand.

"Was that who I think it was?"

Samantha managed a whispered, "Yes." She left him there in the dark corner, and she went out onto the street to face a father who was always too good, too proud, too expectant to disappoint even though she so often did. Blinded by the light as she searched up and down the street, she almost begged the heavens that she would not find him, but then she did. He was sitting on a bench, hunched over as if someone had punched him in his gut. It was her. She had done this to him, his own daughter.

"I'm sorry. I'm so sorry."

He looked up at her with moisture-filled eyes, making him appear defeated and old. Samantha had never seen her father cry. Tears began to stream down her cheeks, each one begging to be seen, each one crying out for help.

"Sit down, Samantha."

Like a beaten, unworthy animal, she slowly eased herself onto the bench, her focus only on the ground, unable to look elsewhere. She saw the ants ambling around the roots and for one moment craved their simplicity, craved the inability to understand the words that were about to come.

"I love you, Sam, but I'm going to be brutally honest with you right now. I introduced your sister to Jacob because he's a good man, a solid man. He'll take care of his own until his dying day. I knew your sister was the type of person to meet him in the middle and not just take from him. You never give, Samantha. You've always taken. I'm your father. It's my job to give. I will give to you until my dying day and never expect anything back. I do that for both my girls. The difference between the two of you is that Haley has never expected it from us. Just knowing that she wanted to make us happy, to please us, was more than enough. She didn't have to do anything beyond that. I never saw that in you, Samantha. You take, and you don't give. You expect from others, yet no one can expect from you. It shouldn't surprise me that when things became hard, you ran. Jacob had nothing left to give. He needed, and you ran."

Samantha stared at him in disbelief. Not because of what he was saying. She knew deep down to her core that it was true, but that someone else saw her so clearly. It was humbling to the point of shattering to see herself through her father's eyes. She was selfish and greedy.

"Sam, I don't know what is going on with you and Seth." Samantha's mouth opened to say words she had not decided on, but she was cut off by her father's hand warning her to stay silent. "I don't want to know. But Sam, when the people you love no longer have strength, that's when you need to have strength for them. Your sister would have. You need to ask yourself, what are you willing to give back when he needs you?" Her father laid his strong guiding hand on her knee before he stood to go. He didn't look back.

Chapter 41

Samantha

Samantha wanted to avoid Seth's phone calls but she needed to cry to someone. Someone that saw her as more even if it was only because they didn't know her well enough yet. She cried it all out, sobbing at times.

"Samantha, I can't believe your own father would paint you in that light. It's your family's fault they never appreciated you for who you are. Have you ever considered that maybe your father never gave up on the idea that Haley would end up with Jacob? He knew she was visiting him. What else does he know?"

"Seth, please. I can't even…"

"Just hear me out Samantha. Maybe you're fighting the wrong fight. Maybe if you just stop fighting you'll see what's right in front of you. The truth."

All night, Samantha sat up thinking about her life, her memories with Jacob. They seemed so real. He couldn't have faked a lifetime of feelings. Or could he? She once thought she knew him better than anyone in the world. She thought about Haley, the sister she was before and the sister she was after

Samantha had betrayed her. She tried to own her part in that but the bitterness was still too strong. She thought about her father's words.

All these thoughts helped her see herself through everyone's eyes, her life through a distant unbiased telescope and where she fell in it. In the end, it was Seth's words that screamed to her the loudest. The truth would show itself when she stopped fighting to find it.

Samantha decided the time had come when she had to choose to let go in order to clearly see if she was deserving of what she was clinging to, if it ever really belonged to her, if she wanted it to. On the way to the jail, she pictured Haley's life with Jacob. Who would they have been? What children would be dancing around their living room of an unimaginable color, a color Samantha was sure she would have hated, even if it was just for the sake of it? She would have nieces and nephews that she would have loved, though. Samantha was sure she would have loved them the way Haley loved Sydney and Ryan. She hoped so, anyway.

It wasn't even surprising to her when she saw Haley leaving the jail. So faithful. So nurturing. She was there for him even when no one expected her to be. Before this moment, she would have been furious to see her, jealous even. Now it was just concrete sealing her father's words. Maybe Haley had always been meant to be with Jacob—Haley, the one visiting him in the jail, while Samantha was running off to a cabin with another man when things got tough.

She knew what she needed to do. She needed to let Jacob go. She had never deserved him. She knew that now. Her life was a pathetic attempt to live a life that only her sister deserved. Someone, she thought, should have loved her, someone that she could have loved back. It was becoming more apparent; it was supposed to be Jacob. For the first time in her life, she saw what she had taken from her sister. It was time to give it back, if that was even possible. In her heart, she knew she was walking away from a highway accident and telling her sister she could have the scraps of metal burning on the side of the road. What else did she have to offer?

"Haley." Samantha squeezed the name from her clenched throat. Haley turned towards her sister like a deer not sure it should be tamed.

"Samantha. I would have ridden with you if I knew you were coming." Samantha let the obvious fact that she had not contacted her slip away.

"I want to talk to you."

"Okay." An uncomfortable pause settled between them.

"Maybe we can find a seat somewhere." Without speaking, they ambled to an abandoned bench. "I'm not quite sure what I want to say," Samantha said when they finally sat.

"I'll start." Haley began. "I'm very sorry about the other day at Mom and Dad's. I didn't mean to sound so ugly. I don't even know where it was coming from."

"Yes, you do."

"Yea, I guess we both do," Haley confessed. "I guess I should tell you I heard you were having lunch with Seth." Samantha looked open-mouthed at her sister. Even though she had no right, she felt betrayed.

"How?"

"I at first overheard Dad talking to Mom. I didn't, in his defense, give him much choice but to fill me in."

"Did he tell you about our conversation after?" Samantha pleaded for a no.

"He just said you followed him out, and you talked. He didn't give much detail about that." Samantha relaxed just a little.

"Do you hate me? I mean, do you still hate me for ending up with Jacob?"

Haley stared out at the few trees sporadically growing nearby. Samantha knew she was choosing her words wisely. She prayed they would be kind.

"Growing up with you, I gave you everything I could. I loved you so much. But you made friends so easily, that you didn't need me for long. I always needed you. You were the best friend I ever had and sadly, I have to admit you still are."

Samantha's eyes filled with tears. She was a terrible best friend to the one person that was so deserving of friendship.

"I watched as you drifted away from me thinking someday I would be important to you again, that in adulthood we would find that bond again. When I started dating Jacob, I somehow thought it might be part of our bonding. I would have stories to share. I would be more interesting. We could maybe even go on double dates."

Haley paused for a bit and Samantha could hear her raspy breathing that was about to overflow into a cry. She regained her composure.

"Sometimes in life, we mistakenly give fate too much credit. When I found out you were seeing Jacob, I sat back and watched. Yes, at first, I was angry, really angry, and then I thought," Haley laughed to herself, "I thought it was part of a plan that finally someone would have their chance with you and come running back to me. I really liked him, Samantha, and you just swooped in and took him like he was just another quest and not a whole line of possibilities for me. I imagined my life, my children, my dreams so quickly with him that I knew it was fate that brought him to me. When he chose you, for the longest time I waited for fate to bring him back to me. I should have fought harder before it was too late."

Both women sat in silence for a moment, both contemplating a future where Haley had been braver, more determined.

"I'm so sorry, Haley." Silence fell between them for a few long moments. "Did you tell him? About Seth?"

"No, Samantha, that's for you to do, or not do, I guess." Haley stood and walked toward her car. As she reached the point where she was barely audible, she spoke over her shoulder, "Just do the right thing for once. Just do the right thing."

Samantha watched as her sister disappeared. Could she? Was she prepared to do the right thing? What was the right thing?

Samantha was crying when Jacob approached the table. It's strange how someone looks so different when you are saying goodbye. When you feel in some ways forced to say goodbye. He was a stranger, yet so familiar. Almost like he appeared on their first dates after they had already touched, but she was still not sure if she had the right to touch him again. Everything was more beautiful, new, precious. Her sister's words rang in her ears. She had given up her rights to him the minute she left for the cabin with Seth. Jacob deserved better.

Samantha saw how he studied her all the way to the table, a small panic arising in his eyes. He would know something had changed inside of her. He must have sensed that they were in trouble.

"Jacob, we need to talk," Samantha uttered, still not knowing what she was willing to say.

"Samantha, please, please, let me talk."

"Jacob, you don't understand. I need to speak first. I need to tell you-"

"I beg you, Samantha. Don't say anything. Every day I wake up, and I see these walls. I don't even want to lift my head off of the Godforsaken crappy pillows they give us. Then I think of you and the kids, and I get up, and I go through the motions knowing that they can't keep me here forever. Even if I am found guilty, I will come home to you eventually. We will be a family again. It's the only thing that keeps me going. Please don't take that from me." Both of them, sobbing, reached for each other.

"Jacob, what about Haley?"

Jacob loosened his grip and looked at Samantha as if he had never met her.

"What are you talking about, Samantha? What does she have to do with anything?"

"I saw her leaving. I know she comes to see you often. She has always been in love with you. I know that now. What if? What if, Jacob, the reason we are together is because I didn't want you with her? What if I hadn't interfered? What if I had not smiled at you, begging for you to notice me? Maybe everyone would have been happier. I never had anything to offer you. I don't make money. I'm not that brilliant. I can't play the piano. I have nothing to give you. I stole you away from someone who would have offered you so much more than I ever could."

Jacob smiled through his tears. "I'll always remember that moment. The moment you attempted seduction like a little girl trying on her mother's makeup. I was in love with the woman I imagined what lay behind that smile from the second I saw you. I watched you stand uncomfortably in crowds of middle-aged people, staring down at your drink like it was salvation. I wanted to be that drink in your hand. I wanted to be what you clung to when you felt out of place and insecure. I wanted it to be my hand you found in a crowded room, my eyes you sought out to say, 'Everything will be okay.' I want to be that again someday, Samantha. It's all I wanted since the day I met you."

Samantha stared at him in amazement. How did he so easily see the flaws she tried to bury? How did he love her anyway?

"It wasn't the smile I remembered for days to come. It was the insecure young woman I saw behind it. You thought you owned me by your confidence when you really owned me by everything I felt I could offer you, like a smile because you couldn't stop yourself from smiling, a smile without ulterior motives. You never stole me from your sister. It was all about patience after that night, but I knew someday we would be together."

Oh Lord, she thought, *Jacob, from the first moment may have been a better person than I ever dreamed of deserving, but he was always what I needed. And for some unexplainable reason I didn't have to steal him from Haley because he had always wanted me.*

When Samantha lay in bed that night, she thought obsessively about Jacob's words. He loved her for what he could offer her. Right from the start, he was only concerned with what he could offer her. She felt acid rise in her throat as it often did lately. She made herself sick. How come he didn't see behind the person she was before it was too late? He would have run from her, a person always seeking to obtain something from someone, always trying to fill the void, her human, insatiable void, by taking, taking, taking.

What had she done? Once again she cared more about her emptiness than anything else. Her husband, her children, her responsibilities. Jacob's words made her question if it was love she felt for Seth, and made her sure that even if she did, that she shouldn't. Was it just that she needed him because, once again, the giant gaping hole inside of her, an ache crying out to be healed, to be noticed ruled her decisions. Her tears dripped down the sides of her face, puddling on her pillows. She had never felt so empty.

Chapter 42

Samantha

November fifteen loomed painfully in the future, the day the trial would begin—with only weeks left for her to decide who she was and who she wanted to be. Samantha avoided her parents, her sister, her friends. Not one of them would lead her to her truth. The truth could be found only in her children and in herself, and yes, she admitted to herself she wasn't done with Seth yet.

As the days passed, the power of Jacob's words mingled with the feelings she had while lying next to Seth in the cabin, both equally strong. She didn't want to lose Jacob, but ending her relationship with Seth too abruptly would leave her aching for him for many years to come. There had to be closure. Or at least that was what she told herself during each encounter. If she went back to Jacob, it would have to be with her whole heart. She would be the woman he deserved. Even Samantha heard the insanity in her logic, the logic that in order to find her way back to Jacob, she needed to keep seeing Seth.

She would walk down the hallways, running her hands along the walls as if caught between a hello and goodbye. The nearly bare wall gave way to a picture taken on the shores of North Carolina. Their matching khakis and white shirts glowed in the setting sun. She remembered the day well. The picture didn't show the squabble that Sydney and Ryan had had just moments before.

They looked like a million other families that had sat on the off-limit dunes to let a photographer catch the sun illuminating their time and place in the universe. It was their still life photo taken before things begin to spoil, before the sun burned too deeply to hold still in one place, before the waves came and washed the prints of the day away.

How could one person, one event, cut such a hole in a picture that seemed so finished—a picture that had been walked past a million times and taken for granted that it would be there the next time she passed by it. The way an arm gently draped across a shoulder, posed yet still real. A smile that was so familiar, every crease, every crooked angle, every tooth slightly off color yet so human, so beautiful. A family of imperfectly perfect people that came together to form her world, her everything. The accident, maybe that was the hole, but Seth, what was Seth? He was the question mark in the middle of it all. He was the question mark begging for an answer. Did Samantha want to fix it?

Was there a reason for her desires, or did the universe just enjoy setting up temptations? At what point does something become a love story rather than an inexcusable evil? Was every feeling of love and desire for someone else after two people had spoken their vows to each other completely inappropriate, or could they have a purpose?

Samantha remembered a time not long before that she would have, without hesitation, said yes. They were only evils, and anyone with any morals could avoid them. The whole neighborhood knew of the young couple in the front cul-de-sac that went through an ugly divorce. She was friendly with the woman, but not friends—the perfect closeness that allowed her to know bits and pieces and be able to judge without guilt.

Samantha enjoyed waiting at the corner with the other mothers and adding whatever gossip she could to the small bit of excitement in the air. The woman was a teacher at the middle school her children would attend and became just a bit too friendly with the principal, who was married as well. Scandalous behavior that Samantha used for her entertainment. Samantha remembered crawling in bed with Jacob and feeling as if she could never be touched by such temptations. Temptation could never find her tucked away in the comfort of her home. It was so much fun to judge.

Now she avoided the neighbors. They probably enjoyed her distance since quiet whispers could be difficult to hear above the din of kids and traffic. Maybe they had seen Seth pulling up to her house. Maybe they hadn't. Either way, they had other fuel for the gossip about their family. Now she wondered about that neighbor. How did temptation find her? Was her husband negligent to her needs? Did she fall out of love? Did she just lack morals and strength? It's funny how different things appear when viewed from the base of the pedestal.

Somewhere inside that neighbor's heart was a hole that she filled by falling from grace. Yes, no matter the story, her neighbor was wrong. Samantha was wrong. But in her angry, childish defense, she asked the universe, begged the universe one question. What cruel world would create an emptiness that could only be filled by falling into darkness?

Samantha hated Jacob for shaking up the reality she was trying to crawl back to eventually. She was something in that reality, something that mattered. She was a pretty great wife and mother, or so she thought. Maybe she wasn't writing articles on marriage and parenting. She wasn't PTO president or even class mom. She sometimes had processed meals and wore cotton and not lingerie to bed, but she was still good at her role. Now she wasn't sure what she was anymore.

What if she had met Seth some other way? In a grocery store, a work party, a friend's husband? What if she had been happy when she met him? Would she have still started craving him as if he were the air she needed to survive? Why did she have to meet him when she was so weak and so painfully lonely? Maybe because she was meant to fall in love with him, or maybe this was the test of her life? Could she truly leave what was once everything to her?

Outside, the rain pelted the windows. It was a day of memories and longing. Momentarily, she put the idea of chores in the farthest parts of her mind. Lost in her distant world, she heard the sound of the doorbell struggling to get her attention. Still in slippers and lounge clothes, she sluggishly walked down the foyer to see who had braved the weather. On the other side stood a dripping wet Seth. Apparently, the rain was not helping his landscape business. He had never stepped foot in her home, and she wasn't quite sure she wanted him to cross that boundary, but with little hesitation, Samantha opened the door.

"Seth, I can't believe you came out in this weather."

"Anything for you." He smiled. She smiled back politely, not sure it was really for her at all.

"Well, come on in and get dry." He stepped into the foyer. The rain dripping off his jacket was sure to leave watermarks on her polished floor. She would try to erase them later. "I'll get you a towel."

When she returned, he had removed his shoes and coat and was looking a bit too familiar with his surroundings.

"So what made you come out in this?"

"I needed to see you. So much is about to happen. I just want to soak up whatever time we have before…"

"I know. Well, actually, I don't know. I don't know anything right now."

Seth set the towel down after wiping himself off the best he could. He wrapped his arms around her, and she let her head rest on his chest.

"That's what I'm becoming terrified of, Samantha. I'm afraid of losing you. I'm afraid you'll feel obligated to forget about us."

She wanted to scream that it wasn't just obligation. She loved Jacob, but somehow, in some strange way, she felt unfaithful telling him she was in love with her husband.

"Want some coffee?"

"Yes, please." He paused. "We never really talk about it, the accident, the trial. Maybe it's time we do."

She silently put the coffee on to brew, her body tense and nauseated by the idea of a conversation so painful to both of them. Seth was already sitting at the kitchen table, once again too comfortable. Did he know he was in Jacob's seat? Samantha slid into her own as if trying on a new outfit. They both watched the rain pelting the window as the coffeemaker began spitting out the first hot drips of coffee.

"Should I begin?" Seth offered.

"Sure, since I have no idea how to."

"Well, first, have you spoken to your father again?"

"No, it's kind of hard to speak to him after he..." She caught her breath, not realizing how hard it would be to say the words out loud again. "He let me know that he wished Haley would have ended up with Jacob, that she was pretty much a better person."

"Distance can be a good thing sometimes."

"Can you seriously blame him for feeling that way when he caught me sitting next to you like I was?"

"It's still a cruel thing for a father to say. I'm sorry, Samantha."

"My life has always been a competition, it seems, a competition that I could never win until it came to Jacob. Let's move onto something else."

They both let silence fall between them as they drank their coffee and glanced again at the array of birds on the feeder, silently thanking them for their distraction.

"Maybe there are even better things in your future. Maybe we were meant to be sitting here at your table drinking coffee and watching the birds together," Seth offered.

"Life is pretty cruel if 'meant to be' means destroying everything in its path to make it happen."

"Agreed. To be honest, I don't know what to wish for anymore. I want justice. Ava was my wife." He stopped momentarily, testing the sound of Ava's name being spoken aloud in Samantha's home. "She was an incredible mother. I never saw her lose her patience or be too tired to read a story or to stay awake with them until they fell back to sleep. She never complained. Being a mother was all she ever wanted."

Samantha felt the sting of jealousy but fought to move beyond it. "I loved her, Samantha. I adored her. We were happy." Again he paused. Samantha could not look at him, but she heard the pain in his voice. "My children, they won't even know her. I show them pictures, and I tell them stories about her every day. I don't want them to see their mother as a stranger. It's all I can do to keep her memory alive."

Samantha felt her heart began to heave. Suddenly, she was an outsider to both her world and his. Why had it never occurred to her that Ava was still alive in their home, that she was still so alive to Seth? Maybe because she didn't want to believe it. How could she ever compare to Ava, to Haley?

"How do I not want justice, Samantha? How do I not want him to pay for taking her away from us?" The first tear rolled down her cheek. He must have looked at her then because his voice turned more to panic. She heard his chair being pushed from the table suddenly.

"Oh my God, Samantha, I'm so sorry. What was I thinking? I can't talk to you about this."

She felt herself melt into his arms, and she let the tears fall. His lips began catching her teardrops with soft kisses and mumbled apologies. She felt herself being lifted and gently set back down on the couch. Without thought, she began kissing him, desperate for a closeness only he could give. They became lost in a passion of pain and need and want, pulling each other as close as possible, leaving no room for the world to squeeze between them. They lay together in silence, defeated and exhausted.

It wasn't fair, she wanted to scream, how badly one could need another soul and how the same fate that created the need also made it impossible. The ache was too hard to bear. Samantha curled more tightly into Seth's arms, allowing her tears to roll onto his chest. She knew he was crying, too. Their bodies melted together like a warm comforter forcing away the cold, and they drifted off to sleep.

Samantha wasn't sure how long they had slept, but when she felt him begin to stir, she knew the air had shifted. Seth was quiet and almost cold. He began putting on his clothes, still damp from the storm. Something was off, almost dangerously bordering awkward.

Finally, Seth spoke, "So will you tell him?" The question completely threw Samantha. It was as if he had brought Jacob into the room with them. She could almost envision his face, emotionally crushed seeing his wife, her hair messed from Seth's touch.

Even though she was sure she knew what he was talking about, she asked anyway. "Tell who, what?"

"Are you telling Jacob about us?"

"I don't know. I haven't thought..."

"I think you should."

Samantha stared at Seth's face as his jawbone found the rigid stance it held in the courtroom so long ago.

"Why?"

"So he knows we both took something from each other."

Samantha's body went numb as Seth finished dressing.

"Seth, why would you say that?" Samantha begged, crushed.

"I need to go."

Before closing the door behind him, he called over his shoulder. "See you at the trial,

Samantha." He paused for a moment. "I hope it gives us all closure."

Samantha stared at the closed door for what seemed like an eternity, feeling more naked than she had ever felt before.

Chapter 43

━━ ━━ ━━ ━━ ━━ ━━ ━━ ━━ ━━

Samantha

For days, she waited. She didn't want to speak to Seth, but she wanted him to at least try. She wanted an apology. She had been a fool to believe he loved her. Karma. All she wanted was to be forgiven, to be loved. Instead, she hurt the one man that had ever truly loved her. As she loaded her car with groceries, she glanced once again at her phone. Nothing. The silence was killing her. It was as if he had played a sick joke, and she was waiting for him to jump out, laugh, and yell, "Gotcha." But no one was jumping out.

She backed up slowly, knowing she needed to focus. Her brain was in a million places. Each day, she found herself being forgetful, making stupid mistakes. She stopped at the stop sign waiting to pull out. Just enough time to check again. Nothing. She pulled out carefully. Broad Street was always annoyingly busy.

After several moments, she was able to pull out and slide into the uneven rhythm of traffic. The stop and go of it drove her nuts. The phone beeped. Was that the email sound, text sound? She couldn't remember. Quickly, she glanced down. It was only but a moment. When she looked back up, all she saw were brake lights. Panicked, she slammed down hard, making more of a squeal than necessary.

Had the woman driving the car in front of her looked back at her, Samantha was sure she would have seen nothing but disgust and anger in her eyes, but the mom was busy, busy focusing on the tiny person too small for Samantha to glimpse in the backseat. The *baby on board* sign slightly swaying in the window screamed at Samantha. How quickly she could have hit them. How easy it would have been to have hurt that baby… Jacob, she had to see Jacob.

The next day was Saturday, and for the first time she was excited, genuinely excited to take her children to see their father. Jacob could see it on her face as he entered the visiting room. She watched as a shadow lifted from his face. No, she would not tell him today either. Maybe some day, probably, but not today. She met him halfway and hugged him tightly as if he were returning to her from a much nobler experience. His scent was different now, but maybe more real. There was no cologne to cover the real Jacob. She pulled away and looked at him. It was the real him. Stripped of everything. There was no job, no social stature, no suit. It was just him, and she realized how very much she loved him. Jacob pulled her back into him.

"Oh my God, Samantha, it's so incredible to see you." He had seen her only a week before, but not really; she had been missing for a longer time than that.

"Jacob, I just want you home. I want my family back." The kids were wrapped around them as well after only a moment.

"You never lost your family, Samantha. No one can take that from us."

Not today, she thought again. He doesn't need to know today.

Later that week, Samantha scrubbed her house. It was a surprisingly warm fall day, so she opened the windows. A meal simmered in the crock pot. She was happy. Something she had learned not to take for granted. Occasionally, her mind drifted to Seth, but she pushed the thought away. It had been almost two weeks since he walked out her door, and she was beginning to think she honestly wouldn't see him until the trial. By that time, she should sufficiently hate him; she should have had enough time for the obvious truth to become her new reality.

When the doorbell rang, Samantha assumed it was some unexpected delivery, but instead found her mother standing there with fresh flowers.

"I thought you might need some cheering up."

"Thanks," Samantha said as she accepted the flowers and kissed her mother on the cheek. "I'm surprised you want to speak to me after the conversation I know you had with Dad."

"Samantha, a mother doesn't just turn her back on her child because she's struggling with her decisions. In fact, that's exactly when I want you to know I'm her for you, to listen. I offered that before, when you went away for the weekend. I'm not blind, my dear."

"Mom, how can I open up to someone who would never mess up, who would never betray their husband? You and Dad have had the perfect marriage. How can you possibly understand?"

"Samantha, there are no perfect marriages because there are no perfect people. That includes me, Samantha."

"Somehow, I think I would rather have this conversation sitting down. Let me get us coffee."

Liz followed her daughter into the kitchen and watched her shaky hands pour the coffee and place it on the table.

"Well," Liz began, "I don't have much of a story to tell if you're thinking of a scandalous affair."

"Thank God."

"But I have learned a few things in my years. Some people have had affairs because two weak moments aligned and some people have never had an affair because they didn't. There was a man once, whom I prefer not to mention, that I fell in love with. One can argue that that is worse, but I'm not sure. I wouldn't want your father to have faltered physically or mentally. They would both crush me. But what I learned in that short time, was that I wasn't immune, even in a seemingly perfect marriage. If our two weak moments had aligned, maybe everything would be different for our family."

Samantha began to cry. "I feel so ashamed of my weakness. I would have never thought I would have been one of those women."

"Samantha, I'm not saying it's okay, but I want you to know we were not born into this world the finished product God wants us to be. Maybe instead of looking at it as a weakness with no purpose, think of it in a way a creator looks at a project. We are all just the cement, gravel, and sand before the water hits it. We so easily cave to pressure. We change form with the slightest resistance. Then the water comes in and for a while it appears to have made everything muddy sludge until it is allowed to finish its work. In time, that muddy sludge hardens to something more stable than it had ever been, concrete. You're just becoming more concrete, more dependable and sure of the person you are meant to be."

The tears flowed freely from both woman as Samantha allowed her mother to hold her as she did as a child. After a few moments, Liz wiped the tears from Samantha's eyes and stood to leave.

"Believe in yourself Samantha. I have always believed in you." Samantha walked her mother to the door, and with a final embrace said goodbye.

The sound of her cell phone buzzing, brought her back. With renewed strength, she didn't fear who was on the other end because he had lost his hold. There was nothing he could say to make up for the way he left her. There was nothing he could do that would undo that memory. She quickly glanced at the phone to confirm it was him, and then put her phone on silence. After that, Samantha busied herself throughout the house, picking up socks deposited as Sydney and Ryan had run, and finding dishes in rooms where they weren't allowed to eat.

She had only a short time left until they were home and ready to start the cycle over. Even the mundane chores made her happy. Just as she spotted a half-eaten box of crackers sticking out from under the couch and began, without actual annoyance, mumbling, "Ryan Truax, I know this was you," the doorbell rang. She tried to straighten her hair in the hallway mirror before answering.

Seth stood before her, looking almost as miserable as she had felt for days before. The sight of him looking defeated only gave her more power.

"Samantha, please let me in. I need to talk to you. We can't leave things like this."

"I don't know what you could possibly have to say to erase what you did."

"I know. I know. Just please let me try." Samantha moved to the side, and Seth slipped in like a child afraid of punishment. He turned to face her in the hallway and was met with crossed arms and an expressionless face.

"I can't explain what happened. I was so happy to be with you the other day. I meant it when I said I love you. I do love you. One minute I was laying there so happy, and then this black cloud went over everything, and I felt so guilty. I felt guilty for moving on, for loving someone, for allowing myself to stop thinking of Ava. It was like I let her go, and I wasn't ready. Not only did I let her go, but

I also slept with her murderer's wife. I felt like a traitor. I felt like she was watching me, and it overwhelmed me. I needed to do something to prove I loved her, and unfortunately, all I could do was to say something hateful to you. Do you understand that at all?"

Samantha stared back at him allowing him to feel the discomfort he deserved. Yes, she did understand. Desperately, she wanted to say something ugly to show her love as well. She did understand the guilt. She understood it all. But he did not.

"His name is Jacob. He is not a murderer. He made a terrible mistake and is now rotting away in a cell while his wife betrays him. He's a good man, Seth. Maybe you will never be able to accept that, but he's a very good man. You would have liked him if things were different."

They stared at each other, and she felt the wall begin to form between them. There could never be a them. Samantha didn't have to ask him to leave. He turned toward the door and disappeared, leaving Samantha with too many emotions. One of them, she had to admit to herself, was relief.

Chapter 44

Samantha

It was time to remember who she was, or at least was capable of being, before everything crashed, throwing her so far off track. Fall wreaths were being hung. Mums were being planted. Grocery stores were displaying an abundance of candy.

Somewhere inside her was a piece of her mother she had tried, for reasons she could not explain, to ignore. Today though, it was exactly the piece of her she needed. It was the piece of her that believed in herself, saw possibilities, saw who she could be if she only allowed it to happen.

Suddenly, she was struck with an urge to revisit the place that so many years ago made her doubt herself, to feel second to her sister and her sister's gifts. There was an answer there, and she was going to find it.

"We're going on an adventure today, kids." She could see their ears perk up, and she chuckled to herself at how baffled they would be when she told them they would be visiting a nursing home. "First, we need to buy candies and mums."

"Why do we need mums for an adventure?" Ryan may have actually had a tone of disgust.

"It's a surprise. I'm taking you to a place I used to go with Grandma and Haley when I was a little girl."

"Will we like it?" Sydney asked.

"Someday, you will. Someday you may even want to take your own kids there."

"So that means I won't like it today." Ryan was definitely disgusted.

"How about you tell me later what you think of our adventure." Samantha could predict the comments, but it didn't matter. It was something she needed to do.

After buying the essentials, they pulled into the nursing home. Samantha had called beforehand, so the staff were expecting them. Sydney and Ryan both looked at her as if she were crazy, but she lifted her chin and forged ahead. They each carried a mum they placed near the entrance to brighten the atmosphere. Her mother would be proud, but for some reason, she didn't share her plan with her.

"Why are we here, Mommy?" Ryan's voice had now turned to panic.

"We are here to brighten someone's day." Samantha carried a bag full of smaller bags that Sydney and Ryan had stuffed with candy in the backseat. She was sure to find some empty wrappers back there later.

"But Mommy, what do we do?" Ryan begged.

"You say hello? Most of them will lead the conversation."

"I don't get it. Why do they want to talk to me? I'm just a kid, Mom," Ryan asked.

"They want your time, your attention. Sometimes that's all anyone wants, just to know you thought they were worth your time. But just in case, you also have candy." Samantha smiled as she handed him his first bag to pass out.

Samantha didn't need to see the eye roll. She knew it was there as she heard the mumbled, "I don't even know them." Forge ahead, she told herself.

Samantha stopped, and somewhere inside herself she felt an elderly woman from long ago smile. She got it. Her little tiny blushing self finally got what the woman was trying to tell her. She wasn't, at that tender age, feeling proud of anything she had to offer because she had not yet figured out that offering herself was enough. That's not what made her blush.

She realized now that she had been embarrassed for another reason. It was not being content with the fact that her gift wasn't to be in front of the crowd playing the piano or coming home with straight As. Her gift was herself, the hand she had to offer, the smile she had to spread, and she thought she was too good to give such a small gift.

She didn't realize that we were not all meant to be noticed by the world, but we were all meant to be noticed by someone. We weren't all meant to be the one on stage, but we could cheer that person on, and that should be enough if we weren't too proud to accept it. Maybe there would still be a way to give that gift to the people she loved. Maybe they would still want it. Maybe.

The afternoon went as she suspected. There were some awkward moments and some genuine smiles from both the residents and her children. She would claim the day a success.

The kids crawled into the backseat with an almost empty bag. They quietly began opening the remaining candies and eating more than Samantha would normally allow.

"So what did you think?"

Through full mouths, she heard a mumbled, "It was okay." She knew that was all she could expect, and that too was okay. She smiled to herself and glanced at them in the rearview mirror.

"So are there any Snickers left?" Samantha put out her hand and one magically appeared. Chocolate had never tasted so sweet.

Chapter 45

―― ―― ―― ―― ―― ―― ―― ―― ――

Samantha

One week left until trial. Their lawyer was preparing them for the fight of their life. Samantha knew in the last texting and driving case Judge Murphy had sided with the driver when sentencing. She also knew of the backlash from the public. Their lawyer had warned them this could work against them when Judge Murphy decided the sentence. The world was becoming less forgiving of such a controllable negligent behavior. Truth be known, Samantha might have been rallying beside them if Jacob's future were not at stake.

If convicted, Jacob could be looking at over a decade in prison. Would there be anything left of them as a family? Samantha was losing hope, and some days her vulnerability still surfaced, but there was no denying that Seth's words had changed her. They were a slap in the face from a universe that was sick of seeing her still battling youth's jealousy and selfishness. In the moments when she sat naked and alone on that couch, she let the sting sink in and flesh out the corrupt parts of her soul. Were they gone? Absolutely not.

The ability for her frail character to waver during her challenging, lonely moments discouraged her. Life, she was finding, was not as much about the moment a person adamantly makes a decision, but, in reality, is all about the follow-through. How many great business ideas lay dormant on tables? How many sober alcoholics celebrate with a drink? Every step she took had to be leading her back to her husband, to forgiveness of everyone—Jaocb, Haley, herself. But if one checked the percentages, moments of determination and inspiration were more capable of fizzling into nothingness than ever reaching fruition. She could not let her family fizzle into nothingness.

Daily she received texts, just to say he was thinking about her. Seth missed her. Maybe. But it didn't matter because in reality she would never know the truth. Seth had proven to be a person she could never trust, so when late at night a smell, or a vision, tried to intrude her mind, she tried to meld the memory with her more recent conclusions.

The Friday before the trial started, Haley came over with their parents carrying lasagna, garlic bread, salad, and plenty of wine. She found herself a teenager again, but less jealous. When Haley sat down at their pathetic keyboard and started playing some after-dinner pick-me-up songs, Samantha found herself smiling. When the children started dancing around the living room to the beat Haley created, she found herself dancing with them. When she looked up from their smiling, intoxicating faces, she saw her parents had joined in as well. The fire glowed, the music enlivened them, and the laughter took them to a place they had not been in too long. Home.

Haley tucked the children in while Samantha got the dishes together to send home with her parents. Once again, Haley would stay the night, as they liked to indulge more than her parents did. Samantha could not help but notice the ease in which Haley left her husband home alone. It was a perfect night. Haley came down with the glow of motherhood, a glow she would not get to experience on her own. Still, she smiled as if she held the secret of happiness inside her.

When Haley eventually asked if Samantha had decided to do the right thing, Samantha replied that she was working on it. Haley responded with a smile, sad and understanding.

The sisters sat and talked until Samantha went on a bit too long about an old memory and turned to find Haley fast asleep curled up in her chair. She watched her sister, her friend, breathe contently, soundly. Samantha had the overwhelming feeling that she needed to understand her if she were to understand herself.

It was one more feeling, another thought that tainted the lens through which she viewed her life. She often felt she was a girl trapped in a bottle watching herself on the other side. In the beginning, the figure was so distorted, she didn't even realize who she was looking at through the glass. Just a figure, staring back at her hoping to connect, trying desperately to tell her something.

For so many years, too many years, Samantha had searched herself wondering who she truly was, until one day she realized she was a lesser version of the girl on the outside of the bottle, free —a girl who was confident and powerful, a girl with purpose and desire, a girl not contaminated by life and temptations and weaknesses.

She wondered if Haley saw herself through the glass and strived to be that person or if the two images, the one she was and the one she hoped to be, were so close she could barely tell the difference. Could her glass be so clear and thin that her two identities were almost synonymous? Samantha could only sense that somewhere inside of herself was the strength to be her better self. The self that was calling to her from somewhere beyond was begging to be discovered.

On Monday morning, she entered the courtroom with all eyes on her family. Some looked her over in anger. Some looked her over with pity. She wanted not to care. She wanted to lock eyes with her husband and form a bond no one could destroy, but she wasn't sure she was strong enough yet. Their eyes could still destroy her. Her determination was still like a baby fawn learning to walk. The smallest bump could send her stumbling.

"All rise," the bailiff said, and like diligent students everyone rose. She could feel Seth's eyes on her, and she stared hard at the familiar shape of her husband. He was wearing a suit. Such an old, comforting sight. He looked almost like the man that hugged her goodbye on that fateful day.

The words, "You may call your first witness," rang out like words before a fatal battle. Let the games begin. The crowd would watch as people slowly slaughtered her husband, and she could only stand by helplessly. The arresting police officer was the first to take the stand. Once again, she heard the accident described in detail. Once again, she heard discussion about the texts. Who sent them? What did they say? Did he respond?

Without permission, her head turned toward Seth. It was easy to lie to herself and say it was to show that it didn't bother her. She knew. It wasn't a surprise that her sister had been the one texting him. But she found herself searching his eyes for concern, for an apology. It was pouring out of him, so fiercely she felt weakened. She looked away quickly.

The day was emotionally draining. And after she watched Jacob being taken back out through the side door, she hurried with her family to the exit.

"Samantha. Samantha, please wait."

Her family looked not toward the sound of Seth's voice but to Samantha's torn face, not knowing how to react. She could almost read their minds as they tried to decide whether to protect her or give her space.

"Excuse me. I only need a minute." She turned away from them without making eye contact. Desperately trying to remain defiant she said, "Seth, we have nothing to say to each other anymore. Please, stop trying to talk to me."

"I can't do that, Samantha. This week, it's going to be hard on both of us. Why can't we just try to take away some of the pain? Just a drink together. Anything is better than nothing." His eyes pleaded.

"Seth, you said it all that day. You want to hurt him when you haven't even considered how much he is hurting. And to make it worse, I was a part of causing him more pain. I get it, Seth, I really do. Your anger. But not the rest. How could you have faked all of that just to cause more pain?"

"So I mean nothing? All this has been nothing?" Seth reached for her hand, which she allowed, "I never faked a minute with you. I just allowed my other feelings to overshadow what we have."

"Had."

"Please, Samantha. Don't give up on us because of a few words. These are the hardest times of my life. I have feelings beyond what I thought I was capable of feeling. Pain so deep I feel like my heart is bleeding some days. Anger, like there aren't enough words to scream. I never knew they could be so strong. But I never faked my feelings for you. I promise."

Samantha slid her hand out from his. "The fact is Seth, it doesn't matter. I have to choose my family, and I think you would have done the same." Samantha turned quickly and headed for the door.

***

That night she dreamed of Seth and cursed her mind for arousing such deep emotions. In the dream, he was calling to her, begging for her to help him. The tangled silhouette of a body lay behind him. She woke up gasping. Quickly, she turned on the light to chase away the demons. What was love, anyway? Where did it come from? Was it evil or good? She struggled because she felt both. Either way, she was hurting someone. Reaching over, she grabbed the pillow that had not been touched in months. It became both of them, Jacob and Seth, and she held it tightly until her heart calmed enough to let her drift back to sleep.

The next day at trial, Alexa Rogers took the stand. Her vigor for destroying Jacob may have diminished some in the months since the accident, but not by much. When asked if she saw the man who had hit Ava Johnson in the courtroom, she pointed her judgmental finger at Jacob, condemning him. She made him seem like a cocky, erratic driver, and Samantha could not help but wonder what she would be thinking if Jacob were not her husband.

The cross-examination did not seem to diffuse the steam created by her testimony. Samantha's palms lay pressed together in silent prayer on her lap. She could feel the sweat forming between them as each moment seemed to cause more and more damage to her husband. Her prayers were not being heard, but then would God really listen to her now? It was much harder judging her husband when she carried so much guilt herself.

The second day, there were more witnesses. that Samantha had yet to hear since the nightmare began. Several people had stopped to help by the time the ambulance arrived. Each one recounted erratic driving, Jacob leaving the scene, then running a questionable light before some would say karma hit him hard at the next intersection.

As each day passed, she became weaker and weaker. She knew she had not been eating or sleeping the way she needed to, and it was catching up to her. Like a ghost, she walked into the courtroom on the day Seth would take the stand. There would be wine in her future. In fact, she wished she had thought of having a glass beforehand. Desperately, she needed something to numb her from the pain she was going to feel.

The courtroom seemed warmer than normal, and she searched for escape like a hostage. She felt the drips of perspiration trickling down her neck and moistening her collar. Swallowing became impossible. Her father stood on one side and her mother on the other. Haley was shadowed behind her father. She was more like him than she had realized when they were young. Her father stood firmly, refusing to reach for her hand when they called Seth's name, but she felt her mother lift her limp hand in hers and hold on in her always understanding way. Both the avoidance and the understanding added to her pain, making her both beg and bow internally.

The questions were stale and impersonal at first,—just the facts. Yes, Ava was his wife of ten years. Yes, she was a mother of two children. Their names she had heard many times before, but the pain in his voice he had kept hidden from her almost always. There was an increasing obsession building inside of her to meet his eyes. Now was the time. He had to understand her choices. *Remember me*, she would have begged if he looked her way. Remember that he had sworn he loved her. *Please,* she would have begged, *don't hurt my family*. But Seth would not look her way.

Samantha, realizing that she was an outsider to his world, looked down at the floor to try to ease some of her pain. His voice, though, could not be ignored. The way it cracked, the pauses he took to compose himself, the pain she could hear that cut too deeply, made her want to run from the courtroom. She wanted to run from everything and everyone. That was impossible. Again, she forced herself to think of Jacob and the pain Seth's testimony was surely creating. Maybe if she thought hard enough, she could steal some of his pain away and ease him in some way. That too, she knew, was impossible.

After what seemed like an impossibly long testimony, Seth stood like a young defeated boy and returned to his seat. From the corner of her eye, she could see an arm reach around him. Was it his mother or Ava's? She would never know.

Jacob was the last one to take the stand. His lawyer desperately tried to paint a picture of an innocent citizen forced into a nightmare by circumstances and weather conditions. Samantha thought he had done a good job, but her moment of hope was quickly stripped away from her when Seth's attorney stepped up to the plate. The picture of Ava's body covered in a sheet was still set up as a backdrop to remind the jury of his crime. He was asked about the yellow lights. Strike one. He was asked about his speed. Strike two. He was asked if he thought he may have seen Ava and reacted more quickly had it not been for the texting. There was an unplanned silence before he could utter the word, "No." Strike three. They all felt it.

Haley came over with their parents. Between the three of them, they had dinner covered. Samantha was thankful for that and for the fact that no one expected her to be a conversationalist. They fed the kids, read them stories, and tried to make life appear normal. After that, they cleaned up every last morsel of dinner and disappeared into the night. She wasn't even sure she had thanked them, but she was sure they didn't care. The final day of trial awaited her, and she climbed into bed to somehow find a way to replenish the energy life had sucked out of her.

The courtroom was somber. No hope creeped in through the minute cracks. Samantha looked around the room at the other half—the half that would cheer as her world shattered. How could they not care at all about Jacob's family? His children? The judge came to the front of the courtroom and the last day began. Seth's pain lingered, Samantha was sure, in every juror's ears as the lawyers began their closing arguments.

Mr. Sinclair stood and faced the jury. "Ladies and gentlemen of the jury, the prosecution has the burden to prove beyond a reasonable doubt that my client, Jacob Truax, is guilty of hitting Ava Johnson and leaving the scene knowing that he hit her. You have heard from many witnesses that saw Jacob leaving the scene. Jacob does not deny it was he who did indeed hit Ava Johnson.

But how can a witness know what Jacob experienced in his car? We have experts looking at the accident records and can confirm that Jacob would have felt the hit, but cannot confirm that Jacob would have known what caused the bump. Even the witnesses confirm that the rain was coming down heavily and have used that to help depict my client as an erratic driver due to the fact that visibility would have been affected. If witnesses are confirming these conditions, how can the same witnesses know that Jacob would have known what he hit?

"Yes, it has been proven that Jacob glanced at his phone and even sent a quick reply, but this trial is not about texting and driving. This trial is about a possible, and I repeat, possible hit-and-run. The law would not, despite anyone's feelings on the subject, send my client to jail even if that were the cause of Ava's death. We must dismiss that from our minds. What you need to decide is if the prosecution truly proved beyond a reasonable doubt that Jacob Truax knew that he had hit Ava and then continued on his route.

"Jacob Truax, by all other accounts, has been a model citizen. Yes, he had a speeding ticket. What percentage of the population has not had a speeding ticket? This man," he paused to glance at Jacob, "this father of two young children, this husband to a young wife, is respected in his place of work not only due to his work ethics but because of the person and friend that he is to them.

"We have heard from many character witnesses to account for this. Why would a man who has it all, drive away from an accident? Why would he give it all up just to get to work on time?

Accidents happen. Even terrible accidents like this one. Jacob, by all evidence of his character, would have stopped. Can you honestly say, beyond a reasonable doubt, that you think otherwise? It is not up to the police or the witnesses to determine guilt or innocence. You do. Let's send Jacob back to his children."

Samantha contained herself. She so wanted to stand up and cheer, to grab Jacob's hand and stroll out of the courtroom and back to their home. Mr. Sinclair had nailed it. Even as she watched Seth's lawyer stand, she had no worries. For the first time in a very long time, she had no doubt he was coming home.

"Ladies and gentlemen, Mr. Sinclair has painted a very respectful picture of Jacob Truax. He has managed to take a reckless driving ticket down to a minor speeding ticket with a quick dismissal of the actual facts. It would be easy to also dismiss the fact that witnesses watched him running yellow lights and texting.

"Mr. Sinclair is correct that, unfortunately, texting and killing someone does not have the punishment today as it will undoubtedly have in the future, but can we discount these facts. No. These are facts, proven by many witnesses. These witnesses were visible to Jacob. He tried to outrun Alexa Rogers. He put the phone to the side when he saw her looking. He was frazzled and late for work. Irritated by the rain. Jacob Truax was not, in that moment, the person people speak highly of at work. He was the person that you watch on the road, waiting for an accident to happen. And then it did.

"Ava Johnson will not be the mother of her two children. They will never know her except through pictures and stories that her once-devoted husband will tell them through the years. In that moment, when Jacob Truax forgot who he was and became instead an irrational driver thinking he could hide his driver identity behind the steering wheel of his car, safe in his bubble so no one would know him, he hit Ava.

"He hit her because he was being unsafe. In that moment, when he knew he just changed everything, when he knew the side of him he hides from coworkers, his children, maybe even his wife, the side he buries when he walks through the door of his home and of his office, took over. That is when Jacob Truax decided to do one more irrational thing. He ran. I am asking you, the jurors, to find the defendant, Jacob Truax, guilty of vehicular manslaughter."

Samantha found herself staring at the jurors. Was there a chance they were remembering what Mr. Sinclair had stated about Jacob's history as a husband, a father, a successful businessman? Their faces were stone as they looked at Jacob. The prosecutor's final words—reckless driving record, erratic driving, texting, hit and run, loss of a mother and wife—would fuel their fire. Samantha felt the darkness deep within her. She knew what they were thinking.

Chapter 46

Samantha

Court had dismissed late the day before, and Samantha was prepared to wait for the verdict. In fact, she was thankful for the wait. All night she had paced her house with a wineglass in her hand. Each sip had only burned her stomach. Her parents and sister had sat quietly whispering in the living room until they all decided it was best to rest for the following day. There would be no sleep for her.

Occasionally, she sneaked into the children's rooms to watch them breathe soundly and hoped their dreams would be sweet for them. She had spent longer than usual with them reading, hugging, and reassuring them in a voice she was sure was not at all reassuring.

Less occasionally, she had let herself hope that Jacob would be standing right there beside her in just a few hours. She would hold him all night, not caring if she became hot, tangled in his body, or if her arm fell asleep, or if he breathed so hard in her face that she felt he sucked all of the oxygen out of the room. Samantha knew she would stay firmly planted next to him until the sun sprang through their windows announcing the beginning of a new day.

She remembered seeing two o'clock before she sat in her favorite chair. The sound of a blue jay fighting for his spot on the bird feeder awakened her, so beautifully dangerous those blue jays seemed to be. Funny how nature could disguise such ugly qualities behind a colorful surface.

Sydney and Ryan were still asleep. How were they to sit through their school day? If only she could know the outcome. What she would give to see their faces if the jury would only come back with a no-guilty verdict. She could see the picture in her mind that would be in tomorrow's paper.

Jacob would be holding Ryan in an arm while the rest of their hands connected them together. Their smiles would show the world that the jury had made the right decision. Their family deserved to be together. They were not criminals. Unfortunately, Samantha could not know the verdict beforehand, and the image of her children hearing *guilty* was too hard to bear. She showered before waking them, wanting to be prepared to run out the door if the verdict came in.

She walked them to school looking ready for an interview, stiff, ready to be challenged. On her way back, the image of Ava's face on the large poster board invaded her mind. The words of the defense attorney rang in her ears: "I am asking you, the jurors, to find the defendant, Jacob Truax, guilty of vehicular manslaughter." The weaker plea of their attorney whispered in the background, "It is not up to the police to determine guilt or innocence. You do."

The ringing phone met her as she entered her home. It was time.

The news crews were already setting up camp outside the courthouse. Microphones were shoved into her numb face as she pushed past the crowds. How did she get to this place in her life?

She settled in next to her family after giving supportive hugs and kisses. There was nothing anyone had to say to each other. They were all lost in silent prayer. Jacob entered again from the side door. He dared to look at her with hope and a small smile. A tear formed and settled in the corner of her eye, prepared to fall.

"All rise."

She saw her husband put his hands on the table in front of him to help his now-feeble body find the strength. He was so beaten down. The man before her did not resemble the man that would burst through the door each evening ready to embrace the two overzealous children that always managed to beat her to him. She would wait patiently behind them to greet him with her own embrace. Moments that were so commonplace then and so very distant now. If only she had known what was about to come. She would have held on longer.

Just like in the movies, the judge asked the jury if they had reached their verdict. The selected jury announced that they had, and the bailiff carried the verdict to the judge and back to the juror Samantha reminded herself to breathe after moments of forgetting.

"Would you please read the verdict."

"We the jurors find the defendant, Jacob Truax, guilty of vehicular manslaughter."

She could hear Jacob weeping in front of her. She could hear the celebration of Seth's family. She could see the bailiff's hand leading Jacob away as he begged forgiveness with his eyes. But she could feel nothing.

Chapter 47

Samantha

Samantha sat with pen in hand trying to find the words she needed to say to Jacob. She would wait for him. If it took fifteen years, twenty years, she would wait for him. Be strong, she told herself, but the thought of so many years alone began to feel like her own prison sentence. She was right back to her original feelings: anger, fear, loneliness. The sounds of Seth's family celebrating in the courtroom cut through her.

She stared at the page. She had written only the word *Jacob.*. Sydney and Ryan had cried so hard when they learned the news. Samantha assured them that Jacob would always be their daddy and that they would always visit him. She assured them he would always love them, and nothing could change that.

Wouldn't that be the same for her? How could she ever stop loving him? She would be taking the children to see him as often as possible. Would she be able to keep their love alive enough through weekend visitations in a cold, sterile room? It was not what she ever thought could happen to them, but it had. She made herself believe for the moment that she would adjust to their new reality.

Next to her, her phone began to vibrate. After watching it shift across the table like a live creature, she picked it up without looking at the screen. Something told her before hearing his voice who it would be.

"Hello, Samantha."

"So do you feel you got the justice that you wanted?"

"I think we both know it's more complicated than that."

"I don't know anything anymore. I don't know how I'm going to get my kids through this. I don't know how I'm going to pay my bills. I don't know how to manage my life alone."

"Samantha, we're both alone."

She was silent. How could she not remember his loss too? How could she get her justice for what life had done to her?

"I'm sorry, Seth. You may not understand this, but I'm beyond worrying about making you mad. My husband, yes, he chose to look at his text, but he never chose to kill Ava. He would never choose that. But people—you, the jurors, the judge, all the people in the courtroom—did choose to take my husband away." The line was silent.

"So." She waited. "I guess that means I pissed you off."

"No, Sam, I'm not pissed. I hear what you're saying. I really do. You may not believe me when I tell you this, but it kills me that you're suffering. I never lied when I said I love you. How can I not care about what this is doing to you?"

"Listen, Seth, I'm tired. I don't feel like talking to you this soon."

"This soon? Does that mean there's hope for us?"

"Seth, all I know is I'm trying to understand everyone right now, why people do the things they do, why they say the things they say, and I'm trying not to be buried in all my attempts at understanding. All I know is that I don't hate you. If this weren't my family, then I would understand. I'll try to remember that, but beyond that, I just think I need to figure things out, and you can't be a part of that."

The next morning the phone rang before anyone had gotten out of bed. Again, it was Seth. She regretted saying she didn't hate him.

"Seth, really, you cannot be calling me all the time. I told you I need time to sort out my life."

"I want to prove to you how much I love you."

"What? Seth, what are you talking about? I am not…"

"Stop talking, Samantha. I have a plan."

Curious, Samantha rolled her eyes but told him to continue.

"I can help Jacob get a shorter sentence." Samantha sat straight up.

"What? How? Would you really do that for us?"

"I would do that for you." She couldn't help but cry.

"Tell me how," she begged.

"I can stand up for him at the sentencing hearing. I can tell them I forgive him and that I know it was an accident. I can tell them that I don't want another family destroyed."

Samantha began sobbing. "Do you think it will work?"

"Yes, Samantha. I think it will get him home sooner."

"But Seth, you know if Jacob comes home…"

"I know. I know. That's how much I love you."

"Thank you, Seth. Thank you. You know I loved you too." She felt she owed him that and at that moment all she could feel was love.

"I need you to do something in order for me to do it."

"Anything."

"You need to have Jacob put me on his visitation list. I need to hear from him that he's sorry before I can fight for him to be released."

"I'll go see him tomorrow."

"Call me after." She heard the phone go dead and jumped out of bed ready to take on the world.

Samantha went without the children. She didn't want to give them hope again just to crush them. While she waited for Jacob to enter the room, she found herself wringing her hands until they were almost purple. She could not wait to tell Jacob.

He came to the table quickly as if he sensed her excitement, his curiosity obvious. Without a thought, Samantha grabbed him in a full hug and excitedly said, "Seth is going to help get you out early."

"What? Slow down. Seth?"

"Yes, Seth is going to help." Somewhere mid-sentence she noticed the familiarity with how she spoke of him. A small bit of energy was drained from her body as fear replaced it.

"Seth? The husband? How? Why?" Jacob stuttered.

Panicked, she searched her mind for the answers. She hadn't thought this through. "I don't know. He called the house. He said he didn't want our kids to be without their father."

"Are you serious, Samantha?"

"I wouldn't kid about this, Jacob. He's going to stand up for you at the sentencing hearing."

Jacob grabbed Samantha again and held her tight. "Oh my God, Samantha. This is unbelievable."

"I know. There is just one thing you need to do."

"What?"

"Put him on the visitor's list. He needs to speak with you. He needs a formal apology."

Only momentarily did his smile fade and then it grew again. "Done."

Chapter 48

———————————————

Seth

Seth sat in the cold room made of cinderblocks, spinning his wedding ring around his finger and waiting for Jacob to appear. He wished there were a glass partition between them, not knowing how Jacob would react to his visit and the message he came to deliver.

The look on Jacob's face was one of confusion and mistrust, mixed with only the slightest bit of hope. Apparently, life had been too hard on him for him to maintain the excitement Samantha ignited. Seth could almost see Jacob's mind trying to make sense of the image in front of him. His face was drawn in and beaten by life.

Could he do this? Before the accident, there wasn't a sliver of his soul that would have enjoyed what he was about to do to another man, but now he let that sliver grow as he stared into the eyes of his wife's killer. Was Jacob really thinking he would be forgiven today? If so, he would be gravely disappointed. Seth waited until Jacob sat down and then allowed an uncomfortable moment of silence to form between them.

"I needed to talk to you about something." Only silence. Seth cleared his throat. "I would like to help you at your sentencing."

"Samantha told me. I have spent the last few days asking myself one question. Why?"

"That's a good question to ask yourself, isn't it? Why would I want to help the man who killed my wife? It could be what Samantha thinks. That I don't want another family destroyed, but the truth is, I don't really care that much about your family."

He let that soak into the crumpled man in front of him. "There are things you need to know and accept." Silence and another clearing of the throat. "It's time you start thinking of your children."

"I've never stopped thinking of my children, of my family."

"You've been away from them too long. They need their father."

A little hope returned to Jacob's eyes, more spark.

"Even though I would like to see you rot in here for years, there's no need for your children to suffer because of your negligence. There's no need for your kids to be raised without both parents in their lives the way mine will be."

Jacob stared. The hope dimmed as the daggers hit their target.

"I will speak at your sentencing and ask that your time be considered served. Maybe they can do probation or community service or whatever they do, but I will work at getting you out of here."

"Thank you." It came very forced. Seth could easily tell.

"But there's a condition." Seth was sure Jacob stopped breathing as he considered the possibilities. "You need to leave Samantha."

"What!" Anger rose in Jacob's throat. They both turned to look at the correctional officers, who had been watching them attentively. Jacob lowered his voice. "I'm not leaving my wife."

"Before you go on, you should probably know that she has already left you."

"What are you talking about?"

"She's in love with me."

"Samantha is not in love with you. She couldn't be."

Seth cut him off. "But she is. We've been seeing each other for months."

"She's just lonely." Jacob's voice cracked without permission. "She just needs someone to talk to."

"She needed more than that." Seth found an evil inside of him that he embraced.

"What?" Jacob uttered, defeated.

"She loves me, Jacob. She may feel too guilty to tell you herself, but she wants to be with me." It felt impossibly exhilarating taking from the man that had stolen everything from him. He watched as Jacob's jaw tightened and wished for a moment he would come at him. He would love to physically knock any future hope of happiness out of his mind.

"You bastard."

"This is your doing. I'm offering you your children. If you leave Samantha, then I speak in your defense at the sentencing. If you don't make it happen as soon as the holidays are over, then I file a civil suit and take you for everything I can."

Jacob stared into Seth's uncompromising eyes for an eternity before saying, "Fuck you," and walking away.

Days later, Seth would receive the call he expected. Jacob would leave Samantha.

Chapter 49

Samantha

How could she say no to lunch? Hadn't he just saved her family? Seth boldly pulled up in front of her house. Maybe he felt their meetings could be explained now that he had spoken with Jacob. Whatever the reason, Seth had insisted on picking her up. Samantha had been watching from the window so that she could rush out of the door as soon as he arrived. She jumped into his car as if it was the getaway car after a bank heist and waited for him to floor it so they could escape any watchful eyes. Instead, he took his time.

"You look beautiful this afternoon. But then you always do."

"Thank you. So where are we going?" Panic rose inside of her. Why were they still sitting in front of her house?

"What are you craving?"

The form of two women pushing strollers rounded the corner.

"Anything, really." The women were closing in on them. "Shouldn't we get going?"

"Well, I have to know where we're going first, don't I?"

"Let's go to Sunset Grill." It was a popular place, but out of the way. She never ran into people she knew there.

"Where's that again?" Was he toying with her? Why was he acting so brazen? The women were close enough to make them out now.

"Just start driving, and I'll give you directions."

She tried to smile through it, to pretend she was happy to be there with him. The two women were passing. Maybe they wouldn't notice them. Samantha knew them but not well. Just two young mothers out looking for the latest gossip to entertain them while they walked. She hated them for that even if she knew she wasn't altogether that different from them.

He put the car in gear, but not before one of them spotted her. Their eyes locked momentarily and sure enough, after mumbling something to her walking partner, she glanced her way as well. All Samantha could do was look away.

"Did you know those women? They seemed to know you."

"Seth, everyone thinks they know me now."

"Well, you can't let those things bother you."

Samantha knew it was best to be quiet. She couldn't let the afternoon turn ugly. Her family needed him.

"So, are you going to tell me how things went with Jacob?" Somehow it was relieving to be able to say his name to him.

"You're right. I think I probably would have got along well with him under different circumstances. He seemed like a decent person."

"Thank you, Seth."

"Just stating the facts."

"I'm sure you got the apology that you wanted. Jacob was probably more than happy to tell you how sorry he is for everything. It had to have helped both of you."

"You know, I did feel a lot better after speaking to him. I think maybe everything is going to work out just fine for all of us."

Samantha breathed a sigh of relief that she had been holding in for months. They were getting out of her neighborhood, and she felt her body ease into his seat, feeling safer than she had felt in a very long time. It was a shame, really, that there would be no room in her life for Seth when all this was over. How long would it be before she stopped craving the warmth of his company?

Lunch was comfortable. She felt in some ways like they were two friends. It was a new feeling, a good feeling. A pressure had lifted, allowing her to speak with ease and get to know him just a bit more on a level beyond the giddiness and adrenaline that shadowed a calmer, more real self. It was after all, what she first sought when met Seth. Forgiveness for her family, not just her, but all of them, that the hate that clouded them could somehow disappear. Maybe this lunch was just one step closer.

Across the street, there was a mini putt-putt course. Without approval, he drove immediately there. She told herself that she owed him. Jacob would understand. Seth handed her a small green putter and a matching ball. Her laugh was more natural, his smile more real. They were the only two on the course, being that school was in session, and it was quite chilly. The time went too fast and too slow at the same time. In her mind, she was saying goodbye to something she should have never begun.

When they pulled in front of her house, he was more cautious this time of the people around them. "Well, at least we don't have onlookers."

Samantha let out a small uneasy laugh. She felt his hand slide around hers, and she looked up.

"I'll always love you, Samantha." He leaned in and kissed her goodbye on her forehead.

"Goodbye, Seth." Samantha felt like skipping into her home that once again held her future.

Chapter 50

Samantha

Jacob's sentencing hearing would take place after a couple of excruciating months, but Samantha could already start picturing their new future. She would forgive him. She already had forgiven him. And hopefully, she prayed, he would forgive her. She didn't want to tell him when he was still in jail, but he needed time to heal. Everything needed to be behind him when he came home to them. Getting ready to see him, she felt almost exhilarated to get the weight of guilt off herself. She was ready. Any fear, she pushed from her mind, knowing she just had to be brave, or they would not have their new beginning.

She was strong getting ready. She was strong for the drive. But the wait was killing her. Why was it taking so long today? Today of all days, the day she needed to tell him everything. If he waited too long, she might not be brave enough. At the next table, an old man sat reading a book while waiting for his visitor. She was curious to see who would be visiting him. Was the man a husband? Grandfather? Who would be waiting for him on the other side if he ever did get to see the other side again?

Samantha was unaware of her staring until he looked up at her.

"Hello, young lady."

Startled, she responded, "Hello," but quickly averted her eyes.

"And who would be the lucky man receiving a visit from such a beautiful woman?"

He sounded like a gentleman, yet looked like he had spent years on the street. For some reason, she cautiously engaged in his conversation. "I'm here to see my husband."

"Hmm. Very nice." He looked back at his book for a moment. "My wife passed on many years ago, but my son still visits."

So many questions passed through her mind. What had he done? How long had he been here? She knew better than to ask although she got the feeling he would have answered.

"He's taking so long to come out today." Once again she found herself wringing her hands.

"Some days are like that. That's why I bring my reading. I've become quite a reader here through the years. Read the whole Bible front to back three times. Now that's something I never thought I would say. Changed my life, it did."

Samantha's faith was shaky at best, yet somehow the man's own comfort began to ease her.

"How about you? You ever read the whole Bible front to back?"

Samantha thought back to all the Sundays she stood at church counting the minutes until the service ended. "No, I have to admit I have never read any of it."

"Still time, my dear, still time."

"Well, maybe some day." She glanced desperately at the door. Still no Jacob.

"What's making you seem so nervous today, if you don't mind my asking?"

At first Samantha stared at him quizzically and then she found herself testing the waters of the conversation to come.

"I'm here to ask forgiveness and I'm not sure I'm going to get it."

"Forgiveness for what?" The old man closed his book and turned his full attention to Samantha as if he had practiced his preacher skills on many troubled souls.

"Forgiveness for being me I guess, the only me I knew how to be until now. For needing to make a huge mistake before finally seeing who I was."

"Isn't that always the case? We need to completely mess up before we realize our own weaknesses. But that's part of the journey. Nothing to hate yourself over if you remember it's part of the process."

"How can you say that? I hurt people."

"Ezekiel 36:26 'I will give you a new heart and put a new spirit in you; I will remove from you your heart of stone and give you a heart of flesh.' Removing your heart. Sounds like a painful process. Some things just aren't learned easily. The main thing is you learned it."

The prisoner let out a laugh, and Samantha found herself staring into his toothless mouth for answers. "By my age I've realized my weaknesses weren't my ending just my beginning. Maybe you wouldn't understand that, dear, but for an old man like me bound to spend a life behind bars, a man who has been very weak in his day, it's very important. It's everything, to not lose hope, to not lose faith, that all of this has a reason behind it."

Samantha stared at the mysterious man, a man that had chosen to do something apparently far worse than Samantha had done and realized that maybe all the pain somehow made sense. "Thank you," she uttered. Jacob entered the room, and she rose to meet him and find a new seat. "It was nice talking with you."

"Good luck, my dear." She smiled back at the thin, decrepit criminal and for the first time didn't feel above any of the people sitting around the dreadful holding space.

She raced to Jacob and embraced him, not knowing what the next embrace would be like or if he would ever hold her again.

"I need to talk to you," she said before she could change her mind. "I did something. I did something terrible, and I'm petrified you're going to hate me."

He stared at her blankly. It was impossible to read him. "Jacob, I've been unfaithful. I'm so sorry. I can't give you an excuse that's good enough. I was selfish and lost. Say something, Jacob. Please say something.

"Jacob, you may hate me, and you deserve to. You're a better person than I have ever been. I always knew that, but I didn't really get it. I get it now. Please don't tell me it's too late." Still nothing came from him but an icy stare.

"Because of you, I know what it means to really love someone and to be loved back. I was just too stupid and selfish to understand fast enough. I'm finally the person you deserve even if I don't deserve you." Jacob stood then and walked back to the door he had just come through.

Samantha wouldn't know how much he wanted to take her in his arms and tell her he didn't care or, at least, that he would learn to forgive her, but he couldn't. He wanted to assure her they would get through it. But it didn't matter how he felt. She no longer belonged to him. She wouldn't know how he would spend hours staring at his cell ceiling wondering when he would ever stop being punished.

That night Samantha walked down the hallway to her bedroom stopping before each picture of the unknowing family, staring so confidently back at the lens as if nothing could shake them, nothing could make them fall, nothing could test them. But test it did. And they did fall, or at least she did.

If only that old man with his gaping horrific smile could know how much she needed to believe there was a reason, that someday there would be a new picture on their wall of a family that very much resembled the family in these photos, but somehow was stronger and better because of it all. That somehow, in the end, these years were not allowed to destroy them.

Chapter 51

─ ─ ─ ─ ─ ─ ─ ─ ─

Haley

Haley told Bradley she would be late getting into the flower shop. He had looked at her with raised eyebrows since it was their busy time of year. She knew, but some things were more important. She sprayed some extra Red Door Spa perfume on before heading out the door just because she couldn't resist.

"What time exactly can I expect you?"

"By ten, definitely by eleven." She didn't look back. It didn't bother her that he was upset, happy, indifferent. It had never bothered her. Somehow Bradley only reminded her of what she felt life had cheated her of, the feelings she tried not to have around Jacob. Bradley could never make her sail through her days, or feel an adrenaline rush just by being near him, or make her excited about the little things that the day had to offer. Everything was just life with him. There were good days and bad days that averaged out to the big revelation that life was just okay.

Haley was nowhere near feeling the way she should about Jacob, but this was not the time to give up the visits. She was trying though, to be the sister-in-law she was supposed to be. She planned on talking about Samantha and the kids and the times they had spent together in the past weeks. He would be happy to hear that they were trying to reconcile and somehow were closer than they had been in a long time. Knowing this would bring him peace, and for Samantha's sake, she would try to clear her mind of the many other thoughts that would try to seep in.

But when Jacob entered, there was a weight on his spirit she knew that no story could lift.

"What's the matter, Jacob?"

"What's the matter? Are you kidding me? Life is what's the matter." His anger frightened her again, yet she was also still excited to share another emotion with him.

"I'm not sure what to say, Jacob, except you can't give up hope. Time goes by faster than we can imagine. One minute you're stuck here, in this situation. The next minute, you will be getting your life back. You'll see."

"You don't understand. I'll never get my life back. I'll never get Samantha back." Haley's mind raced. She left him. Samantha left him. He would see, and someday care, that she would never leave him the way that Samantha did. A window to a life she should have had from the beginning opened right before her.

"Jacob, what happened?"

"I can't talk about it. It could ruin everything. Every chance of me being able to be a father to my children some day."

"Jacob, you can tell me anything. You know that. I would never utter a word about whatever you tell me." Jacob studied her for several moments, and Haley sat quietly letting him see into her soul. Couldn't he tell how much she loved him?

"Seth came to see me," he said.

Haley knew her mouth was agape, but couldn't manage to shut it.

"Why?"

"He had Samantha tell me to put him on my visitor's list. He said he wanted to help me get out of here but needed an apology."

"He's going to help you get out?" Panic and excitement rose inside of her.

"Under certain conditions."

"And what are they?"

Once again Jacob studied Haley. "Did you know Samantha is having an affair with Seth?"

More panic, an ocean of it welled up. She could not look like a traitor. "I knew they had met for lunch. I thought it was weird, but I didn't know anything else. I'm sorry, Jacob. You deserve better."

"Do I, really, Haley?" They locked eyes until her guilt made her look away. "Seth said if I leave Samantha he will help get me out. He's going to speak up for me at the sentencing so I can get home to my kids. If I don't leave Samantha, then he's going after me in a civil trial."

Unbearable waves of excitement and hope took over. "Are you going to leave her?"

"What choice do I have?" He paused as if imagining the future. "I would have forgiven her. I would have fought for us." Jacob stood to leave. "If you tell Samantha, you could wreck everything."

With only a whisper of voice, she said, "I would never do that to you, Jacob." She watched him walk away, and all her determination to be a better sister dwindled as she began to imagine that her day might be coming.

Chapter 52

——— ——— ——— ——— ——— ——— ——— ———

Samantha

There was new hope in each day. Samantha began holding her head higher at the crosswalk, not inviting conversation, but, at least, she was not avoiding it as much. Each step she took was bringing her family back to normalcy. Soon, she believed, life would begin again.

As she approached the crossing guard, she noticed her speaking to a man. He was familiar and out of place. The crossing guard laughed at something he said and then turned to address the first group of children collecting at the corner. The man turned toward Samantha and even though a part of her already knew who he was, she was stunned. Seth was standing there in front of all the other women who curiously observed him. Maybe they recognized him from the news. She was sure they did.

Samantha was pissed at the intrusion into her life, but once again felt like his puppet. She could not let her feelings show. Sydney and Ryan were approaching the corner. They would be in the next group of children crossing the street.

Stay calm, she told herself. "Seth, why are you here?"

"I have a good reason, Samantha. Trust me. I've been thinking a lot about what is the healthiest way for all of us and our children to move on from all of this."

With clenched teeth she said, "Do you think maybe you should have discussed it with me before you show up in front of all of the neighbors and my children? For God's sake, Seth, my children, I haven't prepared them for this."

"It's better this way. It makes it more casual."

"I think I should have some say in things that involve my children, Seth. This crosses a line."

"Relax. I know what I'm doing."

Just then Sydney and Ryan appeared next to them, both of them looking curiously at Seth.

"So are you going to introduce us?" Seth asked.

After giving Seth a momentary glare, she turned toward them. "Sydney, Ryan, this is a friend of mine. His name is Mr. Johnson."

"Hi, Mr. Johnson," they quietly replied.

"I wanted to treat all of you to a little after school hot cocoa. Panera has the best marshmallows around."

"Yum," Ryan announced. Sydney remained silent.

"Seth, that's very kind, but we really need to get back home. We have projects and…"

"Mommy, I don't have a project," Ryan almost shouted.

"Well, there you go. I'm parked right over there, so you don't need to carry those heavy backpacks any farther," Seth said with a smile.

"Seth, we need to talk."

"We can talk over hot cocoa." Ryan was already walking with Seth. Sydney reached out for Samantha's hand. When Samantha looked down at her daughter, she was met with questioning eyes. Probably failing, Samantha tried to communicate that everything was okay.

They each buckled as Seth began the conversation. "So did you learn anything interesting at school today?"

"I learned that Dylan has really bad breath, and if you tell him to stop talking in your face, he'll do it even more," Ryan replied.

"Ryan, that's not very polite to tell someone they have bad breath," corrected Samantha.

"Well, it's not polite to have it either."

"You have bad breath too, Ryan." Sydney finally decided to say something. Normally, their arguing would be embarrassing, but at the moment, Samantha was angry about other matters.

The ride there continued with little facts and fights. Samantha watched out the window for distractions from the torment in the car. They stopped at a red light, and Samantha noticed the cross on the side of the road. The flowers were yellowed and depressing. Immediately, it dawned on her where they were, and she looked at Seth. He was staring at her. In the background, the children continued on about whose backpack was in whose way. There were ways to avoid this section of Broad

Street. He chose this path just to remind her, to add more guilt. She looked away.

Once there, Seth ordered their hot cocoas and apparently asked for extra marshmallows. Like a well-trained host, he laid one down in front of each of them and took his seat beside Samantha. As they sipped their hot cocoas, Seth forged on, forcing himself into their life.

"I have two children too. I have a boy, Connor. He's almost four now. I bet you would like him, Ryan. I also have a little girl named Sophie. She's only two. She's my baby. Sydney, do you baby-sit yet?"

"Not yet. Mom said maybe I could start being a mother's helper soon, though."

"How about a daddy's helper?" Seth asked.

"I guess so," Sydney replied.

Samantha wanted to grab her children and run. Why couldn't she just say a final goodbye and have him understand? For now, though, she had to play his game.

"I'll try to work that out with your mom. It's always nice to make a little money."

"I want to make some money, too," Ryan said.

"Hmm. Let me think on that. Do you do yard work?"

"I used to help my dad bag leaves, but then he would get mad when I jumped in all the piles."

Seth laughed. "Well, most of the bagging leaves time has passed, but I think we can work something out."

"Can I jump in the piles?"

"Sure."

"Seth, thanks for the hot cocoa, but I think we need to get going," Samantha said.

"I agree. It's probably time to hit the books."

"Can we do this again?" Ryan chimed.

"I'd love to," Seth replied. Samantha and Sydney remained silent.

Seth walked them to the door when they reached their house. "Samantha, someday today will make sense to you even if you're angry right now. It's healthier for everyone, especially the children, to see that there are no enemies in all of this. We'll all move on faster and someday when they look back at this terrible time, there will be closure and peace, not bitterness. You'll see."

Samantha, with all the control she had in her, thanked him but asked if he would give her warning next time. With a smile, he agreed.

Chapter 53

Samantha

The children went with her on the next visit to see Jacob. She needed them to ease the awkwardness. To an observer it worked, but she could feel the tension. She was able to share in the giggles and add to the conversations like an unnecessary guest, but at least they were talking. And then it happened.

"We got to go out for hot cocoa with Mommy's friend. He picked us up on our way home from school."

Jacob looked at Samantha as he asked, "Who was Mommy's friend?"

Sydney chimed in, "Mr. Johnson."

Samantha wanted to break eye contact but couldn't. The rest of the conversation was lost on them as they had a private communication with their eyes. Samantha considered telling her children not to mention it, but she knew that if she told Ryan not to mention something that it would definitely be mentioned.

"Dad, are you listening? He said that I could earn money raking leaves and that I could jump in the piles of leaves."

"Is that so?"

Samantha could see the tension in his jaw.

"I had to, Jacob. I have to keep him happy right now. Just till after the sentencing," Samantha said as quietly as she could.

"How happy are you keeping him?" Jacob asked.

"It's not like that, I promise. I just need him on our side."

"What are you guys talking about?" Ryan asked. Both kids looked up at them with frightened faces.

"It's nothing. Just adult talk." Samantha tried to calm them.

"But..." Ryan tried again.

"So Ryan, are you going to play basketball this winter?" Jacob asked.

He was so easily distracted. Sydney, on the other hand, kept her eyes on Samantha.

They ended their visit with hugs and quick kisses. Samantha managed to whisper in Jacob's ear, "I love you, Jacob. Everything I do from here on out is about our future. Please trust me."

She was surprised to hear a muffled, "I love you too," in return.

Chapter 54

Samantha

It had been a couple of weeks since Samantha had seen Seth, but the occasional text would still come through—texts that were sent with no expectation of a response. "No worries, Samantha, you can count on me."

"Thinking of you. Hoping it's a good day." "Things will be better soon."

They began to feel like a daily proverb, sayings that despite herself, she started to look forward to because they reassured her of his promise. It made her feel as if maybe her two worlds would not collide into a cosmic explosion but instead gently glide past each other, leaving both unharmed.

The morning of the sentencing she received yet another promise. "It's time to breathe, Samantha."

Her parents and sister met her on the court steps. The unity of a family, that was what made everything bearable. They took turns giving each other firm supportive hugs before heading inside. Seth was already seated with the family members she would never know. He looked back and gave the slightest smile.

Jacob came in and also looked her way, but it was a much colder look that was quickly diverted to Haley. Something passed between them. Samantha tried to catch Haley's eye afterward, but she stared forward. She felt the way an animal must feel when they sense a hunter lurker in the woods. Her whole body felt alert. What was happening?

Her eyes darted from person to person like a frantic prey, not sure of whom or what to fear. Words. Babble. Legalities. Nothing mattered until Seth stood to address the court.

"Her name was Ava Johnson. We met in college. She actually wasn't aware of me the first time I saw her, or the second, or the many other times before I found the nerve to approach her. When I say approach her, I got stuck in an elevator with her." He paused to chuckle privately at the memory. "It was the most monumental thirty minutes in my life up to that point. I learned many things about Ava in that thirty minutes, but the most amazing thing I learned was that she didn't think she was above me. I can't remember everything she said, but I will always remember her smile, the sound of her laugh, the smell of her perfume. I'll always remember that I left that elevator knowing that someday I would marry her. Someday, we would have beautiful children together. Someday, we would grow old together. That's all I needed to know."

"And it almost all came true. I watched her walk down the aisle toward me. I watched her dress for her first real professional job and then turn to ask me how she looked. I watched her read the pregnancy stick with complete wonder in her eyes. I watched her body change and grow. We held hands together over her rolling belly as we discussed baby names and nursery colors. I watched her give birth to our beautiful boy, Connor, and then I got to do it all over again for Sophie. I could sit here and tell you about a million personal moments we shared that made me love her more every day, but I'm going to keep them to myself."

Seth paused and looked at Jacob for just a moment. "I never knew Jacob Truax before the accident, and I'm sure that I will not ever truly know him, but I'm a father, and on that level I feel we do know each other. I would do anything for my children, and I have no reason to believe that Jacob Truax would not do anything for his. I know that for every amazing moment I shared with my family, Jacob probably has a story of his own. If someone told me Jacob was drunk in the bar every night, or abusive to his family, or negligent in some way, sending him away for years would be easy. But that's not what I've heard. That's not the man I believe him to be.

"Every child deserves their parents in their lives, and although I can hate the man that got behind the wheel the morning I lost my wife, I cannot hate the man that wants to give his family the best. Ava would not want any child to suffer if there was a choice. We have a choice. We can let Jacob Truax return to his family and stop the suffering. I ask that in honor of my late wife. It would be her wish. I am asking for minimal time with community service. Let's not have more children suffer. Thank you."

On the other side of the courtroom there were sniffles but not outrage. Seth must have prepared them. They must have agreed it was what Ava would want.

It was only a short time before the judge was ready to sentence Jacob. The courtroom was silent as he proclaimed that Jacob would be home by Christmas and would serve two years community service and probation.

Samantha began crying uncontrollably. She would have him at Christmas. They would be a family again. She waited for Jacob to look back at her. After too long, he finally did, but all she saw was sadness behind a feeble smile.

Chapter 55

Samantha

Samantha pulled the nine-foot tree from the third-floor storage, slid it dangerously down the stairs behind her, and set it up before the kids got home. They only cared about putting on the ornaments anyway.

With enthusiasm, she baked cookies and had them sitting on the table awaiting decorations. In the background, Christmas carols were being played through the surround sound. By the time she went to pick up Jacob the following day, the house would be aglow with the holiday. She had even attempted a few outdoor lights, although that was always Jacob's thing. He wouldn't entirely escape that duty this year. Even thinking of him cursing while stringing the lights made her smile.

When Sydney and Ryan entered the house and smelled the evergreen candle and saw the empty tree begging for decorations, their already good mood skyrocketed. One more day left of school. Homework was nothing but fun filler stuff they completed joyfully. By the time they settled in, everything was ready to welcome Jacob home.

In the morning, Samantha scooted them off to school and ran out to buy the perfect outfit to greet the man she would be getting to know for the second time in her lifetime. Rushing out of Short Pump Town Center with bags in hand, she got what she hoped to be her final text.

"Everything I've done is to make you happy. To give you and your family what you deserve."

Once again, it was written in a way that left it lingering. Was she supposed to respond? One last time, she told herself as she typed the message. "Thank you, Seth. You will always mean so much to me. I hope you find happiness too."

"Don't worry, Samantha. I will."

This time, she would not respond. She let her mind reject the small amount of dejection it caused that he was so sure he would be happy without her. She was supposed to just be relieved by that. Wasn't she?

It was already getting dark when she headed to the prison. The Christmas lights lit her way, and "Little Drummer Boy" accompanied her in her travels. She pulled into the parking lot and the guards told her where to park and wait. The night was quiet, and the stars shone down on her, showering her with a renewed spirit. She came alone. Life would have its chance to pull him in its array of directions soon enough.

She decided to get out of the car to watch for him even though the bitterly cold air bit at her ears and nose. The silence was broken by the sound of footfalls on gravel. Each step making her heart race with excitement. Then the sound of metal on metal echoed through the night as the guards unlocked the gates and pushed them open. She could see them sway back in place behind the small figure that seemed to be spit out of some creature's mouth knowing it didn't belong in its midst.

The silhouette of the man she somehow knew better and loved deeper than she had ever thought possible approached apprehensively. With each step, he grew larger and larger until he became the size she remembered him to be, strong enough for all of them but no longer needing to be. She had grown too. It was a moment that would be locked in her mind until thoughts no longer lingered there. One more still life to add to the photo album of time, one more pause in eternity where she stopped for just a moment before welcoming her future. She smiled, despite his downcast eyes, still so unaware of the hurdles that lay ahead.

Chapter 56

Samantha

It was different from what she had thought, having Jacob home. He existed silently, alone in his thoughts, smiling only when the children were near. Samantha tried desperately to make it feel like the family she remembered. She made tacos, poured wine, told stories of her day, but she could not breathe life into him. It was as if he was trying to soak it all in, as if he didn't realize it belonged to him again. He still hadn't touched her, and as much as she understood, it made her feel used up and trashy. Would he ever be able to touch her again without thinking about what she had done to him and to her family?

After tucking the children in, he came to their room. Samantha was using their bed to wrap Christmas presents.

"Would you like to help?" She smiled invitingly. "My back is starting to kill me."

Jacob picked up a Lego set and studied it like he had never seen Legos before.

"Ryan will love this." He looked around at the abundance of wrapped presents lying around the room. "Did you leave any shopping for me?"

"There is always room for more presents. Want to make it a date night like we usually do?"

Long moments passed. "That would be great."

"Really?" Samantha sounded a bit too desperate, but she didn't care. "Oh Jacob, I would love it. We could grab dinner, and shop, and maybe even pull off a movie." She was rambling like a high schooler. Jacob slowly edged closer to her, and she felt the scissors slip from her hands. His arms slid around her waist. His eyes met hers. "Jacob, I've missed you so much." Her hands grazed the stubble from the day. She had never wanted him to touch her more than she did at that moment.

"Please be quiet, Samantha." He brushed the presents to the side and shut off the light.

"But, Jacob?"

"Don't ruin it."

She didn't dare speak another word. She would take what she could get. In the dark of the room, she felt his tears drop upon her face. Samantha reached up to wipe them away, but he stopped her. Somehow his tears became more intimate than any other piece of them they could share.

She woke in the morning in a whirlwind of wrapping paper and presents. Jacob was already downstairs. When she found him, he had transformed back to the shell he was before. Studying his home, his world, like he no longer belonged. Where had her husband gone?

She was surprised when he brought up date night again and asked if maybe Haley could watch the children for them. Quickly, she was on the phone making plans and reservations at Magiano's. Haley showed up with Christmas cookies and the movie Elf. Sydney and Ryan were ecstatic. Samantha hugged her sister goodbye and watched as Jacob did the same. With some uneasiness, Samantha noticed the slightest pained look pass between them but knew she would never dare to address it. She had become an outsider to their relationship.

There was so much silence between them whenever Samantha's nervous conversation paused, and then she finally ran out of energy and walked silently beside him. It was then that she felt the gentle brush of his hand as he slid it around hers. She looked at him, but he didn't look back.

"Are we going to be all right, Jacob?"

"I don't even know what that is anymore, Samantha. I guess only time will tell us what we will be." With everything she had, she focused on the feeling of his hand gripping hers. Something was warning her she might never feel it again.

Christmas morning, the children flew into their room. Samantha couldn't help but forget the problems between her and Jacob. It was Christmas, she told herself, and she let the magic take over. Jacob and Samantha never bought much for each other—usually just a small meaningful item and even though she had no idea what to expect from her husband any more, she had bought him a frame and in it was the business card for the photographer she had scheduled to take their family photos.

"I figured you might like a new frame for your desk when you start back." Her palms were sweating, waiting for the response. It seemed as if he was searching for what to say. Finally, he responded,

"That's a beautiful idea, Samantha. It'll be nice getting back to the office after the holidays."

Her space under the tree was empty. There was nothing for her. She choked back the sob of pain that wanted to come out and said, "Well, let's get this paper cleaned up so you can play with your toys."

"But Daddy, where's your gift to Mommy?" Ryan pleaded.

"Do you think I forgot your mother? Not a chance." From his pants pocket, he pulled a small box that immediately screamed jewelry. She took it from his outstretched hand.

"Thank you, Jacob."

"You don't know what it is yet. Why are you thanking me?"

"I don't care what it is." She opened it slowly, savoring the moment. Inside was a beautiful silver locket with a picture of their family.

"Jacob, I love it."

He took the necklace from her hands.

"Let me put it on you."

He gently fastened it and pulled her hair back behind her shoulders.

"It looks perfect on you."

To hide her tears, she wrapped her arms around him and buried her face in his shoulder. She felt the arms of Sydney and Ryan wrap around them, and she stood there until the kids ran back to their toys, and only then did she release her grip and walk away.

Chapter 57

Samantha

Samantha and Jacob walked their children to the crosswalk for their first day back at school. Jacob, dressed in a suit, was ready to return to work. She knew he would be welcomed back. They had all shown their support in different ways through the painful year.

Even so, she no longer cared how people looked at them or if they judged them. All she cared about was the way Jacob looked at his children when he bent to hug them goodbye, and the way they looked back at him. Everything disappeared around them, leaving her alone with her family in a bubble of happiness and peace. She placed her hand, without thinking, on the locket Jacob had given her. They had made it through to the other side of hell, and they had survived.

On the way back to their house, Samantha took Jacob's hand, and he weakly held on to hers. She found herself nervously talking about silly, meaningless things. She was running to the gym. There was a new instructor for a barre class that was quite challenging. She laughed as she admitted she would not be managing the stairs for a few days. Only silence.

She rambled on about the grocery store and buying things for a new chili recipe that used hominy. "Did you know that was a type of corn?" she asked. She thought he shook his head no, but she wasn't sure. Anyway, she was really excited to try something new and would probably make some cornbread. The rambling took them into the house, where an eerie silence settled over them. Jacob took both of her hands and let his eyes search her.

"Samantha, I'm sorry. I tried. I really tried."

"What are talking about, Jacob?" Samantha asked, panicked.

"I tried to forgive you. I really did. I know you have been through so much because of me. I know, or at least I think I know, that you always loved me. Maybe you truly regret it." Tears were welling in her eyes, and Jacob looked away letting her hands drift from his. "I can't forgive you."

"What? What does that mean, Jacob?"

"It means I've got an apartment, and I'll be going there tonight."

"Oh my God, Jacob. How can you do this to us? How can you do this to our children? They just got you back. Please, I'm begging you. Don't do this to them."

"I'm sorry." Jacob walked upstairs and returned with a suitcase that at some point he had stashed somewhere. "Tell the kids that I'm picking them up to take them to dinner. I'll find a way to break this to them." And then he was gone.

She had heard at one point that each life leaves an imprint. It's not just the people you touch but the way they lived their lives because of you. When someone creates pain, the ripple effect may go on for generations of unborn grandchildren struggling to find internal peace because of the scars of their parents caused by scars of their parents. That night when she lay in bed, after wiping tear after tear from their innocent faces, she thought of the scars she left on her children. The memory of this day would haunt them forever and form an injured self they would stumble through life trying to heal, bumping into innocent generations on their journey. She had done this to them. She would do anything to heal their wounds, to erase the memory of the day, the year. If only the universe could tell her how.

Chapter 58

Jacob

Jacob picked up the children and tried to have as little interaction with Samantha as possible. Just watching her walk them to the door and give them a hug goodbye was too much for him. He knew he would crumble in front of all of them if he stayed any longer than he did.

"Why isn't Mommy coming to dinner with us?" Ryan asked as they rode to Friday's.

"She's going to get some things done while I have some time alone with you. It's been too long don't you think?" He didn't want to start in on the necessary conversation until later on in the evening.

"She seemed sad. I think she wanted to come," Ryan added.

"Maybe another time, Ryan," Jacob replied as he peered in the rearview mirror at the two of them. Sydney was watching with a questioning and knowing expression all at once. She was always too aware for a girl her age.

As they took their last bites of their shared dessert, Jacob knew he couldn't hold out any longer.

"Kids, I have to talk to you about something."

Sydney's eyes already had tears which made it even harder for Jacob to hide his emotions.

"It's been a really hard year on all of us. Some things in our life got a little bent and they look and feel different now."

"Huh?" interrupted Ryan.

Jacob struggled to find the words. Nothing was right.

"Your mom and I, we were like this strong brick home in a storm. Each time something slammed against us, we stood strong, but then there were these really strong winds we didn't expect and they, well, they just caused too much damage. The storm won."

"You're confusing me," Ryan replied.

"Ryan, he's telling us him and Mommy are breaking up."

Ryan at first sat silent, and then he lay his small head in his arms on the table and started to cry. In a rare moment, Sydney put her arm around him and whispered consoling words in his ear. Jacob slapped some money on the table, took Sydney's hand and picked up his son. The three of them headed to the car where their tears could fall in private. When he got to the house, he hugged them goodbye at the door and turned away as soon as they entered.

All the way home, he tried to tell himself that they would be okay. He could still be an amazing father. He could provide for them financially, keep them in their beautiful home, go to every game, see them on some holidays. They could still figure out how to be a family, just a different family.

He couldn't fail them again. He couldn't make them go through another trial and watch as Seth took away their home and whatever else he could manage to get his hands on. In time, they would adjust to the new them.

Chapter 59

Haley

Haley loaded the car with the few bags of groceries she had carefully selected. He would need milk, cereal, frozen dinners. She was desperately hoping he would also need her, being the only other person besides Seth that knew why Jacob sat alone in a half-furnished apartment.

She drove slowly, trying to find the sister-in-law feelings she held for Jacob that were smothered with all the ones she was fighting to free herself of. Haley rehearsed the many different opening lines she had thought appropriate. Maybe somewhere deep down she heard a muffled voice, telling her it was impossible to hide feelings that were overpowering. It was impossible to stand that close to the fire without getting burned.

Balancing a bag on one leg, she rang the bell. It took a minute for any sound to come from inside. Finally, Jacob opened the door wearing only gray sweatpants and a five o'clock shadow. Somehow she forgot every witty comment she had prepared and stood with her mouth hanging open in an unflattering position.

"Are you going to come in?" Jacob asked.

"Yes, if it's okay. I brought some things I thought you might need."

"Thanks."

"How are things going?"

"Great," he answered sarcastically. She wondered why she continued to ask such a stupid question.

Haley began putting things away. "Was it good to get back to work?"

"Actually, that was pretty good until your father came by my office. He has a way of making me feel like shit without saying a word."

"Don't worry, Jacob, he'll get over it. Just do your job. Focus on the other people. Things will start to feel more normal every day."

"Whatever normal is."

"I brought some cold beer, your favorite, Magic Hat #9. Would you like one?"

"Sure." She proceeded to open two.

"So you're staying?"

Suddenly, she felt very out of place but with a bit of effort, she was able to rewrite his tone to mean something more welcoming.

"I thought I would stay for one, if that's good with you."

"Sure." Jacob took a large swallow before continuing. "So what does Bradley think of you bringing me over groceries and hanging out for beer?"

She felt a flush come over her face. "He knows you're family, and that we've been friends through this."

"Hmmm." He took another large swallow. "Want to sit on the balcony?" Jacob asked.

"It's like forty out there. How about staying inside? Not to mention you might be a bit chilly without your shirt." She skid her gaze over his chest, touching him with her eyes. Some unwelcome force made her take one step closer to him.

"So have you talked to Samantha? How's she doing?"

"Well, of course, she's upset and confused. I think she's talking to Seth again, but it's not something she shares with me. When I was over, I saw a missed call on her phone from him." She studied his face intently. He finished his beer and went to the fridge for another.

"So she's never talked to you about it?" he asked.

"Hardly." She finished her beer as well and went to grab another.

"You know, Haley, I think I need to be alone right now."

"Okay."

"Thanks for the groceries." He put his hand on her back. Was he guiding her to the door? "Would you try to talk to her? I want to know what she really thinks of him." He was using her. She was becoming the friend one pretends to like for whatever benefit they can offer. She stiffened a bit, until Jacob pulled her toward him to embrace her. Maybe he sensed her awareness. "Thank you, Haley. Thank you for everything." Or maybe he meant it.

"Of course, I'll talk to her, Jacob. I'll call you after and maybe run some more things by so we can talk." Yes, she knew she had set him up for another visit if he wanted information.

"Sounds great, Haley." Again his hand was on her back and before she could turn to say a final goodbye the door closed behind her.

Who had she become? A woman so desperate for one man that she would be a traitor to her sister? She would allow that same man to make her feel like mud on his shoe that he had been trying to scrape off for years. *Thank you Jacob for guiding to me to the door, a door I will not allow myself to enter again,* she thought to a Jacob that would never listen.

Haley entered her kitchen and dropped her keys on the counter as usual. The house was bizarrely quiet. Only a note lay on the table behind her. She sensed, before she even read it, what it would say. She opened it anyway.

Dear Haley,

I don't make you happy. I never have. It's been years since I have tried, I realize, but a man can only take so much rejection before he shuts down. Go find your thing because I have come to accept that I'm not it.

Bradley

She read it two more times, trying to let it make sense. Certain things were meant to be constants in life. The sun would rise whether or not you stepped outside to greet it, whether or not you planted flowers or bathed in its glory. It would rise whether or not you praised it or shunned it or cursed it. This was a given. Didn't Bradley know that he was a given? Leaving wasn't supposed to be a passing thought in his mind.

Haley heard a small sound behind her. Startled, she turned to find Bradley standing in the doorway.

"You weren't supposed to be home yet."

"Brad, what's going on? I don't understand."

"I think my note says it all, Haley. I'll be back for the rest of my things later." He bent to grab his small bag.

"Wait. Let's talk."

"It's too late for that."

She lifelessly followed him to the door but didn't attempt to stop him. He threw his bag in the backseat and got behind the wheel. Haley watched as the car backed down the driveway and immediately began to wonder if his eyes had always been that blue, if his khakis had always clung perfectly to his backside, if his voice had always had that sad longing in it. What had she done?

Chapter 60

Samantha

Nothing made sense to Samantha. Seth had given them a chance, and Jacob was throwing it away. Looking back, there had been obvious signs that his only concern was for the children. Jacob had been distant to her ever since she had told him about Seth. It made sense, but oddly there was a piece of her that believed if she was ready to move forward, if she was ready to choose Jacob, then he had to want the same. Why had it never occurred to her that she might truly lose him? When Seth went to him, did Jacob know then that he would be leaving her after the holidays? When he placed the locket around her neck, had he been saying goodbye?

Seth's phone calls began to slowly trickle in after Jacob left. He said he heard through a very long grapevine what had happened and wanted to know if she needed to talk. Just as friends, he said. Feeling so betrayed by Jacob, there wasn't much reason to say no. It was only lunch. She wouldn't be running into hotels with him in the middle of the day or prancing around the streets holding hands.

Well, maybe he did hold her hand at the table when she began to cry. Maybe he did let her curl into him to hide her tears. But that's what friends do for each other.

Maybe she shouldn't have agreed to go to his house after dropping her kids off at school, but she felt like a ship lost at sea, trying to find a shore. He was the only light shining out to her. Jacob ended every conversation they had as soon as it drifted from the children. He had become cold. She pulled in front of the house and saw the curtain fall back into place. Seth must have been watching for her. When she rang the doorbell, there was an immediate scramble of feet on the other side of the door.

"Daddy, she's here." She wanted to run. Why were his children home? Again, he was crossing a line she wasn't ready to cross. The door swung open, and Seth stood before her with his son clinging to his leg, his daughter in his arms, and a smile spread across his face. She wanted to slap him.

"I told them I was going to introduce them to a friend of mine today. We made muffins."

She looked at their angelic, smiling faces. "Thank you. That was very kind of you."

A bashful, "You're welcome," was muffled into Seth's jeans.

"Come on in." Inside a candle burned on the counter next to a freshly cut fruit tray and a plate of what appeared to be blueberry muffins. "Would you like coffee?"

"That would be great."

He had set her up. If it had not been rude to the children, she would have turned and walked away. After several moments of shyness passed, Connor was showing off his toys and running by with a flirtatious smile every time he passed. Sophie eventually climbed off Seth's lap and made her way to her pile of toys. Seth's eyes protectively followed her, ready to catch her if she toppled over. Sophie plopped down in front of her stacking cups and beginning to build something. The tower would get to be about five high before tumbling over, and she began to display her frustration. Seth excused himself to sit with her and build the tower to its full height. The frustration gave way to a precious smile before she knocked it down with a giggle.

"Gen, Daddy."

"Again? Anything for my Sophie." Once again he built the tower she quickly destroyed. Samantha didn't want to admit to herself how endearing it was to see Seth as a father.

"Can I build it now, Daddy?" Connor appeared behind them wanting to be the source of his sister's laughter.

"Sure buddy." He stood and messed Connor's hair before returning to Samantha.

It was apparent even at such a young age that the two children adored each other. She thought of Sydney and Ryan and their constant squabbles. She felt a small pang of jealousy as she took ownership of their behavior. Maybe Ava had been a calmer, more loving mother. Maybe this was just more evidence of her inabilities. Almost reading her mind Seth chimed in, "It's not always so peaceful."

"How come I don't believe you?"

"Come over at bedtime when they're tired and cranky." He paused. "I just should be quiet and let you believe that we're perfect."

"At least you pulled it off for a visit. Sydney and Ryan probably fought in the first five minutes."

"I don't remember it that way." His smile assured her he wasn't scared off by them.

She stayed for about an hour before finding an excuse to leave. After being escorted to the door, Seth took the extra step to close in, leaving the possibilities open. She stepped back.

"I wish you had warned me, Seth."

"I was afraid you wouldn't come. They're a big part of me. I want you to know them, too."

"I don't know what to say. I did enjoy meeting them, but I wasn't ready. Everything inside me feels broken right now. How can I move forward with anything until I fix it?"

"I'm broken too, Samantha. I need fixing too."

"Then what are we doing?"

"Maybe we're fixing each other."

"Or maybe we're hurting each other."

"I don't think so, Samantha. I don't. Give it a chance. Please, Samantha."

"Bye, Seth."

"Is that a maybe?"

Over her shoulder, she uttered, "I don't know what it is."

On the drive home, she thought about the roads in front of her. The inviting and exciting choice of giving Seth a chance. The difficult, degrading one of fighting for Jacob. Why was it all so messy? Everything that she had sought to fulfill herself was destroying her.

It was so hard to be who she wanted to be when she so desperately found herself needing love, needing to be appreciated, needing someone to see everything sad inside and loving her in spite of it all. She realized it was impossible to have perfect love because everyone she knew was so far from perfect. For her to expect someone to come in and fix that brokenness inside was asking too much. She had to fix it.

That night she prayed, not for Jacob or the children or their finances. She prayed for herself. She prayed for the imprint she wanted to leave. She prayed for the strength to overcome her very human impulse to screw everything up while seeking an answer to her crumbling life.

She prayed that when her crumbling life gave way, when she found herself standing alone, without her husband, her home, her family, that she would finally be the trunk stable enough to support new growth. Samantha needed to be the trunk that would allow each gift, each hope, each dream she had to grow like branches that could reach out so far into the generations to come that they could overshadow any remnant of the dark imprints she had already created.

The next day she called her sister. It was where she had decided to rebuild, at the very place she had started the destruction. Haley walked into the coffee shop, tentatively, Samantha thought, and was met by her sister's outstretched arms. Samantha could feel the tension melt out of her rigid body. They eased themselves into their chairs and smiled across the table at each other.

"You might just look more beaten up than I do," Samantha began.

Haley took a sip of coffee Samantha had waiting for her. "Bradley left."

"What? Why?"

"Probably because I've been a terrible wife," Haley answered.

"You have not, Haley. What are you talking about?"

"But I have," was all Haley could say.

"I'm sorry, Haley," Samantha said after a moment of silence settled between them.

Haley let out a sad laugh. "I'm not. In a strange way, when I watched him walk away, I started to understand things better. I felt like I was losing a dear friend and I was sad, but if I called him back and begged him to stay, it would be because I didn't want to hurt a good person."

She paused for a moment and looked at Samantha. "I was Jacob's Bradley." Samantha put down her cup knowing the rest would be hard to hear. "Jacob is a good person. He was afraid of hurting me. Returning my texts wasn't to be bad to you or to lead me on, he just didn't want to hurt me.

"Bradley did the right thing. He believed there was someone out there that would not only light up his world, but allow him to light up theirs. I would have never done that for Jacob. My mistake was to think he was the only one in all the world with that ability, and when I couldn't have him, I settled. I'll find my Jacob someday. He's all yours. He always has been."

"So you were texting him a lot?" Samantha asked.

"When Bradley left, I sat in my empty house, and I thought about everything. Why I cared about Jacob and not about Bradley, not enough anyway. Maybe, it was his hair, his voice, his smell. I don't know how one person becomes an addiction with one interaction and someone else, with so much to offer, can offer you nothing. Maybe part of it was having someone find me worthwhile even after they met you. Silly how it takes so long to grow up, isn't it?"

Samantha reached out and hugged her sister. "You were always more grown up than I, Haley." After letting the embrace say everything they didn't have the courage yet to say, they released and wiped their eyes with their sleeves. "I have a plan," Samantha announced. "We're going into business together."

"What!"

"Yes! Don't shoot me down yet."

"What business could we do, seriously?"

"Interior decorating. Think about it. We have Mom, who's a pro. She already told me she wants me to help her grow her business. I really believe I have her eye for things, or at least, I love to shop. You know the business side from running the flower shop. Mom built a good reputation for herself. We will have our own clients immediately."

Haley smiled at her sister and looked down as if searching for words she didn't want to find.

"Samantha, I can't start a business with you right now."

"Why? Maybe I'm not selling it well. See, this is why I need you."

"You don't need me. Samantha, I have to tell you something." She paused for an uncomfortable moment and shifted in her chair. "I'm not your friend. Or at least, I haven't been. You shouldn't trust me. No one should."

"What are you talking about, Haley?"

"I would have taken him back. If he would have me, I'd be with him right now."

Samantha took a deep breath. What could she say?

"I tried to take him back. I called him. I brought him food. I befriended him. For God's sake, I texted him before the accident. I've been trying to take him back since the day you took him from me." Silence. "He's never wanted me. He loves you. He always has, even the day..." She stopped there.

"What day, Haley?"

"Even the day, it was before you were married, when I, Samantha, I managed to make him feel guilty enough to take me out, drink too much, and, I'm sorry, Samantha, but I was with him that one night. I just wanted him to realize he loved me before he became serious with you. I told myself I would back off after that, but through time, I have just gotten worse and worse. It's why Bradley left me, I'm sure. I deserved his leaving me. I've been evil to everyone."

"What do you want me to say to that, Haley? 'It's all right? What the hell?' I need to go."

"Please wait, Samantha. I have to tell you more."

"I don't want to hear it." She rose to go.

"He loves you."

"If he loved me then he wouldn't have left me."

"He would have if it meant getting out of jail."

"What are you talking about?"

"I think you should have a seat. I owe you the truth."

Chapter 61

Samantha

Her whole life Samantha had focused on how everyone had disappointed her. Even fate had seemed to deal her a lesser hand. She had lived like a victim. It began with her parents, who had made her feel second. Then Haley, even though it wasn't her fault, made her feel inferior her whole life. Then, of course, Jacob, who had to text and drive and send their family spiraling. And finally, there was Seth. The savior she clung to that she was sure would fix it all and, instead, used her as a tool for his revenge.

Samantha was done blaming. She thought back to that girl staring at her through the glass, begging her to understand. It wasn't any more their fault than her own. Each one of them bruised each other as they strayed off course, trying to figure out how to do this life thing. How does a parent love each child perfectly when each one is a puzzle? How does a sister not use her gifts just because she might make someone close to her feel slighted? How does a husband, or any person, not err? Small misjudgments that on another day may have only been a slight aggravation and not a tragedy. And lastly, how does a loving husband not feel angry and vengeful when life takes so much from him?

She needed to stop blaming and take ownership. She needed to stop playing the victim. She was not the only one getting bumped and bruised as they tried to live and learn. How many people had she bruised? Her sister, her parents, her husband. What complaints would her children someday have about her as they learned to reflect on the experiences that defined them? In the end, she realized, her need to be loved had always been stronger than her need to truly love.

Yes, it did take a bit of time to let the night Haley shared with Jacob shrivel to the grain of dust it needed to be before she realized the door had just opened, a door back. He hadn't left her because he didn't love her. He would forgive her because he needed to be forgiven as well. Yes, he had been unfaithful to her when they were dating, and with the one person that would cut the deepest. Yes, he lied about it all these years, but was she willing to let one bad decision that happened fifteen years before negate all the years she had spent with him? Considering all the mistakes she had made, she knew her answer. Once everything had all settled in and she had made peace with it all, there was only one thing she wanted, and that was her husband.

She parked in front of Jacob's apartment. Excitement, fear, and happiness overwhelmed her. Using the mirror, she applied her lip gloss for the third time that morning. Her car was parked next to his. He was there. What would the next hour bring?

She refrained from skipping up the stairs in anticipation of good things to come. Instead, she straightened her shirt, lifted her chin, and knocked a bit forcefully on his door. He opened it looking sleepy and worn out.

"So what did you think I really loved more than you?" Samantha said.

"Excuse me?"

"What in our home did you really believe I loved more than you? The couches that are ten years old? The china we pull out once a year? My red-soled shoes? Well, I do really like them."

"What are you talking about, Samantha?"

"You gave me up so we wouldn't lose the house, my Lexus, my stuff. Really, Jacob? Why? Why don't you know how much I love you?"

"So who told you? Haley? Seth?"

"Haley. She told me a lot of things." She saw his eyes grow in shock.

"Samantha, I'm so…"

"No worries. I think I'm ready to move past it now."

"Just like that? What about Seth?"

"He was the biggest mistake of my life except that it made me see parts of myself, really ugly parts of myself, that needed some serious work."

"I always loved you just the way you were."

"But I didn't love myself. I'm sorry it took all this to bring us here, but it did and I think here can be a really great place to start over."

"I couldn't agree more."

Jacob's hand grabbed her more forcefully than she was used to from him. She found herself being pulled through the kitchen. She tried to catch a view of his bachelor pad as he continued to pull her into the tiny bedroom off the living room. Before she could wonder further at his other life, Jacob's shirt was off, and his pants were following. She followed suit and they found themselves staring naked at each other, completely vulnerable and yet completely untouchable, but only for a moment. With a welcome aggression, Jacob grabbed hold of his wife, both of them trying desperately to find the closeness they had been missing.

Chapter 62

Samantha

Samantha once again walked through the hallways of her home. She appreciated the beauty, the memories, the warmth, but she was no longer afraid of losing them. It was a piece of her life, in some ways similar to a country she had visited on her way to other adventures. It didn't own her or define her by its beauty or size. She suddenly felt free to travel the waves of life without fear.

Within a couple of weeks, her mother had Samantha set up with her first decorating job. She poured her time and energy into it and found she loved it, turning old and worn-out into fresh and new. Samantha knew right away it could become addicting. Haley was looking into classes to teach music. A perfect fit, and Samantha felt the promise of good things to come for all of them.

Each week she stopped by the nursing home during her lunch break to bring fresh flowers or to spruce up the entryway. In some way, she felt she owed them something even though no one else in the world would understand her reasoning.

It amazed her how she had dug deeply and found a genuine talent, a gift. It was right there all along. Her eye for stylish charm with or without a high price tag, her mother's genes buried within her, and her nagging hole needing to be filled finally came together. Letting it trickle down to charitable work at the nursing home was a gift to herself.

Maybe there were no words to describe why the door to her soul was found amongst the life warriors glancing backward from wheelchairs and hospital beds. Some were still smiling, some grimacing, but all of them held a story whether or not she would ever be honored enough to hear it. Maybe it made her look at her challenges with a wisdom she hadn't quite mastered.

She carried the flowers in while greeting the patients she now knew by name. After setting the flowers on the table, she reached for Ms. Hubbard's hands—old, feeble and amazingly soft.

"How are you today, Ms. Hubbard?"

"It's a good day, Samantha, a good day. My grandkids are coming in from Seattle and taking me on an outing."

"That's wonderful. I hope you have a great time." A warm tear formed when she looked into the glossy eyes of the old woman that were lit up with joy and Samantha felt a warmth wash over her as she realized she truly meant it. She wanted that sweet old woman to have a wonderful day. Samantha gave Mrs. Hubbard's hand a gentle squeeze, and Samantha felt full.

Hope. She thought, she had heard that word come from a toothless prisoner in what seemed to be another lifetime— man, at the end of a life that should have left him shattered. A man that was still full of hope. She wanted to be him, to keep his state of mind forever, but she knew there would be more bumps and struggles. There would be days she would have to fight harder than others. She was prepared. Some lessons are learned very hard in life, but the hard ones seemed to stick.

The morning of the accident, she had been a shell of a person walking through life, waiting for something to make her feel complete. Yet she didn't fully see what was the root of it. As unhappy as she was with herself, she never noticed her flaws, her part in it when she gossiped at the bus stop or secretly refused to clap for Haley. Wasn't everybody complaining about someone? It was normal she told herself, to be pointing out the flaws of others on a daily basis, a form of entertainment.

The need to feel loved was human, but the funny part she didn't realize was that she had to learn how to love back to see the curtain drop at her feet revealing how much love had always been all around her. After going through hell, after trying in the worst ways to fill her emptiness, she had come to a very real conclusion. It becomes too hard to worry about how empty your life is when you are busy trying to make someone else's full.

After several trips to the car, she had brought spring to the nursing home. The piano in the corner was no longer an ache but an opportunity. Haley's opportunity. She hoped she could find it again someday through her teaching. It was not meant to lie quiet in a corner.

It amazed her how two privileged young ladies turned out to be so battered, bruised, and flawed. They had managed to take all that they were given and allowed it to implode. Maybe that was what life was meant to do to people, tear them apart so they are able to reform into something more real, more strong, more sympathetic. It was what she chose to believe anyway.

Jacob would be coming home for dinner that evening. They had decided to move slowly for the children's sake. They couldn't have everything ripped out from underneath them again, and no matter how much she wanted normalcy, they both knew there was going to be an adjustment period. Keeping Jacob's apartment somehow became a place where they rekindled. In the small confines, they became young lovers getting to know each other again—rebuilding their relationship in the privacy of those tiny rooms.

Seth's texts were dwindling with each lack of acknowledgment of them. Samantha could not be sure if he knew that she had been seeing Jacob. The slow secretive pace was also due to Seth's restrictions. The longer they kept the truth from him the better, even if they now knew he couldn't touch them.

Samantha's business with her mother began to flourish as she sunk all of her nervous energy into shopping and brainstorming. When she wasn't busy in other peoples' homes, she redecorated parts of hers to give it a look of fresh beginnings. She cooked new recipes, ran a million errands, helped with homework, happy to give back in a way she had not been capable of before.

Sometimes when she ran, a memory would come to her, and she would run harder and faster trying to leave it behind her. Some memories were more challenging than others to ignore. How was it possible that she was so easily fooled?

She would sometimes be flooded with feelings of shame and embarrassment, but she tried not to let her mind twist the memories into something easier to take, that maybe under all that hatred, he had cared, even a little. More importantly she had to remind herself it didn't matter how Seth had felt about her or his motives. Her need to be loved couldn't lead her down unhealthy paths anymore.

Samantha finally understood that all along, she had in her grasp what she had craved to fulfill her needs. Yet, she had never allowed her relationships to blossom into what they should have been. She had never fed them, especially those with Haley. Now she could only move forward, hoping that her efforts would some day lead to the kind of relationships they should always have enjoyed.

Epilogue

Jacob officially moved back in at the end of the second month, even though by then his apartment was only for show. It was good and right, and Samantha knew beyond anything else that it was what she wanted. Curled into Jacob's arms under their throw blanket was home. Watching Ryan play in front of the fire with his Matchbox cars, only to stop and stare open-mouthed at some ridiculous scene on the television, or seeing Sydney's eye roll at his car imitations in between pages of her book, filled their evenings. They were moments that had been so commonplace before and now so unimaginably beautiful after they had won them back. Everything was sweeter now, but also, everything was mixed with a remnant of pain, a reminder to hold on and not take anything for granted.

Samantha had begun calling Haley. She of all people knew about being flawed, and she couldn't imagine a life without her sister being a part of it. Haley was selling the house that she and Bradley had shared. He wasn't coming back, and she still insisted it was for the best.

For some reason, Samantha got the feeling that Haley's life was about to begin. The right person would come along and, hopefully for Haley, the persistent rumblings she felt for Jacob would disappear. Somehow, Samantha could no longer bring herself to hate her sister for the unwelcome and inappropriate longings she had secretly held in her heart. She could only hope that some day they would unclench their fist and allow her to run free.

There were still many months remaining for Seth to come after them. Fear became a faint ticking in the back of her mind that she was almost able to ignore. Each day, Samantha went about her business knowing her future was held in the hands of a man she wondered if she knew at all. What were his motives? She wanted to believe he didn't have any and that he was as surprised as she by the relationship that developed between them.

Already she was beginning to receive calls from people she did not know for her decorating advice. When a woman from the West End called, Samantha knew she was going to have to drive dangerously close to Seth's neighborhood, but she couldn't let it hold her back. Promising herself she would not stray from her route, she drove up to a large two-story with a meticulous lawn.

When she rang the doorbell, a woman with, Samantha was sure, implants opened the door. She appeared to be someone who had never cleaned a bathroom or pushed a vacuum in her life, and Samantha would have bet all she had that she had never mowed a lawn. The woman left her neither impressed nor intimidated.

"Hello, I'm Samantha Truax."

After assessing Samantha from top to bottom, she reached out her hand. "It's nice to meet you. Thank you for coming. Please follow me and I'll show you the rooms I would like some help with."

Samantha followed her through a large foyer with an impressive chandelier. The living room was bright and cheerful. Immediately, Samantha decided it was already decorated to her liking. She searched the room looking for something she could improve on and was coming up empty. As she began to feel a small pang of panic, the phone rang. The woman excused herself and disappeared into a room down a short hallway.

Awkwardly, Samantha again scanned the room, feeling for the first time slightly out of her comfort zone in interior decorating. She skimmed her hand over a figurine that screamed expensive, still wondering what she would say.

"So any suggestions?"

She turned quickly at the sound of a man's voice. Seth leaned against the doorway entrance.

"Oh my God, Seth. What are you doing here?"

"No worries. I just needed to see you one last time. You know it's hard when you don't know it's the last time."

"So I take it Miss Implants does not need a decorator."

"No. She's a friend."

"Once again, I'm amazed at your deceitfulness."

"It appears my deceitfulness has worked out pretty well for you."

"I guess time will tell."

"I guess it will." Seth stared at her with eyes she could not read. "So how long did you know?"

"Haley told me a little while after Jacob moved out."

"Hmm," he said with a cocky smile, "so it wasn't Jacob." He pondered silently before continuing. "It's interesting, isn't it, that Jacob confided in Haley."

"Why are you doing this, Seth?"

"I have some decisions to make. I guess I needed help."

"So has this helped?" Samantha could feel her heart pounding in her chest. Her future dangled in the air in front of her.

"I'm not sure."

"It's a shame, Seth, that I'll never know who you were before the accident. Who were you with Ava? Who would she want you to be?"

Seth stood unmoving, not giving away his emotions with any expression.

"Maybe you do know, Samantha, but you just don't trust it anymore."

"Or maybe you are just good at it, making people think you love them."

"Is that what you think?"

"The fact is, it can't matter anymore. I guess it all comes down to what part of Ava's memory do you want to live on, the love you had for her or the hate you feel from losing her?"

Samantha picked up her purse from the table and walked toward the door. Before leaving, she took one look back and stared into his eyes, trying to find something. His face had softened into an almost sadness, but still she could not know for sure.

"Goodbye, Seth." She closed the door without hearing a response.

***

Samantha could see them out her kitchen window. Jacob was tossing a large purple ball to their whiffle ball bat. The size made it almost impossible to miss. It also turned the game of baseball into a game of kickball as soon as the ball left the bat. The batter would scramble to the designated tree bases before Jacob could hit them with the ball. Samantha stopped chopping the onion just to watch them. She found herself thinking about how strange it is, how many moments pass and are forgotten. Sometimes even with reminders, the moment is gone, unable to ever be retrieved again. As she watched them out the window, she knew it was one of the moments that would stick. Her mind had taken a snapshot to be pulled out and gazed upon whenever needed.

The year would continue to tick by as she prayed Seth cared enough to let her go so that her family could re-form into a new and stronger picture. Theirs would be a picture of flawed and beaten souls, of futures dropped and picked back up, of hope and happiness. Expensive retouches would attempt to smooth out the pain of the past, not to make it disappear, but to be less evident when they stared into the eyes of their past selves. Each moment in time life offered, each smile, each tear would be caught in a wooden frame, forever imprisoning it in the album of still lives that would become their story.

THE END

Acknowledgments

I always have to thank my husband, Steve, first because he allows me time to write and always encourages me. I also want to thank my children for their patience with me; Nicholas, Madison, and Emily.

I have been blessed with other family members and friends and sisters who have also influenced me. Thank you to my sister Lisa Cascanette, Kim Stone, and Judy Deon as well as my mother Gail Sheehan, and niece Karrigan Deon.

It's not easy to read a friend's writing and then critique it. Special thanks to my friends who did just that: Jeannie Middlebrooks, Melinda Vanboskirk, and Dori Hall.

Another amazing group of people who have not only helped critique my work, but have shown up at book festivals and set me up as the guest author at book clubs in the area is my amazing book club, appropriately named Between the Wines. This wonderful group consists of the following ladies: Marzieh Abtahi, Meg Balke, Tammy Beckedorf, Kathy Bravo, Charmaine Brooks, Cynde Covington, Peggy Eschbach, Stacy Horan, Katie Keith, Cathy Klein, Tatiana Macdougall, Leah Maltz, Donna Nuckols, Maritza Ochoa, Claudia Oltean, Laurie

Robinson, Holly Ross, Christine Schmitt, Renee Schreck, Sue Schultz, Cecile Spiegel, Lisa Urbanek, Anne Warren, and Gina Yockey. These women have played a huge part in making me believe in myself. Thank you.

For help with the legal questions, I reached out to Howard Maltz, Scott Stolte, and Jason Miller. I tried to be as accurate as possible, but learned the legal system is very complex. I take responsibility for any inaccuracies.

I found one jail that was housed within a prison and used this when envisioning the setting on which Jacob served time. When researching the process, I found different times for incarceration given for crimes committed. I also consulted Paul Cascanette, my brother-in-law, about correctional facilities.

Thank you, Elizabeth Ridley and Robert Bacon, who both completed some of the editing, and special thanks to Taylor and Seale Publishing Company for taking me on as an author.

Other books written by Tracy Tripp

Fiction: *Parting Gifts*

Children's Books: *The Wealthy Frog*

Contact: <u>tracytrippauthor@gmail.com</u>

Website: tracytripp.com

CPSIA information can be obtained
at www.ICGtesting.com
Printed in the USA
LVHW051151160523
747044LV00004B/139

9 781943 789795